**Praise for Afterlight**

"Phenomenal."
*Het Financieele Dagblad*

"Heartbreaking."
*De Standaard*

"Once again, Robben shows himself to be a master of concise, restrained sentences that keep sentimentality at bay. *Afterlight* is an impressive and delicately wrought book about loss. [...] How does he do it? The drama that unfolds in this, his third novel, is beautifully paced and written with a keen sensitivity that steadily tightens the knot—Jaap Robben's trademark."
*Trouw*

"One of the most beautiful books of the year."
*MEZZA*

"Every sentence shimmers and resonates in Jaap Robben's stunning novel about living with a pain that goes unspoken. *Afterlight* is an impressive achievement, a story no reader can forget."
*Het Parool*

"Not a word is out of place, every sentence is charged with emotion. And especially as the novel builds towards its conclusion, every paragraph hits home."
*De Morgen*

"In *Afterlight*, Robben tells the brutal story of what many women had to endure not so very long ago. The result is a beautiful novel, alive with compassion."
*Dagblad van het Noorden*

"One of the subtlest novelists writing in the Dutch language."
De Lage Landen

"Tender and perceptive. Jaap Robben's description of Frieda's life is masterly."
De Ochtend, *NPO Radio 4*

"Through his protagonist's strength of character, Robben speaks from his feminist heart."
*Humo*

"The subtlest of touches bring these lovers to life, in their exchanges with each other and with the wider cast of characters. Robben is a master of dialogue."
*Ons Erfdeel*

"A literary gem that deals with a profoundly moving, unseen history. With inspired precision, Jaap Robben sketches an entire life in impressive fashion."
*Confituur* Booksellers' Award 2023

"Part of what makes *Afterlight* such a powerful novel is the assurance with which Robben allows Frieda's trauma as a young woman to filter through in her later life. [...] He is a sober, sensitive stylist who feels no need to be ostentatious. His pared-down sentences stay with you."
*MappaLibri.be*

"Like Frieda herself, the reader is drawn into a story they will never forget—a story that is wonderfully written to boot."
*Knack*

"I can't remember the last time a novel made me cry. And I suspect I won't be the only reader moved to tears by the touching story of Frieda Tendelow."
*Feeling*

"In this compelling and lovingly written novel, Jaap Robben has captured the harsh injustice inflicted on so many women and their children in the century gone by. It's astounding how Robben, a man in his late thirties, so convincingly inhabits the mind of a young woman and that same woman in old age: remarkable in its truth and depth of feeling."
*Bazarow*

"A gripping novel and a feminist indictment in one."
*Nederlands Dagblad*

"Jaap Robben is a specialist in intimate spaces. A haunting and deeply human story, this book is a monument to every mother whose child was born into silence."
*Friesch Dagblad*

•

**Praise for Summer Brother**

"A deeply humane novel centred on a disabled man, his heroic younger brother and an unreliable, partly criminal father living on an all but derelict site. The book is generous to all its flawed characters, is beautifully written, and humanises lives of abject poverty on the edge of squalor and disaster."
INTERNATIONAL BOOKER PRIZE, jury report

"I just ADORED the novel *Summer Brother*. Bravo, bravo is what I have to say. It kind of saved me in a way."
ELIZABETH STROUT, Pulitzer Prize-winning author

"It's an impressive novel: a deceptively simple story of lives at the margin, with a child's viewpoint perfectly pitched and sustained, it is cleanly written and powerfully imagined. It reminded me of Claire Keegan's novella *Foster*, which has a girl narrator of a similar age, and is an outstanding book. But the challenges are greater here, as Robben deals with all kinds of inflammable material, and does it with such tact and understanding."
HILARY MANTEL

"Robben's background as a playwright is evident in his astute characterisation. [...] He depicts the limitations of a dysfunctional family but also celebrates empathy as a force for good."
*The Guardian*

"It is wild and touching reading."
DORTHE NORS, International Booker Prize-nominated author

"A warm, complex and luminous novel on these profound moments of ambiguity, and on the small, crucial acts of love."
RUTH MCKEE, *Irish Times*

"The central premise of *Summer Brother*, Jaap Robben's evocative coming-of-age novel, longlisted for the International Booker Prize, is that love can thrive in the unlikeliest of places. [...] It is easy to forget this is a

work in translation, so deft is David Doherty's rendition. Robben depicts the limitations of a dysfunctional family but also celebrates empathy as a force for good."
*The Observer*

"Dutch author Jaap Robben's second novel shows us the shedding of innocence. *Summer Brother*, translated by David Doherty, shakes out over a hot summer, during that potent lull when characters so splendidly boil, burst and bloom. [...] *Summer Brother* grapples with the consequences of carelessness and the abuse of power and trust, even if the violation is unintentional [...]. Robben is wonderful at drawing characters with just a few deliberate strokes. [...] Like a photographer shooting a portrait, Robben captures his subjects in *Summer Brother* in a focused close-up."
*New York Times*

"A sensitive yet unsentimental depiction of poverty and disability from the perspective of an abled character."
*Kirkus Reviews*

"The book's language is precise and forthright as Brian observes, and portrays in stark terms, the intense, awkward, and lovely actions of those around him. Sharp exchanges reveal characters who are witty and earnest in equal measure. *Summer Brother* is a harrowing novel about dysfunctional family dynamics and the universal awkwardness of being a teenager."
*Foreword Reviews*

"A tragic tale of generational dysfunction"
*Publishers Weekly*

"*Summer Brother* is a work of rare intricacy that warrants to be read with all the seriousness one can muster."
*World Literature Today*

"Refined and subtle, and at the same time one of the most striking voices in contemporary Dutch literature."
LIZE SPIT, author of *The Melting*

"His first novel, *You Have Me to Love*, was well-received, won prizes, and became a sales success. *Summer Brother* is a worthy successor and has all the ingredients to follow the same path. Robben knows how to write simply and magnificently—I kept underlining beautiful sentences in the first chapters."
*Trouw*

"A writer who crosses the ball with such elegance that there's no need to hammer it home."
*De Volkskrant*

"Subtle and refined."
*NRC Handelsblad*

"Robben's style is deceptively simple. You don't have to be an adult to read *Summer Brother*, yet Robben's imagery, subtle humor, and surprising plot will connect with the most literate of readers. The novel gives a moving insight into a boyhood that gives pause for reflection."
*De Standaard*

**Praise for You Have Me to Love**

"*You Have Me to Love* is an intense and dramatic novel filled with meticulous use of detail and a forensic psychological accuracy. Its power comes from the fierce energy of the narrative structure, the way of handling silence and pain, and the ability to confront the darkest areas of experience with clear-eyed sympathy and care. Jaap Robben handles delicate, dangerous material with subtlety and sympathy, but also with a visionary sense of truth that is masterly and unforgettable."
COLM TÓIBÍN

"I was completely seduced by this novel—it's raw and harrowing and very moving. Robben is a very powerful writer who reminds me very much of Per Petterson."
AIFRIC CAMPBELL

"Beautiful, just beautiful."
GERBRAND BAKKER

"This is a bold, tender and ambivalent narrative, raw and disturbing, with moments of painful beauty; a taut narrative heavy with a convincing sense of dread."
*Irish Times*

"*You Have Me to Love* explores raw and unsettling psychological territory. It is a story that once read will stick with the reader for a long time."
*Literary Review*

"Moving between child-like speculation and shocking realism, Robben's novel transports the reader into lives almost beyond imagining in the contemporary world. With echoes of Ian McEwan and Peter Carey, Robben's tale, already a huge success in the Netherlands, is one to savor and discuss."
*ALA Booklist*

"A small masterpiece."
*Harpers Bazaar*

"*You Have Me to Love* left me gasping, literally, for air. And groping for understanding. A blindingly good novel about the vulnerability of children and the hard truth of the world they inhabit."
The King's English Bookshop

"A promising novelist has risen. Robben lifts you from your life and sweeps you away, with no chance of escaping."
*De Morgen*

"An overwhelming debut about lost childhood innocence, *You Have Me to Love* can be favourably compared to Niccolò Ammaniti's *I'm Not Scared* and Ian McEwan's *The Cement* Garden."
*Het Parool*

"A gripping novel that steadily tightens its hold."
*De Volkskrant*

"Like a record stuck in its groove, it won't let me go."
*European Literature Network*

"From the very first sentence it is clear how well debut novelist Jaap Robben writes. His childishly simple yet highly suggestive sentences make *You Have Me to Love* as stark and foreboding as the island on which it is set."
*NRC NEXT*

"Unbelievable—a beautiful story, light for all its darkness, written in a clear and powerful style. A coming-of-age tale in which Robben merges grief, simplicity, and isolation in a phenomenal way."
*De Telegraaf*

"Robben's clear sentences and empathic use of language read like poetry: rhythmic, probing, and sonorous."
*Dagblad van het Noorden*

# AFTERLIGHT

JAAP ROBBEN

# AFTERLIGHT

Translated from the Dutch
by David Doherty

WORLD EDITIONS
New York

Published in the USA in 2024 by World Editions LLC, New York

World Editions
New York



Printed by Lightning Source, USA



Library of Congress Cataloging in Publication Data is available

ISBN 978-1-64286-147-1

First published as *Schemerleven* in the Netherlands in 2022
by De Geus, Amsterdam.

The publisher gratefully acknowledges the support of the Dutch Foundation for Literature.

Nederlands
letterenfonds
dutch foundation
for literature



Company: worldeditions.org
Facebook: @WorldEditionsInternationalPublishing
Instagram: @WorldEdBooks
TikTok: @worldeditions_tok
Twitter: @WorldEdBooks
YouTube: World Editions

*For my dearest Lucy*

# 1

I see them every time I close my eyes. Louis's feet, sticking out from under the foil blanket. Helpless. Slippers lost in the panic and confusion. His feet, so pale, so naked, as the paramedics slide him into the ambulance.

It's far too soft, this mattress, and my back is all clammy from the plastic cover. I've never been one for sleeping on my side and I doubt I'll sleep another wink in this place.

I squint into the semi-darkness. Tobias forgot to plug in my radio alarm clock, had his hands full setting up that new television for me. Even without my glasses, I can see the little red light. A patch of grey hovers by the bathroom door, my blazer for tomorrow. The same one I wore at the funeral.

I heave myself up to sitting. Milk. Warm, cinnamon sweet.

The switch for my lamp should be dangling here somewhere but I'm damned if I can find it. My hand inches across the bedside table, careful not to knock anything flying. It lands on my puzzle book, my hearing aids. A noiseless clunk as my wedding ring connects with the tumbler of water. At last—my glasses. I unfold them and put them on. The switch is closer than I thought. In this strange room, my familiar bits of furniture look startled by the sudden light. Bare nails still dot the walls.

Louis never let me fetch my own milk. That would have meant tackling the stairs down to the kitchen. And I wasn't going to ask him to get up and make it for me.

My legs slide over the side of the bed. "No stairs here for me to fall down," I mumble to myself. I've tried talking to Louis but somehow it doesn't seem to work.

I shuffle past the open accordion door into the small living room with the kitchenette. Nadine and I stocked the cupboards this afternoon. I try to picture what we did with the cinnamon and sugar cubes. Tobias hardly lets her lift a thing now that there's a baby on the way.

The sugar and cinnamon are most likely where they've always been, at home in a kitchen cupboard. That house of ours, so quiet now, half-empty. I slipped up again today and called Nadine "Sabine." I don't think she noticed. Sabine was Tobias's last girlfriend. *Nadine, Nadine, Nadine.* Louis and I always assumed Tobias wasn't one for children. When he was with Sabine he had even said as much. And with him turning forty-eight this year we had pretty much resigned ourselves. But then he appeared with Nadine in tow and she's a good bit younger.

Louis was overjoyed when they came over to tell us the news. Tears in his eyes. I was very happy for them too, of course. All hugs, he was, even planted a kiss on each of their foreheads. "A gift," he beamed. "That's what it is. A gift!"

I put my mug in the microwave, press a button, and wait. It's a relic of the previous resident, along with her curtains and the fridge. Not much wear and tear. She must have lived here until a few days ago.

The dining table is mine. Brought from home, with two of the four matching chairs. And then there's our sideboard and Louis's electric armchair. A brief compilation of our belongings, standing awkwardly side by side. Only room for three plants on this sill. That was the hardest thing of all. How am I supposed to live without my old Christmas cactus? But it weighs a ton and that huge pot would only be in the way. In the end, it was that or the television. Oh well, Tobias has promised to find it a good home.

No *ping* that I could hear, but the microwave has gone dark. I really want to settle down in Louis's chair with my warm milk, but I think better of it and shuffle back to bed. All evening I've had the feeling some busybody might come barging in unannounced and tell me off for doing something I shouldn't. Or see me in my nightgown and demand to know what I'm doing out of bed in the middle of the night. I'm sure they would knock first, but it's not like I'd hear them if they did. It never occurred to me before that at night, without my hearing aids, I'm deaf to whispers and interlopers. Now the very idea has me on edge.

Through the gap in the curtains I can see the courtyard garden. The black night sky is already turning deep-blue above the rooftops. It's not that I believe Louis can come back, I've never had much time for that kind of thing. Louis has gone for good. But it saddens me to think that if he did, he would never find me here. I don't even know my own address.

I nudge the curtain open a little further, sit on the edge of the mattress, blow over the top of my milk. Still too hot. With the mug safe on the bedside table, I work my way back under the covers.

There's a restless presence, something moving on the other side of the glass. A moth tap-tapping at the top window. Not that I can hear it, but I see it spinning across the pane. It must be drawn to my night light.

"You've got yourself muddled," I whisper. "That's my lamp, not the moon." The fluttering doesn't stop. "What a silly little thing you are." I sip at my cinnamonless, sugar-free milk. It looks like one of those hairy moths with a colourful little petticoat tucked under its grey wings. After another sip or two, I switch off the lamp. The dark shape flits and bumps. "Night then, mothy." I take off my glasses. "I'm going to give this another go."

I must get Tobias to bring my pillow from home. I heave a sigh—and the sugar cubes and cinnamon. Another sigh. I close my eyes. There they are again, his feet. Pale and naked, till the paramedic tugged the foil blanket over them.

"Oh, Lou. Louis, my love."

Right up until it happened, Louis insisted on "seeing to me" without a home help. That was what he called it when hints were dropped that he could use some assistance around the house. A tight-lipped busybody with a binder full of forms sat down at the kitchen table. We only let her in because Tobias had been so stern with us. The level of care I needed put us high on the list for assisted living, she explained, but we were likely to lose out on account of Louis being "in such good shape." She said this in a whisper, our little secret. A conundrum to which she had no solution.

What they *could* do was send someone round to help me out of bed and give me a hand washing and dressing. Three mornings a week, all covered by our health insurance. "How does that sound? Shall we give that a try?"

No one asked me anything. Louis puffed out his chest, crossed his arms, and that was that. "No," he said, with a bluster that was new to me. "Showering is our time together. No one is taking that from us." I felt for his fingers under the table and gave them a squeeze. We spent the rest of the conversation like that, invisibly hand in hand. "I will wash her till the end."

No one had expected me to outlive Louis.

Louis least of all.

* * *

There's someone in my room. Movement, colours. "Tobias?" Someone hands me my glasses, then my hearing aids.

"Good morning, Mrs. Buitink-Tendelow." Young chap. Twinkly eyes and one of those little beards, trim as a tennis court.

For years, I've been plain old Mrs. Buitink, but ever since I moved here they keep tacking on my maiden name. It feels odd, as if they know more about me than I'd like.

“Good morning.”

“Will you come with me? Then we can give you a nice shower.” He holds out an arm. At first, I think he’s wearing long sleeves but his arms are tattooed all the way to his wrists. My feet hit the cold floor. The hem of my nightdress has ridden up and I pull it down quick.

“And what’s your name?” I ask.

“Oh, I’m sorry.” He shakes my hand. “Jamie, at your service.”

The light in the tiny bathroom flickers on automatically and the ventilator starts to hum. My mouth tastes stale, so I keep my answers short and try not to breathe in his direction. The mirror shows me a mad thatch of hair. Cupboard doors swing and slam. Jamie grabs a towel, shower cream, and two dried-up flannels. He’s so at ease, more at home in this place than I’ll ever be.

“Did you get some sleep?”

“I tried.”

“The first night is always the hardest.”

“Is that right?”

“I see it with all the new residents.”

“Can’t see me ever getting a good night’s sleep here.”

“I’m sure you will,” Jamie says, and gestures towards the shower. “Shall we?”

I start to pluck at my nightgown and feel Jamie’s firm hands grasp the fabric. “No, give me a second,” I say. “I can manage.” Only I can’t and he has to help me yank it over my head after all.

“Okey-doke,” he says.

I am standing with my bare back to him. In one swift motion, he slides the incontinence pad from between my legs. I barely notice his touch but feel it all the more and clamp my thighs together. "Okey-doke." It's the prelude to everything he does. So, here I stand, more exposed than I've ever been. Naked but for the red alarm button dangling at my bosom.

Jamie points the shower head at the wall until the water heats up. A cold mist drifts my way and goose bumps shiver down my back. He ushers me into the white chair. I hunch my shoulders, back so bent you'd swear I was trying to curl into a ball. I grow and shrink in time with my breathing. My feet seem a long way off and, with the lad standing so close, the purple veins look darker than ever. My knees with the long scars down both sides. A belly that has to be washed crease by crease. Skin soft as crêpe paper, moles you can dab at most. And my breasts. Oh dear, my breasts. Is it any wonder I keep them clamped behind my forearms?

"Here." Jamie presents me with a flannel. "In case you want to take care of the front yourself." Ever so carefully he points the spray at my feet. "Too warm for you?"

"No, that's fine." I can't hold in my pee anymore but thankfully he doesn't notice. He starts on my back with his flannel. A pleasant surprise. Not a patch on Louis, but just rough enough. I let out a little grunt, but I'm in luck and Jamie doesn't hear. "You're a good lad," I tell him. I don't think he heard that either.

If Louis was too gentle, I'd tell him to imagine he was rubbing a stubborn splat of bird poo off the kitchen window.

"Okey-doke. Raise your arms." I do as I'm bidden. He soaps my armpits and rinses them straight off. "Can you stand up a sec? Then we can do your back." I cling to a bracket he folds down from the wall. The flannel slips between my buttocks. “Are you done with the front?”

“Uhm ...” Louis let me shower a whole boiler long, but Jamie is already turning off the tap. He’s so quick he’s stirring up a bit of a breeze. “Oh wait ... I nearly forgot to lay out your clothes.” In a flash, he flaps my big towel open, drapes it around me and vanishes into the bedroom.

“I want to wear that blazer today,” I call after him.

Cupboards and drawers fly open and shut.

“Which one?”

“The one that was hanging by the bathroom door.”

It goes quiet for a moment. I have no idea what he’s up to in there.

“Are you wearing the white blouse with it? Or is that for another time?”

“That blouse goes with it, especially for today. The trousers are already laid out on my chair.”

Jamie’s head pops round the door. “This one?”

“That’s it.” My other clothes are hanging limply from his arm—underwear, socks, bra on top. I begin to dry the bits of me I can reach. Jamie places the clothes neatly on the lid of the toilet.

“Something special planned for today?”

“How do you mean?”

“With you getting all dressed up.”

“My son is coming to collect me this afternoon.”

“That’ll be nice.”

“Hmm.”

“Won’t it?”

“Yes, it’s just that ...” I can’t reach my feet. Jamie takes the towel, goes down on one knee and looks up at me expectantly. “We’re going to scatter my husband.”

## 2

We had just finished a round of gin rummy. I was sweeping the cards together and Louis was putting on the kettle for our bedtime cup of tea when, out of nowhere, he said, "Perhaps I'll get out more when the time comes."

"What time?"

He still had his back to me.

"What time do you mean?"

"Well, you know. After …"

"After I … after I'm gone?"

He shrugged an apology. Could he help it if the future was set in stone?

"But … I'm still here, aren't I?"

"All I mean is that you don't have to worry. That I'll waste away or whatever." I suppose he was trying to reassure me. Perhaps he was feeling sheepish because I'd caught him looking at second-hand camper vans on the computer.

"Then what's to stop you heading off somewhere now? On your own."

"And who would take care of you?"

"I can get by for a week or so. And Tobias can always pitch in."

And suddenly there he was, lying by the garden path. One ordinary morning. He must have been on his way to the bird table to shake out the bread bag.

Louis, legs twitching on the damp grass. It took me ages to reach him with that stupid walker of mine. I fell to my knees beside him and tried to stroke-shake-scream him back to life. "Duh ... duh ... duh ..." was all he could say. His eyes opened wider with every sound he made, but I don't think he could see anything.

I wanted to call an ambulance, but couldn't get back on my feet unaided. The woman from next door was already straddling the fence. Someone yelled that help was on the way. The neighbour ripped Louis's shirt open—buttons flew up like popcorn—and leaned on his chest. Up and down she bobbed, till the ambulance people came charging across the garden. Someone helped me up and parked me on the seat of my walker. Hands felt Louis all over. "No pulse!" The ambulance people rolled him onto a sheet and hoisted him onto a kind of stretcher trolley, sheet and all. Two paddles were put to his chest, his body tensed and arched. Then it slumped and his hands fell open. He had been sick on himself. "No pulse." They tried again, then wheeled the stretcher through the kitchen and into the hall. The teapot shattered, spitting shards across the kitchen floor. I lurched along behind them, clinging to doorposts, walls, the back of a chair, the coats that hung from the rack. All sorts came crashing down behind me. "Louis!" I shouted. "Louis!" The sight of the ambulance outside our house had drawn the neighbours to their windows. The whole scene was lit in pulsing blue, Louis under a gold foil blanket. "Where are you taking him?" As the stretcher was shoved into the ambulance, I caught sight of the greyish-white soles of his feet poking out from the cocoon of the blanket. Helpless, fallen to either side. "Louis! Louis!" All I could do was shout. Someone had to keep his feet warm. "Where are you taking him?" No one seemed to answer. The doors slammed shut. "Tell me where you're taking him!" There was another ambulance further on, blocking the street. Two paramedics climbed in beside Louis. "You can't just take him from me!" A face close to mine, a policewoman. I saw her lips move but the words were shredded into whistles and shrieks. The sweat had sent my hearing aids haywire, I found out later. "Tell me. Please," I begged. "Just tell me where ..." A neighbour from across the road, a man I barely knew, came up and tried to put his arms around me. I tore myself free but with nothing to hold onto I went over like a ninepin. The ambulance was already moving off. "Louiiiis!" A roar so deep and ugly, it could have ripped through time.

I hope to God he heard me.

Someone helped me into my coat, into a car, clicked the seatbelt and tossed in shoes for my bare feet. I was still in my dressing gown. Someone pulled our front door shut and held up my bag to show me which compartment the keys were in. The car door slammed beside me. Someone ran round, got in, and started the engine. It was Esmé from down the street. Her warm hand gave my knee a squeeze. We sped off and people went back to their lives. I asked

Esmé where they had taken Louis. "To the hospital!" she yelled, at the top of her lungs. "The Ca-ni-si-us!"

The next time I saw him, Louis was on a steel bed with a sheet over his body. The clock on the wall said it was mid-morning but it was unthinkable that this might be a moment in time, a day with a date. Louis looked as if he was asleep, though that was mostly because he didn't have his glasses on.

Brown marks on his forehead led to a shiny patch of grazed skin, bloodless now, among the roots of his hair. He felt cold and oddly familiar. "Oh Lou, Louis my love." I stooped to kiss him. His lips slackened beneath mine, his stubble chafed my chin. This was his body but nothing like the body that had woken beside me only hours before. His hand fumbling beneath the sheet, stroking my thigh. The gentle pat and the kiss on my shoulder before he got up to make the coffee. "Right-o," had been his opener in recent years, "off we go." And he would lever himself up and onto his feet.

I took his hand. No matter how I held it, his fingers no longer locked with mine.

# 3

And now he is ash, enough to fill a blue metallic cylinder. And most of that will be from the coffin. Flanked by Tobias and Nadine, I stand on the close-cropped lawn holding two lilies of the valley in a folded square of kitchen towel. In a while, I will place them on top of what's left of him. The girl from the funeral director's takes charge of the scattering and asks us what shape we want. I say girl, I'm sure she's a woman in her own eyes and has been for years. It's just that the older I get, the younger people seem. Young in ways they can't begin to imagine.

"Shape?"

"A heart, for example? The first letter of his name? Perhaps a cross?"

"Not a cross," I say, looking around at the greyish-white plumes on the lawn. Circles, mainly. The odd letter. Most have already been blown into smudgy patches.

"Mrs. Buitink?"

"Hmm?"

"The shape doesn't really matter, does it, Mum?" Tobias takes charge, his hand on my shoulder. Every time he touches me today, he gives me a little rub. "Mum?"

"No, son, it doesn't matter."

"You might just ..." Tobias shrugs, unable to think of what I "just" might do. But the young lady with the cylinder nods as if she knows exactly what comes after "just." I signal to her to get on with it.

For a second, it looks like something remarkable is about to happen. Perhaps it's her white gloves, her rehearsed gestures. Slowly, she slides back a catch in the handle. She's about to make something appear. A dove. A living creature, far too big for the confines of an urn. And the three of us will applaud and crowd around to peer inside and wonder how on earth she pulled it off. Only none of this happens. Everything Louis once was, everything I once loved, is a spot of dust that steadily grows into a circle. And then the urn is empty. I wait for more to come, but that was it. Everything Louis washed, brushed, combed, flossed and pampered for a lifetime is here on the grass at my feet. Crushed to powder, ready to be blown away. Dead as can be.

Tobias and Nadine shore me up, a hug that judders with their sobbing. I can't see their faces through my tears. I stroke a cheek, kiss a forehead. My lips land on the corner of an eye and I try again, aim a little higher, dispensing comfort I long to receive.

My love. Louis, my love. Where did the days go? All those winter mornings when I peeked from behind the curtains as he set off on his rounds, delivering medicine for the pharmacist. All the times he came home safe.

I place the lilies of the valley on the circle, careful not to touch his ashes. Tobias lends a hand, making sure the two stems are close enough together.

"Does that look about right?" Tobias asks.

"Mm-hmm."

I try to take a handkerchief from my shoulder bag but the zip keeps sticking. Nadine flaps a tissue in front of my face. We sniff and smile at each other through the tears. It's as if the three of us have just plunged into the depths of our sorrow and are standing here dripping on dry land. Tobias holds Nadine close, like she needs to be kept warm. With no place for me in their embrace, he extends his free arm and rubs my shoulder as best he can. I rub my cheek against the back of his hand, the hand of a grown man.

Another hug, another round of sighs. We blow our noses.

Nadine hooks my arm in hers and together we trudge off the lawn. Tobias follows, steering my walker back to the path. He makes a joke I can't quite catch but I chuckle anyway. Their sorrow seems to make way for relief, as if a room has been cleared and swept.

The ash-scatterer accompanies us in her smart midnight-blue suit, keeping a discreet distance. "If you'll follow me." Her gloved hand ushers us towards the way we came in.

Crying has forced my breath deeper, left a hollow space in my chest. I blow my nose, dab at my cheeks, cough and cough again.

Nadine delivers me to my walker and takes Tobias by the arm. "Can you manage, Frieda?"

"Thank you, dear. You two go on ahead."

For every three steps they take, I lag two behind. The young lady in midnight-blue hangs back with me, gloveless now, urn dangling like a kid's bucket from her pink fingers. In silence, she strolls me back to the building at the gates. She has a very natural way of walking slowly. The wheels of my walker leave grooves in the gravel and I plough on like an old nag, panting hard enough to stir the leaves on the trees. A newly laid path stretches off to the side.

I stop a moment.

Breathe.

Some of the wreaths are so poorly put together, you wonder why people pay good money for them. Back in my day at the florist's, a funeral wreath took me the best part of a morning. I have to squint to read the dates on the gravestones closest to me.

"Would you like me to fetch you a wheelchair, Mrs. Buitink?"

"No, I'll be fine." I plough on down the path. She drops behind and I hear the soles of her smart shoes smoothing the grooves in the gravel. Beside a towering conifer on the corner, I have to stop for another breather. Perching on the seat of my walker, I motion to her to go on ahead but she shakes her head patiently. The conifer stands by a gravestone that's all but missing. The tree's roots have cracked the slab and forced it upwards.

"Looks like ... they've been here a while," I sigh, for the sake of something to say.

Eager to fill the silence too, the girl leans over the stone and brushes away a few dry twigs. "Since 1956," she says.

"How long is it there for ... a grave like that?"

"It depends on the family and how much they want to pay for the plot. That's one reason why most people nowadays opt for cremation. So as not to inconvenience those left behind."

"Is this where the older graves are?"

"'Older' meaning ...?"

"From 1963, say."

"Most of those are over that way." Her hand flutters in the direction of a lane lined with tall beeches. "Not that there are many left. The old graves are cleared and new ones take their place. Are you looking for anyone in particular?"

I give a short, sharp shake of the head.

"A man or a woman?"

Tobias and Nadine have reached the end of the path and look round to discover how far behind we are. They hug. Or Tobias hugs Nadine, more like. She only reaches his chin.

"I can look it up for you." She fishes her phone from an inside pocket. My heart throbs in my fingers, white specks swarm before my eyes. She swipes, types, shakes her head. "I'd have to ... Here are the ..." A tap on the screen, and her finger and thumb slide apart to make something bigger. "There are only a few graves left, from early 1963. And someone was interred in a family plot in the summer of 1963." She points over her left shoulder. "I can take you there, if you like."

"There's no need. But thank you."

Before the ash-scatterer can say another word, I'm up churning gravel again.

"I'm coming," I shout to Tobias.

"Sure you can manage, Mum?"

"Yes, son. Your old mum's not as fast as she used to be."

"Shall we stop off at Villa Brakkesteyn for something to drink?" Tobias asks, folding away my walker and stowing it in the boot of the car. “Or head over to the old Thornse mill? They’ve opened a nice little restaurant there. Then again, we could drive past some of the old haunts, if you’d rather.”

“A cup of coffee would go down nicely. I’ll let you two decide where.”

“No trip down memory lane?”

“We’ll save that for another day, all right?” That was something Tobias and Louis liked to do from time to time. Take a drive past the homes we were born in, to see whether the current residents had made any changes, rounded off with a trip to Tobias’s old primary school. All well and good, but most of memory lane is long gone.

“How are you doing?” Nadine says. She keeps asking me versions of the same question.

“Oh,” I sigh. “I’m managing.” With her coat unbuttoned, I can see the curve of her belly. She rubs along the waistband where her trousers are starting to pinch. Our eyes meet and I give her a quick smile.

“By the way, would you like to drop by the house?” Tobias pipes up.

“The house?”

“We don’t have to hand in the keys until the end of the month, so there’s still plenty of time. I can pick you up after the weekend if you like.”

Once we’re all in the car, he asks, “All set?”

I nod.

Suddenly, I’m overwhelmed by the idea that we’ve forgotten Louis, that we can’t just drive off without him. And, though it was what he wanted, I feel desperately sorry that there’s no headstone with his name on it. That now he is nowhere.

Nadine's face appears between the headrests and she puts a hand on my shoulder. "Does it feel okay?"

"What?" God only knows what feeling I'm expected to put words to now.

"You know, the way things went. With the ashes?"

It's one question too many. To stop myself from snapping at her, I stare at the lane of beeches in the distance. "Yes, dear." I pat the hand she's put on my shoulder. "Now tell me, how are things at work?"

# 4

And before you know it, I'm back at my new window. In Louis's chair with its remote control. No will to watch TV, too tired to go to bed, so here I sit, watching the grass grow. A blackbird hops across the lawn and pecks at worms for its little ones, cheeping in a hidden nest. The sun is hanging on but twilight is already gathering among the rooftops.

It's the shadow that catches my eye first, beside me on the floor. It looks like last night's moth, moving across the glass in the top window again, zigzagging wildly, as if it's being steered by a tipsy pilot.

"Hello again." It's the size of a tiny bird. "Are you a hawk moth?" I'd like to think I've dredged up the right name for a moth this size, but it might be the only one I remember.

I have to stand up straight to get a better look, as it taps on the window like a messenger at the gates. It's only now I notice the webs in the corners.

"Watch yourself," I say. I raise my arm but I can't reach that high, and it's hardly likely to scare the little creature off in any case.

At a window across the garden, a silhouette raises a hesitant hand. "Hello, hello," I say, and give a proper wave. She waves back with renewed gusto.

The moth keeps tapping against the glass. "I'll get

those corners cleaned up tomorrow," I tell him. "Tobias can fetch me that rod from home and I can use it to open the window."

I've barely said the words when the moth starts whirring in place, caught in a web. "No, no, no." A spider twitches and shoots across the strands. I thrust my arm in the air again but I'm not even close to reaching the window. I grab the TV guide and whack the glass, hoping the moth will pull free in its fright. It's no good.

The lights! I cling to the sideboard, then shuffle from dining table to kitchen counter, switching off every light as I go. The window becomes an orange-blue rectangle. The moth struggles in the web. I give the handle of the sunshade a whirl, but that's no use either. The moth hangs motionless for a second or two, then tries to whir itself free again. The spider bides its time.

I reach for the phone.

"Good evening. Reception. What can I do for you, Mrs. Buitink-Tendelow?"

"There's a moth at my window."

"A moth, you say?"

"Can you send someone over quick to chase it away?"

"In your room?"

"No, on the outside."

"Ah ... on the outside ..."

"Mm-hmm."

"So it's not actually *in* your room?"

"No, but the poor thing is ..." I don't want the receptionist to think I'm off my rocker. "It's ... uh ..."

"Best ask the nurse when she pops in tomorrow."

"But it's making me nervous."

"In that case, why don't you close the curtains? It'll be bedtime soon anyway." I can tell by her voice that she wants to get off the phone.

"It's a hawk moth. And the spider ..."

"I have to take another call, Mrs. Buitink-Tendelow. Good evening."

I can't bear to see the moth struggling, so I do as I'm told and close the curtains.

I lie down on the bed, close my eyes and wait for sleep to come.

# 5

There were times when I wondered if I even existed before I met Otto.

The sky was painted the freshest blue I had ever seen and an orange sun teased long, crisp shadows from everything it touched. I think I was already in love that afternoon, though I made my way down to the frozen river alone, with no one in particular on my mind. All the dirty snow had been shovelled and scraped aside but white dunes lingered in quiet corners among the ruined houses, whipped into shifting shapes by the wind. For weeks it had been so cold that even the lamppost clocks had seized up, each one telling a different time. A good excuse to be late home for dinner, though admittedly needing an excuse to sidestep my parents' mealtime regime at the age of twenty-one was a sad state of affairs.

I skittered my way over Grotestraat, down towards the white expanse of the river Waal. Kids rushed around me, yelling for all they were worth, each one desperate to reach the next frozen puddle first to crack the ice with the heels of their shoes. Most of the puddles were of their mothers' making, soapy water they had slopped into the street.

"Look! More ice," I shouted. "Over here!"

"Yaay!" They raced towards me.

“Uh-oh, not so fast,” I said as if I knew something they didn’t, and held them at arm’s length until the last little tyke had caught up. With a swish of my hand, we all started stamping.

It was early March 1963. After almost ten full weeks of freezing temperatures, a thaw was due the next day. It had been cold so long that people had lost the will to moan about it. But with the forecasts promising spring, everyone was in high spirits and determined to set foot on the frozen river one last time. That afternoon would be my first.

I had expected a smooth surface, but in places the river was rough as a ploughed field. Ice had been driven up around the moored barges, and over by the Waal Bridge, sheet had piled on sheet to form what looked like the ruins of a winter palace.

Swarms of people had descended on the old gasworks near the railway bridge, where the quay sloped down to the river. Students from one of the fraternities had strung oil lamps from one bank to the other to afford people a safe crossing even after sunset. The thick, white ice was worn, pocked, and cracked, but still treacherously slippery. Within seconds, a harsh cold was nipping through the soles of my shoes, shrivelling my feet in their nylon socks. I shuffled forward a step or two, then gazed around, smiling for all to see. Not that anyone was looking. Fathers were hauling sleds loaded with up to four children, a procession of couples in black coats inched arm in arm towards the far side. Everyone was clinging to someone out on the ice. Even the shivering nuns had each other to keep them upright.

At the first of the arctic pile-ups, a newly engaged

couple were posing for a photo. The girl had been helped onto a chunk of ice, while the boy stood stalwart at her side doing his best to be a man. For every couple, the slipping and sliding was an excuse to touch more than decency would otherwise allow. Hidden hands were clasped in pockets, contours bundled up in thick coats were cautiously explored. On the ice, giggling and tickling exceeded quayside quotas. A sudden lull in the affectionate banter didn't mean a couple had plunged through the frozen surface. Most likely, they had disappeared behind an upturned ice sheet or the bow of an ice-locked barge to steal a kiss.

I clambered over a wall of ice and squeezed through the smallest of gaps. The snow of recent weeks had turned hard and grainy as sugar. My feet were wet as well as cold by now, dark rings spreading through the leather of my shoes, and I could just picture my mother glaring down at them with pursed lips and a slow shake of the head. I plodded on regardless. Slabs of ice had surged together, driving each other higher, and it was child's play to slip away unseen among those odd little peaks.

Something deep inside the ice rumbled, a sound like stones thundering down a quarry. I stiffened. When no cracks appeared, I clambered on. Soon the only voices I could hear were children's shrieks deadened by the cold air. A minute more and I was alone with the panting of my own breath and the creak of my footsteps, occasionally interrupted by sounds from the ice.

The sun sought me out in a clearing among the stacks and warmed me gently. The ice lay smooth and dark, a sign that hardly anyone had been there before me. The thought of metres of black water beneath me sent a queasy ripple through my insides and I wondered if there was a word for fear of depths. Perhaps the river was frozen solid. Hesitantly, I scuffed and skidded into the open, a sort of pond where I could have skated in circles. The icy ramparts hid the quay from view and, turning my back on the Waal Bridge, I could see only white, edged with gold from the setting sun. My very own North Pole.

Then came shuffling and scratching. His shadow appeared first and he followed, pawing his way through the ice wall. More coat than man, scarf pulled up over his nose.

"Welcome," I said, as if inviting him in.

"Oh, I'm sorry," the coat said, startled. "I hadn't expected to find anyone here." He tugged down his scarf to reveal his face. Ice crystals clung to his eyebrows. Gloved hands slapped streaks of snow from his coat. "I fancied a ramble, but I had no idea it would be so hard to find the quay again."

"It's not so far," I said.

"Well, that's a relief."

With the sun almost gone, the shadows reached full stretch. I had stared at the white glare so long that the dusk came as speckles, not a gradual swoop.

"Beautiful, isn't it?" the man said.

"What?"

"This. It's how I imagine the North Pole."

"Mm-hmm," I agreed.

"Just once, I wanted to feel like the only person on the frozen river."

"And?" I asked. "How did that go?"

He gave an enigmatic chuckle; he had seen something beyond words.

"I've seen it too," I said.

The conversation we stumbled into was as instantly forgettable as the chitchat with customers at the florist's. Yet even after all these years, I remember every detail. The sliver of wrist between his glove and his sleeve. My surprise on seeing his greying temples when he took off his woolly hat for a moment. How his pointed nose only became handsome when I saw his whole face. The promise of a joke on the curve of his lips. I only came up to his chin, but our shadows on the ice were face-to-face. If I had leaned forward just a touch, my shadow would have kissed his on the cheek.

"Shall we?" he asked. Just like that, he and I had become "we."

"Shall we what?"

"It will be dark soon."

We clambered along for a while, one behind the other. The steeple of St. Stephen's gave us our bearings, and before long the quay came into view. The headlights of a turning car swept their beams across the ice. The light seemed to cling to us and we turned to each other to shield our faces from the glare. One moment, two, then a sheepish grin before we shuffled on.

When we reached a flatter section, the man produced a silver flask from his inside pocket. "Looks like we've survived our expedition." Relieved, he unscrewed the top and, before putting it to his lips, held it out to me. "Fancy a quick nip?"

"Why not."

"Are you sure?" he asked, pulling a face. "It's old genever. The hard stuff."

"Don't you like it yourself?"

"No, if I'm honest. But it keeps a body warm."

I put the cold metal to my lips and tilted a dribble into my mouth. "Woo-eeee," I gasped, rubbing my breastbone as if that would make a difference. "It's like swallowing fire."

"Exactly!" he grinned. "Couldn't have put it better."

A swarm of young daredevils were the only ones left on the river. A policeman had appeared and was ordering them off the ice, but the louder he barked, the less the boys listened. It gave us both a chuckle. The youngsters knew no cop could catch them in this winter labyrinth.

Scuffing and sliding, we neared the spot where I had first stepped onto the river. Not arm in arm, but he was close enough to catch me if I fell. My feet were two dead weights and I had long since lost touch with my toes.

At the foot of the slope, we looked around. The cop had given up the chase and by the look of it the boys had scrambled ashore further along. We were the last to leave the ice.

"Can you manage?" the man asked. He held out his hand. "Thanks," I said, and let him help me over the smooth basalt blocks, though I was well able to negotiate them myself. As we reached the quay, I held onto his hand longer than necessary. In the dark of evening, we turned and took one last look at the Waal. Whipcracks sounded deep within the ice and the white river seemed to offer a last glimmer of daylight.

"Special, isn't it?" he whispered.

"It's lovely," I said. "And we're probably the last to see it."

"See what?"

"The river. Standing perfectly still, like this."

Mist was rising from the grainy snow. The students' lamps still lit a path across the ice, like low-slung stars.

"Tomorrow the ice will crack and burst. The river will be off and running."

"But now it's here," he said. "Before our eyes."

"Maybe that's why it's so special."

He smiled.

I did too.

It grew too cold to idle. We looked at each other's lips, into each other's eyes. Another smile, smaller this time, almost earnest.

"I'm Otto," the man said.

I nodded, understanding what he hadn't said.

"Bye, Otto." I neglected to trade my name for his.

We were heading in different directions.

"Bye then." Otto raised a gloved hand. I replied with my mitten. For a while, I could hear the creak of his shoes in the snow. Then it stopped. He turned again. Up went my mitten. He waved back. In the shadow of the warehouses, he vanished, only to reappear in the lighted circle beneath the next lamppost. Until he was gone for good, lost down some side street or other.

Otto.

In the days after, I saw him everywhere. But each time it turned out to be another man, often one who looked nothing like him. And so, the following

Sunday, I took another walk down to the Waal. The frozen surface looked intact. But as I came closer, there were waves among the white. Shards bobbed, ice sheets ground together, slabs spurred each other on. Now that it was flowing again, the river made haste, eager to atone for months of stasis. The sheltered spot where we met had long since washed away.

None of us could have known it was the last time the Waal would freeze over. What did any of us know, back then?

# 6

"What are you doing sitting here in the dark?" Tobias is standing in the doorway, bag slung over his shoulder. No Nadine this time. "It's a lovely day, Mum."

I told the nurse I had a splitting headache and that the light only made it worse. Not an excuse that will wash with Tobias. Today's programme consists of writing thank-you cards to everyone who got in touch after Louis died.

"Don't you feel well?"

"Didn't get round to it," I mumble. "That's all."

"What, too busy to open the curtains?" The runners groan across the rail as Tobias tugs them aside. The spring light is raw and unsettling. I can't bring myself to look up at the web straight away.

"I picked up your post. The cards keep coming. Every time I drop by the house, there's another pile on the doormat. I've made arrangements for everything to be forwarded before long."

"Put them on the table, son. I'll look at them later."

"Shall I make us a cup of tea?" He gets started before I can answer.

For a second, I think the moth must have escaped after all. But then I notice the white cocoon of spider's silk high in the web. A long, lifeless tuft.

"Toby?"

"Hmm."

"Would you do something for your old mum?" He'll do anything for me when I put it like that.

"Course."

"Could you get rid of that dirt in the corner of the window?"

"Where?"

I point without looking.

"I can't see anything."

"On the outside. You can probably reach if you stand on the ledge and open the window."

"Since when did a spider's web bother you? When I was young, you'd even let moths into the house when there was a cold spell." He lays off the questions and steps onto the sill to open the top window. His supple fingers pluck the web from the corner. "What do you want me to do with it?" Three steps and he's at the bathroom door.

"In the little bin, love," I say, so I can take it out and look at it in a while. But then I hear the toilet flush, so that's that. Tobias bounds back into the room with those long limbs of his.

"Got to know any of the neighbours yet?"

"A few."

"Oh yes?" he asks brightly.

"Well, no, not really."

"There are so many new people here for you to meet. A whole corridor of potential friends. Maybe even someone you used to know?"

"These four walls will do for now." He stands there looking so helpless that I want to say something to make him feel less responsible for me.

"What do you do all day, here on your own?"
"I sit here and think."
"About what?" He glances around as if my thoughts might lie scattered on the floor.
I shrug. "Nothing in particular."
"Mum," Tobias says. He thinks I'm keeping something from him.
"I sit here mulling things over, and hours go by. It happens when you're older," I tease him. "One day you'll be sat in a chair staring into space, thinking about nothing in particular." I can see in his face that he's having none of it. "It's something I've done for years but without Louis around to break the silence, one memory spirals into another."
"What kind of memories?"
"Things that happened long ago. Nothing special."
Tobias comes and sits beside me. "About Dad?"
"Of course, son." I pat his hand. "Of course. About Dad."
I work my way to the edge of the seat and try to get up.
"Where are you going?"
"To fetch the biscuit tin."
"Leave that to me." Tobias is already at the kitchen counter.
"Now tell me," I say, trying to sound as interested as possible. "How's Nadine doing?"
His smile nearly cracks his face in two. "Good," he half says, half sighs. "Couldn't be better."
"I'm glad to hear it."
"Shall we look at what I brought over?" Tobias picks up the linen bag. "Lots of sweet people with kind words for you."

A sad sack of post. We sit down at the table. I slit the envelopes, look at the tasteful pictures on the cards, peer at the names and lay them to one side. I'll leave the kind words for another time.

Tobias flaps his iPad open and his fingers dart across the screen.

"Nadine finished copying the addresses from the condolence book onto the envelopes."

I must look puzzled.

"For the thank-you cards."

"Yes. Yes, of course."

"I need to ask you about one or two of them. And there might be a few people I've overlooked."

"Yes, well, let's see."

"Jeannette and René? Was that Dad's colleague at the pharmacy?"

I nod.

"What was their surname?"

"Huivinkx."

"And they didn't write down their postcode."

"Gosh, I couldn't tell you that off the top of my head."

Tobias drums away at the screen, conjures up a postcode from the internet.

"Can you do that here too?"

"Do what?"

"Internet."

"Mum," he sighs. "I get that computers aren't your thing. But you must know by now that I have internet wherever I am?"

"Yes. Yes, of course. Even here ..." It still feels odd to be going about your business in a room that's swimming with invisible facts and figures.

"And there's an address here with no name," Tobias continues. "Krayenhofflaan ..."

"Oh, that'll be Grietje."

"Google's got nothing on you!" Tobias laughs. "You've got a search engine in your head."

Everyone is to receive a card with a picture of Louis on it. Tobias dug out a snapshot from years ago, one he took after a walk in the Hatertse Fens. Louis and I barely took any photos of each other in recent years. I couldn't find a single one of him at any rate.

"And there's a letter from someone who wasn't at the funeral. A woman called Johanna." Tobias hands me an envelope.

"That's the couple we met on holiday in Salamanca, years ago."

"I don't know them."

"Yes, you do," I say. "From Heiloo. After he passed we had his card stuck on the fridge for ages."

"Oh, right," Tobias says, so we don't have to dwell.

"Give it here so I can write something extra on her card."

Not that it'll be much. I have a hard time holding a pen steady these days. I thank Johanna for her letter and tell her it was a shock and that it still feels unreal to have lost Louis. And that I'm sure she must know how that feels. *Louis was always very fond of you*, I add. *And we often talked about you and Paul.* It's only when I scribble my name at the bottom that I realise I've written the card to them both. *Dear Johanna and Paul.* I never could get used to writing her name without his. I cross Paul's name out in a panic, but of course that's no good either. I take a new card and leave out the bit about Louis always being fond of her. Instead, I write that I hope to visit her again one day.

"There." I lick the envelope and press it shut. "Do you have Johanna's address here somewhere?"

Tobias is tapping furiously at his screen.

"Hard to find?'

"Hmm ..." He frowns and continues typing. "Sorry, had to deal with an email from work."

"What, now?"

"Yes, I'm sorry."

"Oh, that's all right, love."

"Things have been piling up these past weeks."

"Are you sure it's not too much, taking care of all this today?"

"No, not at all. Now, which address did you want?"

"Johanna and Paul's. There's nothing on the envelope."

Another snippet of information is plucked from thin air. "Okay. We're done, I think."

"Thank you, Toby."

"Unless there's anyone else you want me to look for?"

I shake my head. But just as he's about to slide the iPad into its sleeve, I ask, "Could you type in Otto Drehmann?"

"Who?"

"Otto Dreh-mann." I take a sudden interest in my fingernails so Tobias can't look me in the eye.

"Sure, hang on."

I wipe my palms dry on the tablecloth.

"Drehmann? With double *n*?"

"That's right. And *Dreh* with an *h*, I think," I say as casually as I can.

"Is it his address you're after?"

"No, no. Just look him up."

Tobias glances to the side, then continues typing. "Nope, nothing."

"Hmm." I look over his shoulder, relieved and disappointed at the same time.

"Nothing at all?'

"Only a Professor Drehmann, but he's in the States, Pittsburgh. That won't be him, will it?"

"I don't know. Can you see how old he is?"

Tobias gives a slow shake of the head and swipes across the screen. "There are a couple of articles listed. That's about it. No photo. Nothing."

"What does he teach?"

"Applied Physics. I'm not sure what that is in Dutch."

I pat his hand and tidy up our little stack of envelopes.

"Ah ... that's more like it," Tobias says, out of nowhere. "This should be him. Not the greatest of photos. Looks like our Professor Drehmann retired years ago." He holds his iPad up to my face.

Otto looks back at me from the screen. I take the device from Tobias's hand to get a better look at him, but the image becomes grainier the closer it gets. It's his face, I'm sure of it, only years older. Thin hair retreating across a pink scalp, a serious expression. The room around me begins to sway gently, with every breath the walls seem to bulge outwards and get sucked back in.

"I can't make it any clearer," Tobias says. "But let's see ..." He wants to take back his iPad but I'm holding on too tight. "Mum?"

"I-it's him," I stammer, and let go at last.

"Really?"

I get up before Tobias has a chance to read my expression.

"Would you like to send him a card too?"

"No, no. That was enough."

Otto, Otto, Otto. On my own son's iPad.

"Is anything the matter, Mum?"

"Tired," I sigh. "I'm just a little tired."

"Why don't you have a lie-down?"

"Yes, that's what I'll do."

Tobias takes me by the arm. The curtains over by the bed are still closed. The pillow is cold.

"Could you bring me my pillow from home?"

"What did you say?"

I'm too spent to scrape the words together.

"Do you want me to fetch someone in?"

"No, son, I ..."

"Has it all been a bit too much for you?"

"Yes," I reassure him. "All a bit much."

## 7

"Good afternoon," I heard Gemma say. She was sitting in the window of the florist's where we worked, busy with the spring decorations. I only looked up when the bell at the door tinkled. "Good aft—" I recognised him instantly. Otto. Still more coat than man. Ot-to, Ot-to. He hadn't noticed me. I flew over to the revolving rack on the counter and began rearranging the cards. Meanwhile he sauntered around the shop, inspecting the flowers in their buckets. His brown suit and narrow tie gave him the air of an older gent, though he couldn't have been much over thirty.

Customers were supposed to wait for me to assist them, but I left Otto to his own devices. He squatted by the buckets, picking out flowers here and there. Carnations, mostly. He had the beginnings of a bald patch. I couldn't remember a man ever coming into the shop and picking things out for himself. Usually, they stood there looking helpless and mentioned the occasion they needed something for. I could often tell from their expression who was lying and had misbehaved in ways that only a bouquet would put right.

And then Otto and I were standing across from each other with only a shop counter between us.

"Shall I add a touch of green to those?"

He was still focused on the flowers.

"Otto?"

He pulled back with a kind of a happy shock. "Hello! So here you are," he said, which made it sound like we had arranged to meet. "I didn't know that you ..."

"No," I laughed like a fool.

"I never really pass this way. I just happened to be ..." He rested a hand on the stems of the carnations. "I hadn't expected to find you here."

Gemma carried on sticking flowers into an enormous block of green foam, though I could tell she was all ears.

"Are you planning to surprise someone?" I asked to allay her curiosity.

"No, nothing surprising." His tone was almost soothing. "These are for my parents' grave."

"Oh, I'm sorry. How sad."

Our eyes met for a moment.

"That's all right," Otto nodded. A polite little thank-you nod. "It was quite some time ago, so ..." He shrugged. "I try to go every few weeks. I'm an only child."

Gemma abandoned her window display and began shifting buckets that didn't need shifting.

"Gosh," Otto said, reviving his twinkle of surprise. "Fancy meeting you here." His gaze roamed around the shop. "I've been keeping an eye out, you know." Gemma had abandoned all efforts to blend into the background and was standing behind him, staring wide-eyed to get my attention.

"And here you were all along." Afraid he might say

more, I filled the silence by tugging on the roll at the counter's edge and tearing off a length of paper. I spread a layer of lace fern and placed his flowers on top.

"It was a lovely day," he whispered.

"It was that." I reached for a couple of laurel twigs. "It will be a lovely bouquet."

As a finishing touch, I stapled a black ribbon to the paper and slid the flowers across the counter towards him. "Here you are."

Other customers had entered the shop and were making it clear they wanted helping.

"Thank you." Otto raised the bouquet to eye level. "It is lovely." I recognised that suppressed smile of his from our afternoon on the ice, lips pursed, corners of his mouth not quite curling. A mouth on the verge of a quip and then thinking better of it.

I walked off to show the next customer the flower buckets and Otto headed for the door. At the window, he stuck the bouquet under his arm and reached out with both hands to capture something that was tap-tapping against the inside of the window. He peered intently into his cupped palms and released his catch as soon as he was outside.

"Goodbye, sir," Gemma called after him. Turning to me, eyes wide with curiosity, she mouthed, "Who on earth was that?"

Years passed before it dawned on me that Otto didn't pay for his flowers that day. Louis and I were long since wed by then. I remember the kitchen of our house on Uilenborgstraat. Tobias was already a toddler and Louis came home with a bunch of carnations for

Mother's Day. He had forgotten to take the price off and I laughed louder than I meant to.

"What is it?" Louis asked.

"Oh, nothing to bother about," I said lightly. "Nothing at all."

"Don't you like them?" Louis peered at his bouquet, wondering what might be wrong. "Did I leave the price on?"

"They're lovely," I said, covering the label with my hand.

"Honest?"

"Honest."

Louis poured me a sherry, cracked open a beer with his lighter and sat down at the kitchen table. It must have been a Sunday afternoon. Tobias still went down for a nap in those days.

"You like carnations, don't you?" Louis continued his line of questioning.

"Louis, love ..."

"Hmm?" The bottle was halfway to his mouth.

I ran over and kissed him so intensely that he rocked back and forth in a daze when our lips finally parted. "Frieda," he grinned, "you never cease to amaze me."

* * *

The dark skies made it feel like twilight, though it was well before teatime. As soon as we had closed up, Gemma sprinted off on her bike to beat the downpour. The afternoon had been one long interrogation about my encounter on the ice.

I hurried over to the bus stop but had to wait as the

traffic lights let through a flood of cars. Everyone was in a rush to get home as quickly as they could. The cars were followed by men on bikes, from the university by the look of them, satchels swinging from their handlebars. I waved to a pregnant mother. She didn't see me, but her two kids—one on the front and one on the back of her bike—waved back excitedly. I had a special place in their little lives: once a week, their mother let them come into the shop and pick a flower each. Though the lights had turned red, a baker's delivery boy sputtered past on his moped. At last, I was able to dash across.

"Excuse me." A voice behind me, the clunk of a car door. At first, I had no idea the words were directed at me. "Madam ...?" A hand on my shoulder. I turned around and all I could do was smile. It was Otto.

"Hey."

"Hello!" He sounded surprised to bump into me again.

"Madam?" I asked, jokingly. "Do I look like a madam to you?"

"Sorry, 'Miss' would have been better. But I still don't know your name." He held out his hand. "I completely forgot to ask."

"I'm Elfie." A firm, cold handshake. "Have you been waiting here long?"

"Happened to be passing."

"Passing?"

"No, that's not true. Not passing at all."

"You were waiting for me?"

He gave a reluctant nod, like a little boy caught red-handed.

"How long?"

"An hour at most, I'd say."

"An *hour?*"

"I didn't want to miss you again. It was on my way. And I wanted to apologise."

I was so dazed to see him standing there, I didn't even ask what he wanted to apologise for. He came out with it himself.

"I got such a surprise, this afternoon. I didn't know what to say."

"Oh."

"And I wanted to ask you your name." A raindrop hit the paintwork of his light-blue Simca like a splat from a seagull. One, then another, then a whole lot more. "Get in, get in," Otto yelled. He yanked the car door open and reached over to unlock the passenger's side. In the time this took, I was soaked. I jumped in and slammed the door behind me. My hair was dripping and my skirt had sucked up the cold and damp in a matter of seconds.

"It can't hurt, can it?"

"What?"

"To wait for you here."

I shook my head. "I'm glad you waited."

Perhaps the rain thrumming on the roof meant he didn't hear me. In any case, he didn't answer. The water streaming down the windows reduced the outside world to pinpoints and patches. Red brake lights, the traffic lights jumping from one colour to another. A patch of brown dashed past to shelter from the cloudburst under the awning of the florist's.

And here beside me was Otto.

Extraordinarily close.

Otto.

'Where were you heading?" he asked.

"The bus stop." We practically had to shout to make ourselves heard.

"Can I drive you home?"

"Home?"

"I thought it might save you another soaking." His every advance came with a dose of common sense.

"Are you sure you can spare the time?"

He was already starting the engine. "If you want me to, I'd be only too pleased."

We took turns glancing to the side, giving each other time for sly examination, sharing shamefaced little smiles when our eyes met. He hadn't changed a bit since our encounter on the ice. And yet he somehow looked completely different from how I had remembered him.

The windscreen wiper groaned with every sweep. Up ahead, a married couple were trotting along under an umbrella. They always got off the bus at my stop and never failed to say hello to me as I got on. I raised a hand but of course they didn't see me. Had they wondered where I was today? A truck was heading towards us and I recognised Verkuijlen the butcher at the wheel. In the distance, I could just make out the bus I had missed. It stopped so often that it wasn't long before we overtook it. Further on, I looked up at Gemma's third-floor apartment. The lights were already on and, just as we passed, she drew the curtains. "Gemma," I murmured. No one saw me, no one would have expected to see me in this light-blue car, sitting beside this man. Beside Otto. I had to keep looking to make sure he was there. The lampposts flickered on one by one, a faint orange-pink that grew steadily brighter.

"Turn right here," I shouted over the din of the rain. "Then straight on until you reach St. Annastraat."

Otto's eyes were fixed on the slippery road. Whenever he caught me looking, the corner of his mouth curled ever so slightly, but he continued to stare straight ahead. His thigh was so close to mine and his hand kept reaching for my knee, only to land on the gearstick between us. That was when I caught sight of his ring finger. The gold was dull but caught the light as gold always does.

"Where to now?" Otto asked.

"Just up here." I pointed to an empty parking space not far from my house. Otto steered the car smoothly to a halt. I tried and failed to keep my eyes off the ring.

"Right then." He switched off the ignition and rested his hands on the curve of the steering wheel. Then he saw what I had seen. I half expected him to feel caught out and cover one hand with the other, to stammer some excuse. But he looked down as if his hand was missing a finger, a scar that had stopped hurting long ago. "Yes," he said quietly. "That's how things are." He fell silent for a moment and seemed to have nothing else to say.

I smiled to let him know it was all right, that I understood, and that this was as far as we would go.

"I must get on," I said. "Or they'll start to worry."

"And you? Do you have ...?"

"What?"

"Children ... a husband?"

I held up my bare ring finger.

"Yes, I'd noticed."

"And?"

"I found it hard to believe."

"I still live with my parents."

Otto nodded, digested my answer, and then looked deep into my eyes for the first time. "It was special. On the ice that afternoon. I wanted to tell you that."

"I thought so too."

"You've been on my mind. Often."

The rain had stopped, apart from the patter of drops from the tree we were parked under. Our breath and our wet clothes had clouded up the windows.

"Thanks for driving me home."

I had my hand on the handle but still hadn't pushed the door. We looked at each other's lips, at the same moment, just like that afternoon on the frozen river. "Do you think I might be permitted to kiss you?" I asked, before the thought had even formed.

He smiled. Permission granted.

Our wet coats rustled as we leaned close enough for our lips to touch, a frugal little stamp at best. Then another and my lips parted a little. By the third kiss, his had parted too. A hesitant bite at the other's open mouth. As if he wanted to give a kiss but didn't quite dare to follow through. His tentative tongue, the soft, warm taste of his mouth made me almost hungry. I put my hand on his neck, thumb behind his right ear, and pressed his mouth firmly to mine.

As we let each other go, I gave his earlobe a gentle pinch. Our noses brushed, his pupils were wide. "I have never done this with anyone else," Otto whispered. He touched his mouth, as if to make sure that I had left his lips intact.

"Me neither."
"Can I drive you home again sometime?"
"Yes, that would be nice."
Sometime turned out to be the next day.

"Ah, Elfrieda," my mother said. I was minutes late at most, but I could hear the worry in her voice. "Let's not keep your father waiting with an empty plate. Elfrieda?"

"Mm-hmm."

Until the day they died, my parents only ever called me by my full name. No one else did. I was so used to Ellie and Elfie that Elfrieda always felt so straitlaced and formal. A reminder of the woman they expected me to be.

# 8

The day after Otto had driven me home, I shut up shop to find him waiting for me again. I turned the key in the lock and, before I could take two steps, he had got out of his Simca. “Elfie!”

“Hey!”

We lingered by the car, exchanging looks, then turning away like a pair of bashful toddlers. Stealing glances, as if our kiss could still be seen on the other's lips.

“Happened to be passing again?”

“If you'd like me to drive you home,” he offered hesitantly, “I'd be happy to oblige. I'm not sure I trust those clouds.” His sentences often came with an excuse attached. “I only came by to ... I happened to be passing, so ...”

Another day passed and there he was again, mainly to let me know that he'd be busy the day after and unable to give me a lift. “But Monday's no problem, assuming that suits you, of course. Would you like me to?”

I nodded, I couldn't stop nodding.

And we kissed, we couldn't stop kissing.

The days soon grew longer and brighter, leaving no place for twilit kisses in a car parked round the corner from my parents' house. Instead, we drove through the polder and all the way out to the brickworks at Vlietberg, deserted once the workers had knocked off for the day. There our kisses grew longer, found each other's ears and throats. After, his Simca hurtled along the streets and canals so we wouldn't be late for our lives at home. Gradually, our excuses began to run out.

In exchange for my promise to sweep the shop clean and tell all the next day, Gemma agreed to leave work early and swore to keep her giggly mouth shut. I smuggled Otto through the backyard and into the warehouse. There, among the funeral wreaths I had worked on that afternoon, we fumbled and fondled. His hands found their way under my sweater and kneaded my breasts, and I was bold enough to reach down and stroke him through his trousers. His mouth close to my ear, Otto asked, "Will you ..." The rest was lost in a baffling moan.

"Will I what?" I held his face between my hands.

"Take a walk with me this Sunday?"

"A walk?" I hooted. Of all the propositions that might have come my way in this darkened warehouse, a walk was the last thing I'd expected.

"Along the beaches by the Waal."

"Are you sure?" I tugged at the ring on his finger. "On a Sunday?"

"Yes, I'm sure."

I could have kicked myself for asking. The excitement drained away, as if I had snapped on the warehouse lights. I had let her into his thoughts and now she might as well have been waiting outside in the car, a presence that had briefly slipped his mind.

"Sunday?" I asked brightly.

He nodded.

"What time?"

"After lunch?"

"Can't wait!"

His lips formed that little curve I had come to know, but his eyes wanted no part of the smile. This was how he looked when he was with me and thought of her.

# 9

"Toby, it's your mother here."

"Hey, Mum." He's in the car by the sound of it.

"Hello-o, Frieda," Nadine shouts.

"Hey Nadine, so you're there too?"

There's a metallic clang in the background.

"Is this a bad time?"

"No, not at all. I wouldn't have picked up otherwise. Only I might have to hang up when it's our turn."

"Are you working?"

"We're in a queue," Nadine chimes in. "At the recycling centre. Looks like everyone's decided that today's the day to get rid of all their old junk."

"The housing association wants us to take up the carpets ... And I'm in the middle of clearing out Dad's old shed."

"Oh," I say. "Oh, I see."

"They'll be giving us frequent dumper points next," Nadine giggles.

"Toby!" I butt in. "Next time you come over, could you bring my pillow? I just can't sleep on that spongy thing they've given me here."

"Your pillow? I'll try to remember."

There's a drone and a screech, a truck pulling up and braking.

"Is that all you wanted?"

"And could you bring over that Biedermeier chest of drawers? The one by the coat rack. Your dad was none too fond of it, but I'd like to have it here. I think we can squeeze it in beside my bed. And it'll give me room for an extra plant or two."

It goes quiet at the other end.

"Toby?"

"Uhm ..."

"Do you know the one I mean? I used to give it a good polish with beeswax every so often, remember? We kept the keys and the car insurance papers in the top drawer."

"I know the one you mean."

"No rush, mind. Just whenever you get round to it."

"That might be a bit of a problem."

"What do you mean?" I have visions of wood splintering in the jaws of a giant machine.

"We gave it to a friend of Nadine's."

"Ah, to a friend. Oh well, in that case ..."

"I thought you didn't want anything else from the house."

"Nadine, would you mind asking your friend to part with it for now? I mean, she's welcome to it in a while, when I'm ... you know, in a while. If that's all right?" Another pause comes down the line. "I promise not to keep her waiting long." No response, so I fill in the chuckle myself.

"I can ask," Nadine sighs. "It's just that ..."

"She's painted it," Tobias says.

"*Painted* it? But that was cherry wood!"

"Well, now it's lime green."

"That was my chest of drawers!" My hand tightens around the phone. "You can't just go giving my things away."

"I'm sorry, Mum. But you were pretty clear about what you did and didn't want. And besides ..."

"Besides what?"

"I mean, they're only things."

To you, maybe. I bite my tongue.

"Fair enough," I say, as casually as I can. "There's nothing to be done." The silence tells me the air hasn't cleared, so I add, "They're only things."

"Mum, I have to go. We'll talk later."

"One more thing. The Christmas cactus. You haven't got rid of that, have you?" There's a bit of a commotion down the line, the rumble of a deep voice. "Is someone else in the car with you?"

No answer.

"Hello?"

"No, no," Nadine says. "We're at the front of the queue. The man's directing us to the right container."

"You're not going to throw away my cactus, are you, Toby? That plant is older than you are."

"No, Mum." His patience is wearing thin. I've used up my last question. "Do you know what that monster weighs? Two grown men can barely shift it. We'll need a forklift. And there's definitely no space for it in your new room."

## 10

Our hedge could use a good clipping. I pause on the pavement and take in the sight of the house. Nadine hooks her arm through mine and we toddle up the path.

"Is it nice to be here again?"

"Mm-hmm."

"And it's a bit of an outing now too, I suppose."

I reach into my bag to dig out the keys, only to realise I parted with them weeks ago. "I have to ring the bell at my own front door." Nadine flashes a lipsticked smile and runs a hand across my shoulders.

"What was that?" Tobias asks, jiggling my key in the lock.

"Nothing, son."

I look up at the window of his childhood bedroom and see it stripped bare. Downstairs, all the curtains are still in place. The gaps on the sill come as a shock, left by the three plants I was able to take with me. The rest are wilting in their pots. I'm distracted by the familiar rattle of our letterbox as the door opens, bulldozing advertising leaflets across the mat. One white envelope. Tobias bends to pick up the pile and strides off down the hall with his hands full. "Time to make a start on the cupboards."

"Do you want me to tackle the bathroom?" Nadine

asks. "Everything's been cleared out up there, hasn't it?"

"Great," says Tobias. "You're a darling."

"Will you be all right, Frieda?" Nadine asks.

"Oh yes, don't mind me." With nothing left of the Biedermeier but four dents in the lino, I've nothing to lean on. The coat rack has been reduced to a row of plastered holes in the wall, so I keep my coat on in my own house. I shuffle on, and puffs of dust dance towards the kitchen. The place smells both strange and familiar, the way it used to when we came home from holiday. It's been years since I registered that smell and it occurs to me that I never will again. I stop and breathe in through my nose but it grows fainter with every sniff: the smell of damp rising through the trap door to the cellar, a hint of rubber that might be the crumbling draught excluders.

"Mum."

"What is it, son?"

"How about one last look around? See if there's anything you really want to take with you."

It's hard to swallow, their chatter echoing through our half-empty rooms, our furniture scraping across bare floors, the thud of their shoes on our stairs.

"Watch out, Mum."

"What?"

"That doorpost might be a bit tacky."

"Oh."

"The housing association insisted we give the woodwork a fresh coat of paint." Tobias shakes his head. "You must have paid fifty years' rent on this place and they still want it looking like the day you moved in. Madness." Tobias reels off everything he's done so far, the rooms he's already emptied. He looks at me and I realise that he's hoping for a pat on the back. "Thanks, son. You're doing a great job." I shake my head. "My goodness, there's so much to do."

I wander aimlessly, not really knowing which rooms I'm allowed to enter. Nadine is upstairs seeing to the bathroom with a bucket of hot soapy water, her coat slung over my old armchair. Tobias taps nervously on his phone, puts it to his ear, swears when it goes to voicemail, then sees me standing there. "Mum, could you come and take a look at this stuff?"

On the spot where the dining table once stood, Tobias has herded together an assortment of things he's not sure what to do with.

"Fine," I say, though I was hoping to escape into the kitchen. "In a little while." Tobias is doing so much for me, I can hardly refuse.

"Otherwise it'll be packed off with the rest tomorrow."

"The rest?"

"The folks from the charity shop are coming to collect your armchair, the wardrobes and that couch." Even the light fittings have been removed from the ceiling. "And they can have your bed too. Unless this guy decides it's worth his while after all."

"Our bed is still upstairs?"

"It's been online for two weeks and we've had all of one response from someone who was willing to cart it off for free. Only he was supposed to be here half an hour ago."

"Can't the two of you take it? It's a fine bed. Your dad and I always slept well in it."

"Mum, we've already got a bed."

"But what if someone comes to stay?"

"They usually sleep on the futon. And you know our house. We're short on space as it is, never mind once the baby arrives."

Tobias scoops the screws from our coffee table into a sandwich bag and tapes it to the underside of the tabletop. Handy for its new owner.

"Is there anything of Louis's that you want for yourself?"

"Uhm." Hands on hips, Tobias surveys the remains of our things. "I don't really know."

"Don't feel obliged."

"Every single thing in this house must have gone through my hands these past weeks. And I catch myself wondering how much they honestly meant to Dad."

"What do you mean by that?"

"I think life was what mattered to him. You and I. Dad didn't care much for belongings, I reckon. Not like you. You have your favourite teacup, the one Aunty Emma gave you. I know which spoon you like to stir your tea with. And I know the Christmas cactus goes way back. But it was all the same to Dad which cup he drank his coffee out of. To him, they were just things, there to be used. And what would I want with his shoes? Or that rusty old Union bike of his. Do you get what I mean?"

"Yes, son, I understand." I nod, but I can't say I follow him.

"Never mind," Tobias shrugs. "Only ... there I am upstairs stuffing his clothes into a bin bag and then ... I wish we could have some more time together. You know, just sit here on the couch for a bit."

Tobias sniffs and it's only then that I notice he's crying. And of course, that sets me off too.

"I wish Dad could follow me out to the car one last time, that we could stand there chatting on the pavement. He never failed to ask if I'd checked my oil." Another sniff and a tearful smile. "And when it was time to go, he'd say, 'Well then, dear boy ...' The only person in the world I've ever heard say that. And he'd shut the car door behind me and always forget to wave because he was too busy checking my tyre pressure." He chuckles through his sorrow.

"Your father always waved you off."

"Waved me off?"

"He'd always stand there for a while after you turned the corner. Perhaps in case you came back."

"I miss him so much at times."

I want to get to my feet, to comfort Tobias, but Nadine has come down the stairs for a fresh bucket of water and beats me to it. Mumbling words I can't catch, she presses her lips to his hair, strokes his neck lovingly. I watch from the seat of my walker.

"What about his fishing rods? Didn't the two of you go down to the river together when you were little?" Nadine asks comfortingly. "Or his tools?"

"Yes, that's a thought," Tobias sniffs. "If it's all right with you, Mum?"

"Of course, dear. You take whatever you want."

"Oh, yes, and ..." Tobias is hitting his stride. "Could I have his old wallet?"

"That old thing?"

"I found it in the drawer. Did you know he still had our passport photos from way back behind that little plastic window?"

I look out at the back garden. The grass is green and neatly mowed. You'd never know Louis had lain there. In all the time we lived here, we must have walked that path thousands of times, never suspecting it was where Louis would breathe his last.

"Dad's shed is as good as cleared too."

Tobias is fishing for compliments again but I can't muster the words. Instead, I waddle into the kitchen to make coffee. I have trouble getting going when I've not been on my feet much.

A bin bag gapes from the cold kitchen radiator and the counter is in an awful state. Two empty pizza boxes, an open packet of biscuits—not a brand we ever bought—and a half-empty bottle of cola. The tear-off calendar is lagging behind, stalled on the day I left. Happily, the coffee machine is here where it's always been. I wanted to take it with me, but Nadine and Tobias insisted on giving me a new one. Among the clutter on the counter I find a pack of coffee, half-full. I take a filter from the drawer and fill the pot with water. When I turn the tap, it feels so familiar that I let my hand rest there a while.

Without thinking, I open a cupboard to get the sugar cubes. The shelves are still stacked with groceries. It's almost a shock to see the rows of tins, jars, and boxes, waiting patiently for me and Louis to eat our way through their contents. The remains of a loaf have turned greenish-blue with mould. "Ugh." I deposit the puffed-up plastic wrapper in the bin bag and gently close the door on this corner where nothing has changed.

"We were expecting you half an hour ago," I hear Tobias say.

"What's that?" I ask.

He keeps talking. "We have to leave at two. Could you please call me back? Thank you." He must be leaving a voicemail. I steady myself on the doorpost and feel my palm stick to the surface.

"Careful, Mum. I only painted that this morning."

"I barely touched it," I say, clenching my hand to hide the white of the paint. "Do you need to head off?"

"What do you mean?"

I nod at the phone in his hand.

"Oh, that. Nadine and I have to run over to the obstetrician for an appointment in a little while. And I still can't reach that guy who wants the bed." Tobias leans on the window sill to peer down the street. A dried leaf falls from the spoonwort.

"Weren't you going to see to those?"

"See to what?"

"My plants. You were going to find them a home."

"Sorry, Mum. I ... Are you serious?"

"And now they're dead."

"Mum, I ..." He waves his hand like he's tossing something away. "Have you any idea how much I've done around here? Fuck your stupid plants."

Nadine comes sloshing out of the toilet with her bucket. "Anything the matter?"

"Nothing," Tobias says, reining himself in.

I bustle into the kitchen. The coffee is ready. My hands are shaking but I judder three mugs full and manage to get them and a plate of biscuits onto a tray.

On my way back to the living room, I catch the tail end of Tobias's muted rant. "And then she starts on about her plants dying. I should have binned the lot when I had the chance. And that tosser who was supposed to come for the bed won't pick up."

"Look, why don't I go by myself?" Nadine soothes. "You stay here. I mean it's not like it's an ultrasound or anything."

"No way," Tobias says. "I want to be there and I'm not hanging around here for the sake of that fucking bed. I'd just as soon take it to the dump."

"Let me stay." They both turn and look at me.

"Really?" Tobias asks.

"Are you sure you can manage?" Nadine asks.

"I've managed my whole life in this house. An extra hour won't kill me." I shuffle towards them with the coffee. Nadine takes the tray and puts it down on a chair. Absently, she rubs the sides of her belly, then catches me watching.

"I know," she says. "There's no hiding it anymore."

"No," is all I can say. I need to follow it up with something nice. "And why would you want to?"

Tobias plants a kiss on her hair and his hand circles her navel.

"I can wait till this chap turns up and then call an old folks' taxi to pick me up."

There's a buzz from Tobias's trousers and he fishes his phone out of his pocket. "Ah, that'll be him now." He strides into the hall with a yes and an mm-hmm. "Okay. Listen, my mother will be here to let you in. But there's no one to help carry it."

"You see," Nadine slips me a wink. "It all works out in the end." I'd swear she's arching her back so her belly sticks out even more.

"He'll be here in thirty minutes," Tobias says, relieved.

"Hurry along, then. An appointment like this is something you should do together."

I wave them off at the window, then stand around for a bit. No one in the street seems to have noticed I'm back; they're probably more interested in who their new neighbours will be. Louis and I were the last of the original occupants. I poke a finger into the soil of the plant pots on the sill, then turn to the Christmas cactus. It's a little wrinkly, but nothing that can't be remedied. "You could do with a drink." I put my knee to the pot and push with all my might. It doesn't budge. "I can't take you with me, you know."

Carefully, I break off a few sections. Perhaps I can get them to grow in my room. I take a hankie from my bag, wet it under the tap and fold them inside. Just to be sure, I break off a couple more, in the hope at least one will survive.

Out in the hall, I stand dithering at the foot of the stairs. They were one of the main reasons I couldn't go on living here. I look up. "Come on then." I gee myself up and, grabbing the bannister firmly with both hands, drag myself from step to step. Halfway, I have second thoughts, but the prospect of backing down sets my calves trembling. I haul myself up, one more step, then another, stopping to catch my breath along the way.

Tobias's old room is an empty box. I peek into the bathroom, a tile or two still damp from the mopping. I ease open the door to our bedroom. Louis's shoes are still waiting for him by the bed.

Sighing, I lower myself onto his side of the mattress, run my hands across the soft bedspread with its wash-faded colours. I remember the day I bought it: 49.95 guilders at Vroom & Dreesman. "But it'll last you a lifetime," the sales assistant promised. She wasn't far wrong.

I heave one leg onto the bed, drag the other behind it, and lie under the bedspread with my shoes on. Louis's pillow smells mostly of fabric conditioner. I reach for my own and, clutching it to my chest, make a mental note to take them both with me. The feel of the mattress brings on a familiar drowsiness. We slept in this bed our whole married life, with the wardrobe at its foot as our standard view. It never occurred to us to install a television up here. Tobias was born in this room. And we made love here until around five years ago. There was no decision, no grand finale. It just wasn't that comfortable for me anymore and Louis didn't seem fussed one way or the other. More than five years ago, come to think of it. Now that's the kind of thing Louis would have remembered.

The sound of the doorbell rips through the hollow house.

My startled heart pounds in my chest. I must have nodded off. Sighing and puffing, I try to sit up, but the warmth of the bed holds me down. I turn my head slowly, feel the bedspread against my lips, rub my cheek on the towelling sheet that covers the mattress.

A second shriek from the bell. Then the latecomer rattles the letterbox. That used to be the sound of the postman or Tobias fishing for the key on a string to let himself in.

"Oh Lou, my love. How am I supposed to say good-bye to all this for the two of us?" I fiddle with my hearing aids, try to turn them down with the nail of my pinkie. The bell still gets through, so I take the winkles from their shells and lay them on Louis's bedside table. That can be my alibi when Tobias wants to know why I didn't open the door to a man who only wants our bed because it will cost him nothing.

Fruits de mer. Louis's little joke when he handed me my hearing aids in the morning. "Your periwinkles, Ma'am." That had been our name for them ever since that holiday in Brittany, when we struggled to pick those cold, slippery little buggers from their shells. We made love that holiday, I remember. Our hands searching for each other under the covers. Or we'd slot together like a pair of spoons, back when I had no trouble lying on my side. My backside was always a perfect fit for his lap.

In the end, just lying together was enough.

# 11

For some reason, Otto kept pointing out caterpillars that afternoon. To me, they looked like brightly coloured babies' willies and I couldn't help but laugh. Not that it took much to get me giggling that day. Everything Otto said seemed to be hinting at something else. He didn't seem to mind and kept right on blethering. We both knew where our stroll along the sandy shores of the Waal was leading.

Otto pointed out yet another creature among the shrubs. "Look, this will turn into a moth too." We watched as an eyebrow crawled its way up a thick stalk.

"A speckled footman," he said with a straight face.

"A what?" Each name was more unlikely than the last, until I was convinced he was making them up for my benefit.

"I can't help it—that's what it's called."

I poked him in the ribs. "You're pulling my leg."

"And look here ..." His whisper found its way into his movements as he edged some dry leaves aside to reveal two reddish-brown suppositories. "Cocoons. Some lovely broom moths will emerge from these."

Another childish splutter from me.

Out on the river, a reluctant freighter was ploughing its way to Germany, low in the water. We kept pace with its bow, stopping along the way for me to admire assorted creepy crawlies, some as hairy as my father's ears.

Suddenly, Otto let go of my hand. I looked up and saw a family picnicking around a hamper. The father, slumped in a deckchair with his newspaper, turned the tinted lenses of his sunglasses our way.

"Anyone you know?"

Otto didn't answer.

The mother sat on a blanket at her husband's feet, keeping a watchful eye on her little ones as they splashed about in the waves. It was only when she turned to face us that I felt Otto relax. He gave them a cordial "Good afternoon." The man replied with a curt nod and carried on reading.

Bright spring sunshine warmed the loose sand. I paused to take off my shoes and roll my stockings down so that I could stroll barefoot along the waterline.

"Look," Otto whispered excitedly, putting his hand on my arm to stop me. He pointed at what looked like a shiny string of bird poo inching along a willow twig. "Beautiful, isn't it?"

"Yes, it's remarkable."

"Do you really think so?" Otto looked at me so expectantly that I had to maintain the pretence.

"Yes, of course," I blurted out. "Truly remarkable."

When he tilted an oak leaf to show me the little red spots on the underside, I gave his ribs another poke. "Ow." He stared at my hand in a daze, the look of an only child, a stranger to rough and tumble. I pinched him and nibbled at his neck until it made him laugh. He grabbed my wrist and tickled me under the arm. I sprinted off, giggling as I ran. But he didn't follow. I had to come back and run rings round him until finally he set off after me, tie flapping at his neck like someone had let go of his leash.

We wound up by a pool behind a river dune, shaded by blackthorns and willows. As we kissed, I turned my skirt at the waist to make it easier to unfasten.

"Are you sure?" Otto asked, perhaps more of himself than me. I had fantasised about this so often that doubts were the last thing on my mind. But I had never seen a man's penis before, and certainly nothing like the stiffy that bounced into view when Otto tugged down his pants.

"Ha," I blurted out. "He looks perky."

"Sorry," Otto said, and looked down at himself, a little ashamed.

"What's to be sorry for?"

"I don't really know," he stammered. "I suppose because it made you laugh."

I grabbed his shirt and pulled him towards me.

"Are you honestly sure?" Otto asked again. "We don't have to—" I pressed my lips to his to stop him talking. The moment we came up for air, he said, "I mean, you don't—" I planted another kiss on his mouth and felt a broad grin forming. Still kissing, we sat ourselves down. Otto ran a hand across my bra and one of my breasts popped out, while my other nipple played peek-a-boo over the edge.

"Just a sec," I said.

Otto leaned back. "Is something wrong?"

"No, no, everything's fine." I reached back to undo the clasp of my bra and let the straps slide down over my arms. The cups fell from my breasts. Otto was too beside himself to look. Instead, he spread his coat in the shade of the blackthorn. It looked exactly like a pair of wings. I lay down, crossing my arms over my breasts, and felt something hard dig into my back—probably a pen in his inside pocket. Most of my skin had never seen the sun, but the wind seemed even more eager to get to know me. Though my whole body was glowing, I felt goose bumps rising.

While Otto sat beside me undoing the rest of the buttons on his shirt, I peered at the erection poking from his lap. I tried my very, very best not to think of my mother, and then of course I did. "You just have to get through it," she announced one day, during a minute of instruction that was fraught with unease. I must have been around sixteen and we were sitting in the bathroom with the door locked. That's when I knew this was no ordinary talk.

"Keep still, Elfrieda." As she talked, she poked a crochet hook into my left ear and then my right, to make sure I was cleaning them properly.

"You lie back and you let it happen."

"And then what?"

"*Then* what?"

"Once it's happening." Even saying the word *it* felt wrong somehow. "What do I do then?"

The question earned me a few pats on the shoulder. "The man you marry will know. That's not something we need to worry about." Relieved, she stood up and slipped the crochet hook into the pocket of her apron. "You just have to lie still."

For years, I had imagined something pointy being poked into me down below. Something sharp as a nail. And that I had to lie still or risk a puncture.

Otto's deadly weapon turned out to be a sweet, stubby affair. When he lay on top of me, I automatically spread my legs. A curtain of hair fell in front of his eyes and a vein appeared on his forehead.

"Will you be careful?" I asked.

"Yes, of course I will."

I could feel Otto leaning heavily into my hips, his hard penis jabbing at me impatiently.

"You mustn't ... you know ... inside me. You have to be careful."

"Don't worry," he hushed. "I'll stop in time."

I had expected things to happen all by themselves, like pushing off from the top of a slide. But Otto had to reach down to help and seemed to be stirring and slapping against my thighs instead of sliding into me.

"You're too low," I whispered.

"Could you maybe ...?" he groaned. "Help a little."

"Yes, yes, I'll try."

I tilted my pelvis but what he wanted was for me to guide him with my hand. It was the first time I had touched a man like this. His penis felt hard, but soft and warm at the same time. I held it carefully between my fingertips. "Not so fast," I hushed as he entered me. Everything in me tensed, as if to shrink away from that ploughing motion of his. "Easy, easy."

"Sorry, sorry," he sighed.

"And stop saying sorry all the time."

"Yes, sorr—yes, I will," he said, straightening his arms and levering his upper body off me. "Maybe this isn't such a good ..."

"It is. It is." I pulled him towards me. I wanted the warmth of his belly against mine. "You just have to take it slow," I whispered in his ear. "I haven't really done this before."

"Of course."

"Never, in fact."

"Oh." He hesitated again. "Then are you sure you …?"

I tweaked his earlobe to make it clear that his question was superfluous. "Just be careful, that's all."

"Yes, yes of course."

The more patiently he moved back and forth, the more I was able to relax. It was unsettling to feel something inside me, down there. Moving deeper and deeper, touching places my fingers could not reach. There was friction too and I wondered if a few grains of sand had found their way in. Then came a sudden thrust, deeper still, that sent a shock right through me. "Easy, easy." Otto reined himself in until I was able to relax again. I put my hands on his buttocks in an effort to control his movements. "Keep going," I whispered, giving him another kiss so he would have no reason to think I didn't want this or ask if I wanted to stop again. His breath made jerky little noises in his throat and, wrestling free of our kiss, his jaw slackened and he raised his chin to suck in more air. I grew intensely aware of my whole body, the sand around my feet, the pen digging into my back. My nose so close to his. At the same time, I was overcome with surrender. I bent my knees a little, which let Otto thrust even deeper. An overpowering sensation, intense pleasure, beyond intense.

I closed my eyes.

Every breath he took came with a shiver or a moan. I wanted his mouth on mine, but I couldn't reach it. He went deeper, a place that didn't feel good at all but before I could tell him, the feeling shifted, became something else again. And through it all, there was the delight of the breeze playing across my skin. I never knew it had so many hands, so many fingers.

Suddenly, he slid out of me. He rolled to the side, flustered, as if he'd been handed a cup of scalding hot tea and had nowhere to put it down. "What's wrong?" I propped myself up on my elbows. "Why did you stop?"

Otto sat there next to his coat, bum in the sand, clutching his shiny penis. Milky drops spurted from the tip. Shame-faced, he scooped a handful of sand over them. At first, he looked determined to get dressed right away, but all he did was yank his underpants over his backside and tuck his penis in the front. Apparently, it was over. As if we'd been dancing and the music had stopped mid-song. Otto lay down beside me on his coat, pressed his nose to my neck, rested a hand on my stomach. To my surprise, I was holding a man in my arms. A man who seemed to need comforting. I stroked his shoulder and did my best to oblige.

Well then, I thought to myself. That was that. I've made love. I heard the screech of gulls and, off at a safe distance, the squeals of children playing. The sun was higher now, warming my shins. Happily, the breeze was still all fingers.

Clouds sailed calmly by, there was all kinds of buzzing in the air around us. One of the cows that had been standing in the water minutes ago had settled down on the sand and was batting away flies with its tail. A patch of long grass by the pool moved differently to the rest and a hare appeared, snuffling, ears twitching as it tuned into the distant human sounds. He snuffled on in our direction but we lay so still that he couldn't tell us from the blackthorn bushes.

"Are you asleep?" I asked, softly.

"No, no."

As proof, he ran a finger under my breasts and fumbled around my navel.

"What does it feel like?" I rolled onto my side.

"What?"

"When you come."

He shrugged, too ashamed to put words to the feeling. The hare froze and its ears shot up at our slightest movement, but it soon went back to nibbling the grass.

"Does it feel good?"

"Yes," he nodded. We chuckled and, for the first time since our lovemaking, he looked me in the eye.

"Would you like more?" He might have been a waiter with a tray of leftover canapés.

"More of what?"

"More of us," he chuckled. "I could ... if you like. You don't have to."

"What?"

"With my fingers...' He tinkled a piano in mid-air. "I don't know if that's something you enjoy."

"Come here with those lips of yours," I said, and we disappeared into a long kiss.

The slow slide of his palm, down from my navel, was more delicious than the breeze and all its fingers. Dawdling, he plucked at my pubic hair. I tilted my hips to lead his hand further down.

He had barely reached between my legs when the glow returned. Heat sparked by his fingertips, supple, circling. Hands that could hold a butterfly and leave its wings intact. I clamped my thighs together, afraid he might suddenly stop. This choked off his movements, so I moved for him, my breath growing fiercer. I forced his thumb down a little. A shudder tore through my spine and my forehead slammed into his jaw. "Sorry-sorry-sorry." I released the vice around his hand and his fingers got to work, more intensely now. A short circuit tingled in my nipples and across my lips. I seemed to burst open, a feeling so powerful I had to push his hand away. I slumped into a deep sigh.

Opening my eyes, the sight of a caterpillar moseying along a twig made me crease up with laughter, so loud it gave Otto the jitters. "What is it? What is it?" But there was no stopping me and before long the two of us were in fits.

We lay there, panting. I covered myself with my blouse.

"Are you all right?" I asked after a while.

Otto nodded. I leaned on one elbow to get a better look at the stillness that had come over him.

"Sure?"

Otto shot me a reassuring grin, but his eyes were unsmiling.

"I came here with my father one night," he said after a long silence.

"Here by the river?"

"Yes. I must have been around eight years old."

"What for?" All I knew of his parents was that he laid carnations on their grave. He had told me nothing else about them.

"We counted moths together."

"Is that where this fascination of yours comes from?"

"I suppose so."

A passerby would never have known we had just made love. Otto had slipped into his clothes quicker than I had.

"Why did your father want to count moths?"

"That night by the river, I thought it was a one-off. Or that it had something to do with his work. But after he died, we found a box of notebooks down in the cellar. It turned out he had been keeping a tally for decades. Here, on this very spot."

"And?"

"And what?"

"What did you do next?"

Otto gave one of his sheepish shrugs. "I carried on counting."

Wandering back over the beach, the sand felt softer and looser. Ships belching smoke overtook us, bound for Rotterdam. More than anything, I wanted to lean into Otto but anyone approaching could easily have passed through the space between us.

"Look." I pointed at something fluttering through the air to get him talking again.

"Common brimstone," said Otto. "Ten a penny in these parts."

From my coat pocket, I produced an orange I had brought for us to eat, and sat down on one of the warm basalt blocks. It was a few strides before Otto noticed he had left me behind on the embankment. He retraced his steps and crouched beside me, peering at the gulls that pattered away from the incoming waves and back to the waterline as soon as the surf retreated.

"Here." I fed him a segment of orange. The bright sun lit up a splash of tar that had washed up onto the basalt. Though it was soft, it didn't stick to my clothes. I pressed it and left a fingerprint behind. The edges of my nails were white from the orange peel. I held out the last segment to Otto. He took it between his lips but stopped short of kissing my fingers.

"Can I come too?"

"Come where?"

"On your next moth count."

"Yes," he said, surprised. "Of course you can. Are you sure you'd like to?"

I nodded and took Otto's hand, folding it until only his forefinger stuck out. Chewing on the last of the orange, he watched as I guided his hand and pressed his fingertip into the soft tar. Exactly over my own, so that we left a single imprint. I let go. He rubbed the tip of his finger and smiled when he saw there was no tar on it. I don't think he knew that my fingerprint was beneath his.

"It was lovely," I said, softly.

"I thought so too." In the brown of his iris I discovered a green fan, like the tail of a guppy. And then he let me kiss him.

* * *

Across the dinner table, I could feel my mother's eyes on me. I hunched over my custard, afraid she might notice a change. My father scraped his enamel bowl and licked both sides of his spoon. A deep sigh was followed by his standard phrase. "This bowl and spoon can go right back in the cupboard."

"Good," my mother said. "I'm glad you liked it."
Her gaze turned back to me.

"That was lovely, Ma. Shall I make a start on the washing up?"

"It's not the season for strawberries."

"Strawberries?"

"Your mouth is bright red."

"Oh, that'll be the sorbet I had this afternoon," I lied.

"Ah," she said as if she'd discovered some misdemeanour. "I thought as much."

"What?" I couldn't help feeling caught out, though I knew no one could know.

"Nothing escapes a mother's eye, Elfrieda." And she gave me a long, hard look. "Sorbet on a Sunday afternoon ... Well, well."

My father disappeared into the garden to pamper the parakeets in his birdhouse.

"You'll find that out when you become a mother one day."

"Find out what?"

"A mother knows, Elfrieda. A mother knows."

As soon as I got the chance, I hightailed it up to the bathroom for a look in the mirror. My chin and upper lip had been rasped raw by Otto's stubble. So much for my daydreams of warm, soft kisses, but at least his penis had turned out not to be sharp and pointy. I wanted so much to share all this, but who was there to tell?

# 12

Along a country road out towards the brickworks, there was a willow that wept all the way to the ground. This became Otto's new parking spot. Branches trailed across the windows in bright-green streamers, until we were tucked under the skirts of the tree. The love we made was often so fierce, so intense that I had trouble believing it was something anyone else had ever experienced. On the bus to work, my eyes wandered from face to face but not one betrayed a hint of ever having felt the same.

We found positions that touched me so deeply, tears rolled down my cheeks.

At the height of summer, the trusty Simca took us over the twisting dykes of the Betuwe polder to an orchard where ladders were propped against cherry trees. With no trace of hesitation, Otto seemed to know the way to places he had never been. The car rolled down from the dyke over a rutted track. A troop of honking geese were there to greet us and sheep stopped their grazing to eye us up. "Be with you in a sec," came a voice from a cherry tree. The farmer's body was lost in the leaves and branches, only his legs and his clogs were sticking out. His hands appeared by turns, routinely filling the bucket that hung from his ladder. "You're welcome to taste."

"We're in no rush." Otto had a way of talking to people he had never met as if they were old friends.

The fruit farmer filled two paper cones, adding a generous mound on top especially for us. "Never been as sweet as they are this summer," he drawled. "And never as juicy."

"That's good to hear," said Otto. "Worth coming all this way for."

No one else knew, of course, but those ripe, juicy cherries were our doing. As was the swarm of starlings that danced for us above the flood plains that evening.

And then there were the joys of the Forstgarten in Kleve, landscaped centuries before with the sole purpose of being admired by us that day. We crossed the border as *Herr und Frau*. Germany was only a short drive away, but another world where we were known to no one and Otto felt bold enough to walk me through the park arm in arm. We strolled, stood for a while, squinted up at the rustling treetops and marvelled at the crooked branches of the old oaks. We picked up leaves in shapes we had never seen before, and spruce needles fine as a moth's antenna. The paths were deserted. The gardeners had no doubt hidden themselves away and were peeking out at our faces to see what we made of this paradise. The culmination of centuries of work and here we were at last, king and queen come to inspect its beauty.

The Forstgarten was ours.

In other places, entire buildings had been set down for our benefit. Each stretch of water was our river.

The skies we gazed up at were filled with our clouds. And anything not yet beautiful became so when we stopped to take a look.

# 13

"Morning, Ellie."

"Hello, lad." We agreed he'd call me Ellie, though sometimes he forgets.

"I've come to turn this lovely lady into a stunner."

I was out of bed before he turned up this morning. His name has slipped my mind again, but it's the lad with the tattoo sleeves.

"Shall we give your hair a wash today?"

Swaying from left to right, I waddle in the direction of the bathroom.

"My, someone's got her skates on today."

"I want to pop over to the shopping centre before it gets too hot."

"Yes, today looks set to be a scorcher."

I'm hoping to buy a little pot so that my cactus can take root. "Do you know if there's a florist's at the centre?"

"Hmmm, can't say I do." He pats his pocket. "I'll look it up for you once we're done."

"That's sweet of you."

He's the one I feel most comfortable with, probably because he helped me shower after my first night in this bed. Others have washed me more often in the meantime.

"See anything you like?"

I must have been staring at his tattoos again. "You look like a Ming vase."

"This one"—he points to a dragon coiled around his forearm—"I had done on holiday in Thailand." He smells of shampoo, probably from the lady he showered before me.

"And this flower here is for my mother."

"Aw, that's nice." The colours are bright and seem to reach deep into his skin. "An amaryllis."

"Is that what it's called?"

"Mm-hmm."

"It was her favourite flower. I had it done after she died."

"I'm sorry to hear that. Did she die suddenly?"

"I'd just turned twenty." His fingers glide briefly over the tattoo. "But I can't remember a time when she wasn't ill."

He lets me stroke his hand. I stroke again, with my thumb this time, and point at another picture. "What's the story behind this one?" It's a swallow, bulging on his bicep.

"That stands for happiness." The swallow has a twin on the inside of his arm. "A double helping." He smiles.

"Are they working?'

He hums a little laugh through his nose. "Time will tell. They're the last ones I had done."

I can tell he's itching to get a move on, but it's so nice chatting to him after I wake up. Even worth missing my shower for.

"What was your first tattoo?"

He rolls up the sleeve of his T-shirt to reveal a butterfly. "Now I wish I'd gone for something else." He shrugs. "But I'm stuck with it for life."

"Well, it looks just fine to me." He lets me touch the tattoo. You can't feel a thing on his skin.

"Shall we get that hair of yours shampooed?"

He lets me take off what I can manage: my underwear, the nappy. And I let him help when it saves us time, like pulling my nightdress over my head once I've yanked it up. He turns on the tap and hands me the shower head as soon as it's warm so I don't cool off. I take my place in the plastic chair and point the spray at my chest so the water runs down my front and I can pee without much of a fuss.

"Okey-doke," he says. I feel the breeze stirred up by the doors whizzing open and shut. Towel, flannel, shampoo. "Oops, nearly forgot your glasses." With the lightest of touches, he lifts them from my nose and everything goes hazy. Between the running water and no hearing aids, he practically has to bellow before I can hear him. "Here we go!" His gentle fingers raise my chin and he starts to spray my hair, cupping his other hand to shield my ear. Then he guides my hand to the shower head and, as I hold it, a cold squirt of shampoo lands on my scalp. He massages it through my hair.

"Thank you," I say. And with that I mean everything he does for me. "You're a sweetheart."

He steps in front of me. On his way to grab something.

"Okey-doke," he shouts. The shower head floats from my grasp and a wave of foam streams from my forehead. "Here we go," he yells. Out of nowhere a flannel is pressed to my eyes. Everything goes black, the breath choked out of me. "No," I screech. "Let go of me." I fling off the flannel and lash out with all the strength I have in me; I lash out and I hit him. The shower head bounces off my knee and clatters to the floor. "Owww." Flecks of colour, the sting of shampoo. Anger rips through my body, but I mumble, "Sorry. Sorry-sorry-sorry."

Water spatters up my calves. Nothing moves in the haze, so I can't tell where the lad might be. "I'm so sorry." I cast around for his wrist or his arm so that I can pull him to me. I want to undo what I've done, though I'm still livid with him. "Give me my glasses."

"Here." The haze swims into focus, droplets on the lenses. The lad is on his feet, a step or two away.

"I didn't see that coming," he mutters, dazed.

"Are you hurt?"

"It's all right." He feels along his cheek and the side of his head. The ball of my hand begins to throb so hard that I can't understand why it looks the same as it always does.

"What happened there?" he asks.

"You ... you ..." No, I can't blame him. "It was an accident. I ... I wanted to grab something. But without my glasses, I couldn't see. I couldn't see your face in the way." I forget I'm undressed and try to pull the sweet lad towards me, to stroke the pain from his cheek, hold him close if need be. My hands find his hand and I caress his knuckles, his inked fingers. I tell him I'm sorry all over again.

"Don't worry. I'll be fine. These things happen."

I can't let go of his hand.

"Keep that up," he chuckles, "and you'll rub the ink clean off."

"I was only trying to grab something." I repeat the

words until we both start to believe them. "Let me see your face."

"Nah," he says, brushing it aside. "I'm the youngest of four. All boys. You learn to take a knock or two." He picks the flannel off the floor and sprays it clean.

"We still have your hair to rinse."

"Of course."

"Perhaps it's better if you wash your face yourself."

I put my hands to my eyes and rub them hard, but the guilt remains. He jokes around, paves me a way out of my unease. After a life spent fighting off admirers, no wonder I have a right hook that puts Ali's to shame. And if I wanted someone else to wash me, I could just have asked instead of decking him. I hear myself laughing as loud as I can, as if that's going to make things all right again.

Once I'm dried and dressed, he helps me over to Louis's chair.

"Shall I turn on the TV for you?"

I nod, too out of breath for words. The punch has sapped my energy. All I can do is look down at the slack, crooked hand in my lap, a strange appendage rather than a part of me. My fingers, gnarled as roots, seem to grow at different angles from each knuckle. Only the pinkie is straight, sticking out like it wants nothing to do with the rest.

"Anything else I can do for you, Mrs. Buitink-Tendelow?"

I wave my good hand, but can't find the will to look at him.

"See you next time." He lingers in the doorway, scratching at his tattoos.

"When will you be back?"

"Depends on the roster. They only call me in when they need me."

Maybe it's best if he never comes back, if he takes that punch of mine with him, far away from here. He closes the door so quietly that I have to look to check he's gone. Jamie, that's his name. "I hit that lovely big lad," I whisper. "I hit Jamie." The only soul in the world I want to tell is Louis.

## 14

As we drove along the dyke, swallows swooped down to meet us. Out of nowhere, they swerved across the front of the car, skimmed low over the road, and veered off in a crazy display of aerobatics. "That's where we're going," Otto said, pointing to a steeple and a roof or two peeping out above the trees. The rest of the village was concealed among the foliage.

I caught sight of a cemetery up ahead as we turned off the dyke. "That's where my parents are." His tone was so casual that it took me a moment to cotton on. "It looks like a lovely spot," I said finally. I wanted to say more but we had already driven past. Our half-empty suitcases slid across the back seat as we rounded the bends. The boot was full of his moth-spotting equipment, which was unlikely to get an airing all weekend.

We drove through an archway in the medieval fortifications and into the narrow streets. Otto found a parking space on a village square lined with clipped plane trees. We got out and smiled at each other across the roof of the car.

"Shall I wander over and see if they have a room?"

I nodded. It wouldn't surprise me if I said yes to everything he asked that day.

The hotel windows were made up of small panes of

brown glass, some with swirls. Outside, the air was alive with the onset of summer; inside they probably kept the lights on all year. There was death on every wall: dried flowers, antlers with a lid of skull attached, crucifixes above the door frames. The carpet was so thick, Otto and I seemed to creep across the foyer. Each time our eyes met we smiled, an endless game of catching the other looking. At the reception desk, we put our cases down on the floor.

Otto cleared his throat.

Nothing moved.

The little bell on the desk went ting-ting when I pressed it, something I had never done before in my life. Ting-ting. The curtain behind the desk was whipped open and I had a brief peek at the gloomy living quarters behind before it was whipped shut again.

"Good afternoon, Sir. Madam." The hotel owner addressed himself to Otto. "What can I do for you?"

"Do you happen to have a room available?"

"For tonight?" The owner took a reluctant browse through the big book in front of him. He had the look of a man with a cactus down his pants. "You've arrived a little late in the day ..." He flicked back and forth, though behind him rows of keys were hanging on their hooks.

"One night shouldn't be a problem," he mumbled at last. "I only have one of our more luxuriously appointed rooms available. A slightly higher price range." He peered over his spectacles at Otto, who nodded his assent.

"Your name please. For the register."

"Drehmann."

From the breast pocket of his spencer, the owner pulled out a pen and proceeded to screw the top off as slowly as possible. Then, leaning over the register, he said solemnly, "Mr. and Mrs. Drehmann."

"No," Otto said bluntly.

"I beg your pardon?" The owner and I both looked at Otto in surprise.

"Uhm ..." He scratched the back of his head.

"You are *not* Mr. and Mrs. Drehmann?"

Otto swayed from foot to foot.

"Am I to understand," the owner said with a sardonic air, "that you are not a married couple?"

"Oh, but we are," I interjected swiftly.

"Are you now?"

"Only not so long."

"I see, I see." The owner slid the top back on his pen, but did not screw it tight. "Still getting used to the idea?"

"Exactly. Sharing a surname is new to us. That's Drehmann with an *h* and two *n*'s by the way."

All this time, Otto just stood there. A timid little boy whose powers of speech had fallen through a crack between one word and the next.

"Or would you like me to write it for you?" I said.

The owner shut the register.

"What exactly is the matter?" I tried to bolster our position. "Surely you can have no objection to recently married couples?"

"In that case, I'm sure you won't mind showing me your marriage licence?"

"Uh ..." I turned to Otto. "Did you bring it with you?"

I caught the man eyeing up my hand, which I had

placed on the desk. "Your ring finger is still getting used to the idea too, by the look of things."

"I'm allergic to gold," I blurted out.

The owner frowned. Not flummoxed by my bizarre excuse but holding back his rage. "Out," he said at last.

"Apologies for the inconvenience," Otto prattled as he grabbed our cases and made a beeline for the door. I was left standing there. The hotel owner looked away. I was too filthy to even contemplate. "Out," he repeated, shooing me in the direction of my sham husband's retreat.

Otto and the cases were already halfway down the street. The cobbles were wet with drizzle but the sky had cleared again. I ran to catch up and took my case from his grip. He wouldn't let me put my hand in his. Otto was back to being someone else's husband. I could lose myself in him, but he would never be able to do the same.

"I'm sorry," Otto said. "I hadn't seen that coming."

"I understand," I said. There wasn't a lot else I could say.

"Mr. and Mrs. Drehmann ..."

"I wouldn't have minded that name for a night," I said, trying to lighten the mood.

Otto did his best to smile.

"Is it because she's already Mrs. Drehmann?"

"It was a shock to hear that man address you like that. I didn't really know what to say."

I couldn't help it. I found myself blaming her for all this. It was her fault that we were out here wandering the streets.

"Our love can never come at the expense of my love

for Brigitte." He had never said her name before. "I appear to have more love in me than I imagined, love for both of you. Thanks to you, I can be another man. And that realisation has overwhelmed me." There was no stopping him. "I try to keep my life with her unchanged. Things between us have stayed as they were. They may even have become more pleasant. But when ... when he called you by her name, I felt that I had wronged her. As if you were taking her place and I was being forced to deny her. And I ... I just couldn't do that. I'm sorry."

We had come to a stop. Our half-empty cases had become a portent that even this one night together was asking too much. A gold-coloured letterbox flapped open and a pair of child's eyes peered out at us. A ragged band of crows was circling the steeple.

"Do you want to go home?" I asked.

Happily, he said no.

"I'd understand," I insisted, trying to be more understanding than I was.

"No, honestly I don't. But I'd understand if *you* wanted to. I don't really know what else we can do."

Down the street, on a medieval house front that was leaning a little further than the rest, I spotted a sign bearing the word HOTEL in elegant lettering.

"This way," I said.

"Where?"

Otto's hand let itself be held and pulled along, to the surprise of the rest of his body. 'What are you up to?"

"Just come on, will you."

In the hotel lobby, an older woman was running an ostrich-feather duster over a row of statuettes. "Good afternoon," I called cheerily. "We'd like to book a room." The woman got such a fright that she nearly toppled a posh little table. "Let me fetch the manager for you." Otto looked distinctly ill at ease.

"A smile wouldn't go amiss."

"What are you planning to say?"

I pressed my lips to his.

"Welcome," a voice boomed. Our grizzled host was more beard than face and at first glance appeared to be wearing a jumper knitted from his own hair. "What can I do for you?" he asked, taking a draw on his cigarette.

"We'd like a room for one night." I thrust my ringless hand deep in my coat pocket. "A double, please."

"Do you have a reservation, sir?"

I glanced at Otto, who seemed to have no idea what to say. He looked at me, looked at the beard, and shook his head.

"Not that it's a problem. We still have a room overlooking the street. With a view of the steeple." He turned to face the board where the keys were hanging. "And then I have a slightly more favourable room ..."

"The first one sounds fine," I butted in. The beard nodded and turned back to Otto to state the price and the breakfast times. He took another puff and when he exhaled it was as if his beard had caught fire.

"What name can I note down, sir?"

"Tendelow," I said quickly.

"Ten-der-loo ..." The beard leaned over the book in front of him and noted my name in an elegant, sloping hand. A cautious smile lit up Otto's face, but his eyes maintained a pretence of seriousness as he watched the man write us into wedlock. "That's *o-w* at the end and there's no *r* in the middle," Otto corrected him.

"Ah, I see ..." The beard crossed out the *r* and tried to turn an *o* into a *w*. "Is that correct?" He spun the book around.

"Yes," we said in unison.

"Mr. and Mrs. Tendelow," he repeated solemnly, looking up at us. "In that case, I wish you a very pleasant stay."

"Thank you," Otto said. I gave his hand a little squeeze and he squeezed back. There we stood in a hotel lobby, pronounced man and wife by a smouldering beard who was none the wiser.

"Your room is on the second floor, Mr. and Mrs. Tendelow." It was music to my ears. I'd have given anything to hear him say it again.

"We need you to vacate the room by twelve, but there's usually a little leeway." He unhooked a key from the wall and dangled it by its label above the desk. "Now, who is the keeper of the key?" I reached out and slipped the third finger of my left hand through the ring.

"You'll find the bathroom three doors down."

As we climbed the carpeted stairs, Otto made a high-pitched sound I had never heard him make before.

"Mr. Tendelow," I tutted. "Behave yourself."

"Yes, Mrs. Tendelow," he chuckled. When we reached our floor, he hummed a little tune and danced a few steps down the hall, before flinging open the room door with a grand sweep of his arm. Seconds later, we were at each other as if we didn't have the whole night ahead of us. His hands slid under my sweater and I began to unfasten my skirt. Then Otto froze.

"What's the matter?'

"I have a little something for you."

"Oh ..."

"I contacted a former classmate of mine who works as a pharmacist." He turned towards the table and opened his case. "He gave me this." Otto handed me a featureless box, the kind lightbulbs used to come in.

"What is it?"

"Open it. It's just ... I thought perhaps ... It means we don't have to be so careful. No, I mean, it'll help us be more careful." I opened the box to reveal what looked like a doll's cap made of rubber. A ring with a little cup inside.

"I got this to go with it." He handed me a tube of spermicidal cream.

"Lovely," I grinned. "So much for romance."

"Sorry, I didn't mean it to sound like a gift. It was more ... I thought ..."

"I know what you thought," I said. He was the picture of awkwardness, sitting there with the tube of cream and his fly open.

"Shall we give it a try?"

I finished undressing and let Otto watch until I was standing there without a stitch on. Then I tiptoed across the cold floor to the folding screen that afforded a little privacy at the wash basin.

The little box with the rubber cap also contained a set of instructions with an abstract drawing, a cross-section of a woman's body that seemed to bear no resemblance to my own. But I didn't need instructions to know that I had to pop the cap in down below.

I peered through the gap in the screen. Otto had taken off the rest of his clothes and his cock was mooching between his legs, ponderous but still hard enough to bounce around when he moved. He turned and knelt on the bed to turn on the radiator, and I was treated to an unexpected view of his balls dangling between his legs. I wanted to tease him, to defuse the embarrassment more than anything, but I bit my tongue. He turned down the bed.

"Can you manage?" Otto looked over at the screen.

"Yes, don't worry."

As he waited, he looked down and rearranged his bits, which gave me the giggles.

"Does it tickle?" Otto asked.

"You mind your own business," I said. The rubber of the cap felt dry and thick as a snorkel. I could hardly get the rigid little thing wedged inside me and I didn't want to press too hard for fear of creating some kind of vacuum. I took it out and squeezed a blob of cream from the tube along the rubber rim. It may have been concocted to polish off his sperm, but it also made the rubber more pliable.

Another round of fumbling as I tried to push it in again. It occurred to me to brace myself with one foot against the wash basin and—plop—that did the trick. It was an odd feeling to have something disappear up there and become part of my insides.

I stepped from behind the screen and we both looked at my nether regions as if there was some invisible garment to be admired.

"Does it bother you?"

"I can't really feel it."
"Oh, that's good."
"Shall we give it a trial run?"

Otto's cock bobbed its assent. He blushed and pulled the sheet over his lap. I lay down beside him and pressed my cold buttocks against him. We had never made love in a proper bed, I had never breathed the scent of sex beneath a sheet. We kept at it so long that I began to chafe. His hips slapped against my buttocks and we bit our lips to muffle our voices. We had never kissed more than we did that weekend. Everywhere his tongue went, he rubbed me raw with that sharp, almost invisible stubble of his.

Before Otto, I had thought of my breasts as something to be hidden, part of a parcel to be delivered at a later date, intended for someone else. A gift to be opened on my wedding night and not a day sooner.

Since our lovemaking began, my breasts sometimes felt heavier, fuller. As if being touched had made them grow. Or it was the way Otto looked at them, held them, covered them with his cupped palms as he pressed into my back. After all those years spinning fantasies on my own, I felt that my body was in use at last. More to the point, that I was putting it to use. A strange idea that I never dared share with anyone.

I must have dozed off because I woke up in bed alone. The church clock claimed it was mid-afternoon. I had never lain in bed on a Saturday afternoon without being ill. The bells ding-donged in a bright, blue sky. Time was passing, but it had no hold on us. My stomach growled. Luckily, Otto didn't hear. He had pulled on his trousers and was sitting in the creaky wicker chair, engrossed in a newspaper, braces strapped over his bare shoulders.

In that moment, I was deeply aware that another body, distinct from mine, was sitting there, a fuddle of hair around his pink nipples, dark moles on his pale arms. And that nose of his, which seemed to lengthen when he gazed into the distance or looked up to see what was fluttering in the glow of a lamppost. I knew he worked at the university, but I had no idea what he did there. At times, he seemed almost alien to me, yet I was convinced that the little I did know encompassed the rest of him. Above all, perhaps, I loved the person I became when I was with him. The things I dared to do all of a sudden. It made me want to make love to him. To leave my mark and make him my own.

Otto rustled his way from one page to the next, quietly, no doubt thinking I was still asleep.

"Hello, Mr. Tendelow," I whispered. A broad smile stretched his lips and altered the shape of his face. "Hello, Mrs. Tendelow." This was how he looked when he thought of no one but me.

Time caught up with us in the end. I had to return home, where I struggled back into life with my parents. It was like trying to pull on an old sweater which, after each encounter with Otto, seemed to shrink a little more. Before long I could barely force my head through the neck, so tight that it almost choked me to sit opposite my father and my mother and spoon cauliflower and potatoes onto my plate. Perhaps it had always been a child's sweater and it no longer fitted because I had become a woman.

## 15

A phone ringing. I jolt awake.

I must have been dozing. The newsreader is talking at me from the TV screen. It rings again. I reach for the table but I can't pick up the phone. My thumb and the heel of my right hand are stiff and purple from the punch. Swollen, throbbing with pain. I barely slept a wink all night, didn't want to ask for painkillers. Luckily, I was able to hide the damage from the girl who helped me out of bed and washed me this morning.

The phone rings again. I lurch to the side and manage to pick it up with my left hand. Even that manoeuvre sends pain shooting through my other wrist.

The screen says *Tobias Mobile*. I press the green dot.

"Toby!"

"Mum," he says curtly. A man with a purpose.

"Hello, love."

"Uhm ..."

"Everything all right? Nothing the matter with Nadine, I hope?"

"No, no. I ... uhm ... Mum, you hit someone."

"What?"

"You heard me. You hit someone."

I stammer a few scraps of words and finally come out with, "How do you know that?"

"They called me."
"Oh."
"Yesterday. I thought I'd give you a chance to bring it up yourself. But you didn't. It's really knocked me sideways. I had no idea they would call me about stuff like this. They're concerned, Mum. And so am I."
"Toby, Toby listen—"
"Mum, I—" We talk over one another.
I sigh and give Tobias right of way.
"Mum?"
"Hmm."
"What the hell happened?"
"I don't know. Honestly I don't."
"They said you were confused."
"Confused?"
"You couldn't remember that young guy's name."
"Oh, for heaven's sake. He's got one of those funny names. Do you have any idea how many people I see in a week? And half of them are new. Part-time, on call, helping out for the summer ... And they're all called something. If I only had one or two names to remember, it wouldn't be a problem. Besides, I know all sorts about that boy. His tattoos and what they stand for. I know he was only twenty when his mother died."
"What's so funny about 'Jamie'?"
"It's just that it slips my mind from time to time."
"I didn't know what to tell them when they called."
"So what *did* you tell them?"
"That you've been under a lot of strain. Dad dying suddenly like that. It's been hard on you. That kind of thing."

"Well, you got that right."
"Did I?"
I nod at no one.
"Do you think that's what's behind it?"
"Behind what?"
"The punch."
"Punch? So now it's a punch? I don't know why everyone's making such a song and dance. I didn't have my glasses on. I was reaching for something under the shower and that big lump of a lad got in the way. He's not exactly light on his feet, if you know what I mean. I hit him, it was an accident. That's all there is to it."
"Oh."
"'Punch' sounds like I was trying to floor the poor soul. They've got no business exaggerating like that."
"I see, so it had nothing to do with the strain and everything being new?"
"Listen, love ..." I sigh. I want to convince him once and for all, but I'm out of words.
"Would you like me to come over?"
"There's no need to worry, son."
"Did you open the curtains today?"
"Mm-hmm."
"Mu-um?"
"What?"
"Are they open or not?"
"I was just about to ..."
"Don't tell me you're still sitting there in the dark? It's almost half eleven."
"I just haven't got around to it." I try to tug at the fabric in the hope that he'll hear the runners screech, but the smallest movement sets my wrist jangling.

"I'm trying to keep the place cool."

A wordless hiss between us.

"Mum, I'm starting to worry. It's like the other day, when you forgot that man was coming to pick up the bed."

"I already told you, I didn't have my hearing aids in!"

"Are you sure you don't need me to come over?"

"I don't need you to come over. Honest." The best way to reassure Tobias is in his own words. "It really has been a bit much these past weeks. First your dad, then the move. But there's no need to worry."

"So I don't need to come over?"

"You don't need to come over." I picture him nodding, reassured at last. And a little relieved that he doesn't have to give up another afternoon to attend to me.

"Now tell me," I hear myself say. "How are things with Nadine?"

# 16

"Elfrieda?"

The bathroom door was open a crack.

"Ma?" Only half her face was visible through the gap. "What is it?"

"Get in here." Her hand pulled me into the half-light. The door locked behind me.

"What's the matter?"

"Are you pregnant?" Her question was a fist to my gut. "Tell me it's not true, Elfrieda." Before I could stop it, my hand shot up and hovered around my navel. She looked straight at me, eyes wide, pupils sharp as pencil-points. Every line on her face seemed to be carved deeper. "This can't be true."

Sounds came out of me, not even the beginnings of words. "No," I said at last. "I'm not."

"How could you do this to me?" she screamed. "Your father was right all along. A tighter leash was what you needed. Much, much tighter. Oh Lord, dear Lord." She grabbed my wrist and held me there. I could see dizziness gathering in her eyes. "I raised your three sisters to be decent, upstanding girls. And then you, the last of them ..." She clamped a hand over her open mouth as if to hold back a ball that was trying to force its way out of her. "Tell me it's not true."

"It's not true." My voice was thinner than I wanted it to be. "I've done nothing wrong."

"Don't lie! Don't lie to your own mother." She grabbed the lid of my pail, which stood alongside hers beside the toilet. The pails we soaked our towels in every month. "Yours has been empty for six weeks now."

"You've been spying on me?"

Her hand answered, struck me full in the face. "You are bringing disgrace on this family. And yourself most of all!" She spat the words at me. "And I don't spy on anyone. I'm your mother, I have a right to know." She counted the weeks on her fingers. "Four, five ..." Having run out of fingers on one hand, she enlisted the other. "It's at least seven weeks since you've ..." She gave a short, sharp nod in the direction of my belly.

"Why are you getting so worked up?" I snapped.

"*What* did you just say to me?"

"I've been irregular before."

"Who have you been seeing?"

"No one."

"Don't play innocent with me, Elfrieda. First it was strawberry sorbets. Then that weekend away with Gemma. And back too late for Mass on Sunday. I know what you've been up to."

"I've been using sanitary napkins," I blurted out.

"What?"

"That's why my pail is empty."

"Sanitary napkins?"

"I flush them down the toilet." My mother glanced at the white toilet bowl and then back at me.

"I got them from Gemma. She said they were worth

a try." For a second or two, the cramped bathroom was filled with nothing but breathing.

"Is this true?" she asked, more suspicious than angry. "Is this God's honest truth?"

I nodded, kept on nodding.

"Then why didn't you say so?"

"How was I supposed to know that—"

"Night after night I lay awake," she groaned. "I'm so glad I didn't tell your father. It would have been the death of him. And you would have been out on the street in no time." She began straightening the toothbrushes on the shelf above the wash basin, then licked her thumb and wiped two white specks from the mirror.

"You have spared your father and your mother all kinds of shame. And yourself into the bargain." Her red eyes were shining. She hooked a finger under the collar of her blouse and fanned her face. "You had me in such a state, Elfrieda." She lifted up my pail. "So you won't be needing this anymore?"

"I'll clear it away myself." My words came in a deep croak. I propped myself up on the rim of the wash basin.

"I think your father will want a bit more, under the circumstances. For your board and lodging."

"Why?"

"If you're planning on using those modern napkins. They're not cheap, you know."

"I'll pay for them myself."

She bent swiftly and picked something off the tiled floor. Between two fingers, she held up a hair so long it could only be mine. She let it go above the toilet bowl and flushed. "Now I'd better get downstairs quick. Can't have your father at the breakfast table staring holes in an empty plate."

Every drop of water in my body became part of a wave that sloshed around inside me. I sank down onto the toilet and cooled my head against the tiled wall.

"Elfrieda?" my mother shouted up from the kitchen. "Watch the time!"

How long had I been seeing Otto? Six weeks, maybe seven? Even longer, perhaps, since our first walk together. It was true, my time of the month had been irregular. I never kept track, just responded to the tell-tale signs: cramps, a smear of blood. I pulled down my underwear to check. It was clean.

"Elfrieda!" She was at the bottom of the stairs now. "El-frie-da? Can you hear me?"

"Yes, Mother."

"Your bus leaves in a few minutes."

I don't know what rattled me most, my mother's rage or the bright intensity of her relief when I sold her a lie she could believe in.

"What on earth are you doing up there?"

"Nothing. I'm coming."

When I finally rose to my feet, I pulled my cardigan down tight over my waist. I didn't dare look in the mirror.

## 17

Walking to the bus stop, I was keenly aware of myself, of every step. The fact of my breathing, each detail that caught my eye, my heel connecting with the pavement and my weight rolling through to the ball of my foot. Suddenly, walking seemed like an impossible task, yet I kept putting one foot in front of the other. I even made it to the bus stop in time. I nodded to the others in the queue, faces I saw every working day, but it was like playing a part. I heard myself say hello to the driver. Each letter of the word quivered in mid-air but no one took the slightest notice. At the shop, I arranged flowers into bouquets and told customers to have a nice day.

In quiet moments, behind the counter where no one could see, I kept putting my hands on my belly. It was like being a girl again and unable to resist prodding a loose tooth with the tip of my tongue. Perhaps my tummy did feel harder, but then I had trouble recalling how it had felt before. Another visit to the toilet might put everything right, but I was afraid to go too often. The owner, Mr. Vlessing, had put in an appearance that morning. We called him "the doughnut" behind his back.

Gemma and I stood in the yard out back at break

time, puffing away at one last cigarette. There was still a thin rim of shade before the sun was at its highest.

"Ellie?"

"Hmm?"

"Is something the matter?"

"Why?"

"You're so ... I don't know. You've barely said a word to me all day."

"I think I might be pregnant." The words just came out of me. I couldn't believe I'd said them.

"*What?*" Gemma glared at me as if I'd told her I had some awful disease. "You can't be!"

"I might be."

"What do you mean 'might'?" Gemma held my wrist so I couldn't run from her questions. "When was your last period?"

"I don't know exactly."

"You can count back, can't you?"

"I usually feel a cramp. And then it starts the next day. Or the day after. I've never kept track."

"But can't you remember the last one?"

I took another draw on our shared ciggie. I hadn't been expecting all these questions. But then I hadn't expected to blurt it all out in the first place.

"Look at me," Gemma whispered.

I blew a plume of smoke and looked off to the side. Playing for time.

"Is it Otto's?"

I handed Gemma the cigarette but it went unsmoked. She stared until I had no choice but to look her in the eye. "Otto was really careful," I whispered. "He even gave me something to put in before we ..."

I was desperately sorry that I had ever started this conversation.

"A pessary?"

I nodded.

"For how long?"

"Almost every time."

"And the other times?"

"He was ever so careful."

Gemma sucked cigarette smoke deep into her lungs to help her think. She exhaled a slow, steady stream, then said softly, "You can't get pregnant just like that."

"No?"

"We've been trying for a year."

"Really?" I could feel a space opening in my chest.

"The priest even came knocking, asked us whether it wasn't time to start a family."

"So it doesn't happen just like that?"

"Not for us anyway."

It doesn't happen just like that. The words echoed through my head. I can't get pregnant just like that.

"Does this Otto of yours have children with his wife?"

"Not that I know of." It felt like I was betraying his secrets. "They've been married for years. Maybe it's not that easy for him, either."

From the warehouse, we could hear Vlessing's heavy shoes clumping in our direction. "Come now, young ladies. You're not being paid to gossip."

"We're coming, sir." The doughnut only called us "young ladies" when his wife wasn't in the shop.

"Thanks, Gemma," I said quietly and gave her a hug. She kissed my cheek.

"And from now on I want you to tell me everything, Ellie Belle."

"Don't I always?"

"Well, I didn't know you had done the deed, for one thing." She put her mouth to my ear. "Was it glorious?"

"None of your business."

Her laughter echoed around the yard. "Would you like to marry Otto?"

"No hope of that. As well you know."

"If she finds out another woman is expecting his baby, who knows? Maybe Otto would like that too? He's not seeing you for nothing, now is he?"

"I don't know."

"Ellie Belle ..." Gemma gave me one of her looks. Apparently, I had given myself away.

"You see."

"What?"

"You'd marry him in a heartbeat."

"Ladies!" A foghorn from the warehouse. "These buckets aren't going to clean themselves." Scrubbing out the flower buckets was one of those smelly jobs he left to us.

Gemma flicked the cigarette butt away.

"If not, you'll have to marry someone else, and soon."

"What do you mean?"

"If it does turn out you're expecting." Two twittering sparrows landed next to our discarded cigarette. They took a quick peck, then left well alone.

"You remember Jan van Hees, don't you?"

"Mm-hmm." A pasty fellow who looked like he'd been moulded out of fish meat.

"He's nearly finished his national service."

"So?"

"He always had an eye on you."

"I'm not going out with sad old Jan van Hees. Why would I?"

"If this isn't a false alarm, you'll have to do something." Gemma unrolled the hose and turned on the tap. "He's always liked you, and that's halfway to love."

A stink of stagnant ditch rose from the buckets. Gemma squirted bleach into the murky water and held the buckets at an angle for me to scrub. The space in my chest had shrivelled to a solid mass in the pit of my stomach.

"Come on, Bellie," she said when she noticed I was slacking off. "Don't leave it all up to me!"

"Gem?"

"What?"

I needed to hear her say the words again. Out loud, like a promise or a magic spell.

"What is it?"

"You can't get pregnant just like that?"

Gemma gave a weary nod.

"Could you tell me again? Please?"

"You can't get pregnant just like that, Ellie."

In the days that followed, it stopped being an obsession. Instead it lay dormant, until I caught sight of my reflection in a window or the bathroom mirror. Or when the expectant mother came into the shop to let her two children pick their weekly flower. As the kids squabbled their way past the buckets, their mother looked at me like a fellow conspirator and, for a second, I was afraid she could see right into me.

It was a feeling that overcame me again and again, the sense that other people knew more about me than I did myself.

# 18

"Listen!" Otto thrust a finger in the air. Chirps and humming sounds were coming from all directions. In the distance, the dark shapes of the brickworks lay asleep upriver.

"What am I listening for?" As soon as I said it, the sound came again, a kind of cry.

"That's a fox."

"Oh, a fox."

We were parked by the dyke. I was already slapping at my socks to stop the mosquitoes jabbing at my ankles. To be honest, I'd been hoping that "spotting moths" was just a pretext. But then Otto began to unload his equipment from the boot of the car: a big white case, followed by storm lanterns and two tripods with telescopic legs. He slammed the boot shut and a burst of starlings shot out of a nearby tree.

Getting into his car outside the station, I had been lost for words. How could I tell him about the raging panic in my mother's eyes as she confronted me with the pail beside the toilet? Besides, there was probably nothing to worry about. I was irregular anyway, and Gemma had said you couldn't get pregnant just like that. We'd been careful, hadn't we? So, there was probably nothing ... at most maybe ...

Every time I went to open my mouth, it seemed better to wait a minute, then another, and another.

And so we had driven into the flat evening landscape of the polder, its spindly roadside poplars offering precious little to hide behind. Nijmegen's annual four-day walking event was reaching its climax, and it had been easy to convince my parents that I was working late to pack up the hundreds of carnations and gladioli that would be showered on the hardy souls from near and far who crossed the finish line the next day. A pick-up stood waiting in Vlessing's backyard for us to park along the route and sell from the back of the truck. That part of my alibi was true at least.

"This way," Otto whispered mysteriously, a tripod clamped under each arm. The big white suitcase hung from one hand and three storm lanterns from the other. "I know a shortcut." His cheery disposition was unshakeable.

"Do we have to whisper?"

"Come to think of it, no, we don't," Otto said, in a whisper. He disappeared into the bushes, the glass panels of the storm lanterns tinkling as he walked. We made our way along what I took to be a fishermen's path. Otto forged ahead, despite being weighed down by his gear, while I was lashed by blackthorn branches, and my sweater kept snagging on jaggy bramble bushes. I tried to mend it by pulling the woollen strands back into line from the inside.

"This is actually an animal track," he said over his shoulder. Only then did he notice how far behind I was and wait for me to catch up. "Look." Otto placed his equipment on the ground to take a closer look at a twilit bush. On the nail of his thumb, he held up a brown moth for my inspection. "Gypsy moth. They are always male."

"Aren't there any females?"

"Yes, but they're flightless and never stray far from their cocoon."

"Gosh," I said, which was apparently all the encouragement he needed.

"In some species, the female doesn't even have wings. She can only move during mating. In the Veluwe you've got *Lemonia dumi*. The female only eats when she's a caterpillar. As a moth, she doesn't even have a mouth." Otto rattled on, a torrent of chatter that seemed to push me back into the bushes. "There's a rare subspecies of moth in which the female doesn't even emerge from her case. She's fertilised right there, lays her eggs and waits to be eaten by ...?"

Even the wildest of guesses was beyond me.

"By her own larvae!"

I felt the need to breathe through my mouth, but the air seemed to be heaving with insects. "Otto!"

"What's the matter?"

"Why are you telling me all this?"

"Sorry. I just ... I thought you might like to know."

"Can we get on with it?" I wanted air, I wanted space, and things seemed a little lighter beyond the bushes up ahead.

"Are you sure you want to go on?" Otto was trying to read my mind again. "I can take you home, if you like. I mean, I understand if this isn't what you imagined. Maybe it was a bad idea and you think this is some crazy hobby."

"Just get on with it," I said. It was the answer he'd been hoping for.

The path petered out into loose sand and a fly curtain of willow branches trailed across my body. Seeing the expanse of the river helped me get my breath back. Otto plonked his equipment down in the sand. I started towards the water's edge, but he blocked my path. "Sorry," he mumbled. "For getting carried away like that. Perhaps I was trying too hard to impress you."

I let myself be drawn into an embrace, let him calm me. "It's fine," I said. Shame set in and I hoped I hadn't ruined our evening. "I just found it hard to breathe back there."

He whispered in my ear. "You know, there are moths that latch onto each other when they mate. They can spend hours locked together." He tickled me until I burst out laughing.

All the while, worry was churning away inside me. I crouched at the river's edge and trailed my hand in the gentle waves lapping at the sand. The water felt both warm and fresh. Voices out of nowhere made me jump. Men's voices, strangers, unexpectedly close. My heart sank. Surely Otto hadn't invited a bunch of moth enthusiasts along? It took a while for me to trace the sounds to a rowing boat gliding past the breakwaters on the far side of the river. Two tiny silhouettes, small as ants. I couldn't make out the words but I heard the oars drip as they came up and disappeared into the water again. The rest of the surface was so flat and calm that it seemed to be standing still.

"It's like last winter," I said over my shoulder.

"What?"

"The river stopped flowing then too."

Otto had spread three white sheets on the grass. It looked like a spot for a picnic. But then he knotted one corner of the first sheet to a tripod and another to a willow that bent almost far enough to rest its weary head on the sand for the night. Though I didn't want to appear useless, I had no desire to ask how I could help. Instead, I picked up his little tin of pegs and began handing them to him one by one. Soon the three sheets were draped around us like curtains, a tent that wouldn't offer the least bit of shelter. "Almost ready, just a sec ..." From his suitcase, Otto produced a jam jar and a small paint brush. "The light's already fading," he mumbled. "But it can't hurt."

"What?"

"Oh, nothing. Talking to myself. I'm not used to having someone here with me."

"What's in the jar?" Joining in the conversation made things feel more normal between us.

"This is what I use to attract them." Otto strode over to a tree trunk, unscrewing the top as he went. "My secret formula."

Thinking he might want me to be interested, I asked, "So what's in it?"

"Well," he said, coming on all mysterious again. "Every lepidopterist has their own recipe."

"What was that word?"

"Lepidopterist. A grand term for a moth spotter." He held the open jar under my nose. Expecting something appetising, I took a deep, disgusting whiff of mouldy fruit. Otto chuckled. "Half a jar of syrup, a glug of wine, rotten plums. All mashed up until I'm left with this paste. Moths adore it."

"And you whip this up yourself at home?" I teased.

Otto nodded. Absurd though it was, I couldn't help but be charmed by his jar of rotten jam.

"This is how I attract the species that aren't always drawn by the light." Otto ran his fingertips down the side of a tree. "This trunk is still sticky from last time."

Thoughtlessly I said, "And Brigitte doesn't mind you cooking up this gunk in her kitchen?"

"Well, she ... uh ..."

I instantly regretted bringing her into things.

"No, I can't say Brigitte is wild about the idea." He turned his attention to daubing the bark of a tree.

"Can I have a go?"

"You don't have to, you know."

I had already plucked the jar from his grasp.

"Spread it on nice and thick."

The smell of the paste turned my stomach, but I slapped it on with gusto until patches of the trunk gleamed purple. "They can smell it from a good ten metres away," Otto said, like a father talking to a child. "Moths are far more sensitive to smells than we are." As he spoke, he hung apple peel from the lower branches. There was something strangely domestic about the scene.

"Can I ask you something?"

"Of course," he replied, sounding surprised.

"Did you and Brigitte ever want children?"

Otto stiffened. "Uhm ... Yes, of course we did."

In the twilight, it was hard to read his face, though it was turned in my direction.

"We wanted that very much," he added. "Why do you ask?"

"Just wondered."

His body snapped into action again. "Yes, we really did." He continued hanging his apple peel and seemed to have said all there was to say.

"Have I slapped it on thick enough?" I asked, mainly to steer the conversation away from Brigitte again.

"Yes, yes that's fine," he said, without looking. I put down the empty jar and the brush next to his suitcase. Above our heads, bats flew erratic circuits, flapping off towards the river, then looping back abruptly in the direction of the thicket.

"It hasn't been easy for us," Otto said. It sounded apologetic, a sorrow that didn't belong in this life here with me. "So that's why ..."

Oh, I said without making the sound. Then out loud: "Oh." And because I had to say something: "How awful. For both of you."

"Hmm." He had placed his lanterns among the sheets. He slid up the glass panels, fiddled with the wicks and checked the oil.

There seemed to be a new edge to the evening air, a substance that let me breathe more deeply. There was no way I could look at Otto, not knowing what he might see in my face.

"It's a glorious evening," I said.

"Yes, it's perfect," Otto replied. "A perfect night for moths." We both looked towards the horizon. The sun hadn't quite set, spilling pinks and purples across the darkening river.

"Tomorrow will bring a change of weather and the moths will lay low for a day or two. Nights like this are ideal." He fished a box of matches from his coat pocket. "Ready?"

"As I'll ever be."

Otto struck a match and lit the lanterns. The glass panels tinkled as Otto slid them shut, the flames hissed as he increased the flow. Beauty surrounded us. The walls of white cotton lit up and I could feel the heat from the lanterns. We might have been inside our own hot air balloon. A daddy longlegs danced past, casting an elongated shadow at my feet. The flames turned the twilit grass green, made the ragwort bloom deep gold and thickened the shadows beyond the clearing.

"Come," Otto whispered. He took my hand and led me away from the lanterns. "This is a wonderful moment." From a short distance, we looked back at the sheets, hanging like moonlit sails among the branches. The first flutter appeared. "Look." Otto pointed, eyes shining, though he must have seen this hundreds of times. "I've never watched this with someone before."

"But you have," I said.

Otto shot me a quizzical look.

"With your father."

His fingers held mine that little bit tighter. "Yes, you're right. With my father."

There was humming and buzzing from all directions. Everything that flitted through the air seemed delighted to see Otto again. Famished, they threw themselves at the light he had brought them. It was a fluttering collection of curiosities, a motley bunch that hid in shame by daylight and were now overcome with excitement. Some appeared to have been launched from a catapult, others zigzagged or spiralled uncontrollably in the direction of the illuminated sails.

“Over here.” Otto pulled me a few steps back among the bushes. “We’re standing in their flight path.” The knee-high grass swayed and rustled around us.

“What’s *that?*” I jumped.

“It’s only a hedgehog,” Otto calmed me. “He wants to get past.” Otto took my arm and bundled me to the side. “We’re blocking his route.” If all these creatures had turned out to be personal acquaintances of his, I wouldn’t have been the least bit surprised.

“Quite something, isn’t it?” he asked.

“Mm-hmm.”

“Are you cold?”

“No, not at all.”

“Wait here a moment.” Giving the sails a wide berth, he walked off. The grumpy hedgehog scurried on its way, then suddenly froze. All its spines went up and, with an unlikely show of speed, it snapped a daddy longlegs from the grass.

Otto wandered back, holding up a green bottle with a wicker basket attached. “Only I forgot the glasses. Do you drink wine?”

“I’ll give it a go.”

The first swallow pricked and tingled through my mouth. I helped myself to another swift gulp and handed him back the bottle. “Is this what you make that moth paste with?”

Otto chuckled like a naughty schoolboy. “I only give them the best.”

“Aaah!” A moth grazed my cheek and got caught in my hair, humming like a spinning top. I squealed and flapped for all I was worth. “Get it off me!”

“Easy, easy now.” Otto captured the scrabbling itch in my neck. My skin prickled from head to toe.

"A rosy underwing!" he said. "I've never seen one here before!" Otto looked at me, wide-eyed. "Never!" I half expected a round of applause. "Look how beautiful she is." Otto held his hand up to my face and slowly unfolded his fingers. I shrank back, but the moth sat perfectly still. Its wings were drab as every coat my mother had ever worn, only stained with what looked like runny lines of grey paint. "Look! Look!" Otto whispered. He tilted his cupped hand towards the lamplight. Slowly the moth spread its overlapping wings to reveal a deep-red petticoat with two black bands and white piping along the edge.

"Beautiful," I heard myself say. And I meant it.

"She's a rare one. Extremely rare!" Otto looked deep into my eyes. I had become his lucky charm. Carefully, he gave the moth back to the air. "I need to make a note of this."

By now, the white sheets were patterned with living creatures. Otto took a notebook from his case and began to make a tally, occasionally scribbling a new name on a blank line. Mumbling to himself, he went from one sheet to the next. Some moths seemed to be smuggling rose petals under their grey-brown wings.

"And this one?" I pointed out a white moth with black dots, hoping it might be another rarity. The name "ermine moth" got my hopes up but it turned out to be common as muck, as Otto confirmed by showing me tally marks by the dozen.

"I think it's beautiful anyway."

"It is that," he nodded.

Otto went on writing and counting. Sometimes he had to bring his face right up to the sheet to identify the species. We hadn't had many moments when I was able to look at him without him looking back, and I could see him as a separate being. At times it was impossible for me to accept that this man was contained by his own skin; when we were close his presence felt so much bigger than his body.

It took a while for me to notice that the flames were dimming. The first of the moths flew off, streaking the sheets grey. "Watch." Otto turned the fabric towards the one lantern that was still burning. The dirty streaks sparkled like powdered gold.

"Amazing."

"Some moths," he said with a dramatic flourish, "have stardust between their wings." We looked deep into each other's eyes for a second or two. His were wide and bright. In that moment, I think I might have caught a glimpse of his father.

We had to let the lanterns cool before we could pick them up. We moved closer so that we could see each other. He put his arms around me.

"Have you ever discovered a new species?"

He shook his head.

"Wouldn't you like to?"

"The university is full of men who walk around hoping that one day they'll be able to put their name to a theory. Or they spend a lifetime peering through their microscope to find a particle that's gone unnoticed." Otto's cheek brushed mine as he looked at the stars above us. "All those men who scan the skies hoping to see a brand-new speck." He shrugged. "None of it matters."

"Why not?"

"Whether I discover it or not, that species has always existed without me."

I couldn't tell whether I'd been stupid to ask.

"It's like you," Otto went on.

"Me?"

"I didn't discover you. You existed before I knew you."

"I'm not so sure."

"What do you mean?"

"I'm not sure I existed before I knew you." Something touched my arm and I flinched, still dreading an ambush by some creature or other. It was only Otto's hand, searching for mine.

"Perhaps you're right," Otto said. "I'm not so sure I did either."

"Then we discovered each other."

"And we get to give each other a name." Otto looked at me the way I loved most: with his muddle-headed smile. "And if I *had* known you existed ..."

"Then what?" I asked.

Otto took my face between his hands but stopped just short of kissing me.

"Well?" I said in a whispered challenge but all he did was look and look and keep on looking. "Mr. Tendelow?" All I wanted was for the world to be no bigger than the space between his face and mine. "Oh, Elfie," he sighed. He kissed my mouth, then pressed his lips to my cheeks. With every kiss I grew warmer, my tongue thickened and tingled. Otto kissed my throat. I wanted to hitch up my skirt and take him inside me then and there. Start a universe with him. A life in which I was even prepared to brew up that moth mulch of his in our kitchen.

"Come," Otto interrupted our kiss.
"Where to?"
"To the car?" He stamped my forehead with his lips and let me go.
"Uh … fine." After floating between his hands, it took a second for my head to regain its balance and settle back on my neck.

Before long, we were all joints and limbs, squeezed onto the back seat of his Simca like the wreck of a deck chair. It might have been any time of night. My right leg was hooked over the passenger seat, his arm was under my back. As we made love, I could barely feel where my body ended and his began. But his weight soon became too much for me, and pins and needles began burning in my trapped hand. He turned, sank down beside me and tried to find another place to put his legs. This left me all but doubled up, staring at the curve of my belly.
I took his hand and placed it casually below my navel. If something about my body had changed, he was the one—the only one—who could feel the difference. He trailed his hand slowly across my skin.
"Did you put your pessary in?"
"Y-yes, of course," I stammered, surprised by his question. "Always." I had inserted the cap sitting on the toilet at home, first smearing it thoroughly with the spermicidal cream. By this time, the tube was half empty. I had been so careful, I was almost convinced it would work retroactively.
"Does that thing bother you?"
"I barely feel it."
"I'm glad." His fingers circled my belly once more

and then pit-a-patted their way up to my left breast. The fact that Otto had noticed no difference made me feel light as a feather all of a sudden. “Don’t squeeze so hard!” I laughed and smacked his hand. “You’re not kneading dough.”

He took this as an excuse to kiss my nipples. I burst out laughing and felt a trickle of sperm run down my groin.

“Let’s,” I said.

“What?”

And we did what we had never done before: we made love all over again.

# 19

"Unexpected guests!"

"Oh ... uh ... hello."

Tobias comes marching in, hand in hand with Nadine.

"To what do I owe the pleasure?"

"Oh, no reason," Nadine smiles. She's glowing.

Just as well the woman who hoovered my room this morning opened the curtains. I'd have preferred her not to, but then I'd have been sitting here in the shadows and Tobias would have read me the riot act again.

"Well ..." Tobias says, as if he has something up his sleeve. "There might be more to our visit than that."

Nadine leans in for a hug and a kiss. "Hello Frieda, it's so good to see you."

"You too, love." Only the top button of her cardigan is fastened, so it sweeps down on either side of her belly for dramatic effect. I only have to raise my hand to touch it.

"We have a little surprise."

"A surprise? For me?"

"Hang on a sec," Tobias says over his shoulder. "I'll rustle us up a quick cup of tea." He stands at my kitchen unit waiting for the kettle to boil. "I want to be in on this, too."

"Of course," Nadine says. She slides a chair over from the dining table and sits down opposite me. "You should be the one to tell your mother."

"Right then, just let me turn this television off." I reach for the remote with my left hand. I've been trying not to move my right, but it still hurts. Luckily, Nadine is too busy glowing to notice. When I look at her, she arches her eyebrows even higher above her twinkling eyes.

"Here we go." Tobias arrives with three steaming mugs. "We thought you could use some cheering up, so we decided to hop in the car instead of calling." He puts my tea on the window sill and pulls up a chair next to Nadine. "We had another appointment at the clinic this morning," he says with a sly smile to the side. "And they took another ultrasound." I'm concentrating so hard on what Tobias is saying that I forget about Nadine. "Look," she jumps in, unable to contain herself, and holds an ultrasound photo in front of my face. "Here she is."

"Oh." I pull my head back but the headrest of the chair comes too soon. The contours of a small white body, surrounded by the blackness of space.

"It's a girl!" Tobias erupts. "You're going to have a granddaughter!" He leans across me. "And look, Mum, she's waving at you." The nail of his pinkie prods the middle of the white blob.

"Here's her heart," Nadine says, draped over me from the other side. "Drrrrf-drrrrff-drrff, that's how it sounded. It was just amazing." I can smell her tepid breath as it hits my cheek. "Her tiny heart drumming away, so full of life."

"A girl," Tobias says again. "It all seems so much

more real." He pulls Nadine close. "Now we know whose little heart we heard pounding away all these weeks."

I clamp my good hand around the arm of my chair. I know the walls are still standing and the ceiling is holding above me, but everything seems to tilt and slide.

"Quite something, isn't it, Mum?"

"Oh my." I have to force the words out. "This is a surprise."

Nadine can't stop smiling at me. I want to grab my mug of tea for something to hold on to, but with my right hand the way it is, I have no chance.

"Yes," Tobias says.

"Oh my," I say again. "And you've come all this way for me."

They share a quick glance. The one they share every time a name escapes me or it takes me a while to find the bit of paper with my pin number on it.

"There's no need to look at each other like that!"

"Like what?' Tobias huffs. 'How were we looking?"

"Like that ... *that*. As if you think there's something wrong with me."

Tobias shrugs. "We were thinking nothing of the sort."

"All this song and dance."

"What's that supposed to mean?"

"It's a boy or it's a girl. One or the other. That's all there is to it."

"Mum!"

"What's the difference anyway? We didn't know *you* were a boy until you were born."

"Mum, keep your voice down," Tobias says. "I am your only child. And this, this ..." He jabs a finger at

Nadine's belly with such force you'd think he was going to hit her. "Is probably the only grandchild you will ever get to see. And *this* is how you react?"

"A phone call would have sufficed."

"What on earth has got into you? Do you think you're the only one who's lost someone? I lost my father." He slams a fist against his chest. "At least Dad was looking forward to being a grandfather."

Nadine mumbles something vaguely soothing and keeps a protective hand on her belly.

"It's all about you and your grief. Meanwhile we've been working day and night to strip the house, clear out all your crap and get you set up in this place."

"That's no way to talk to your mother!" I scream.

"Oh, give it a rest!" Tobias shoves his chair out from under him and it slams into the table. "Come on. We're leaving." He's already scooped up Nadine's coat.

"We can't leave like this," Nadine gets to her feet to calm him. "Stay a while," she whispers. "You've hardly touched your tea."

A sudden silence fills the room. My heart is pounding in my ears. Tobias rubs his eyes, runs his fingers through his hair.

"Please," Nadine says and hands me my tea. "Let's all just take a moment."

I have to hold the mug in my left hand. But it's shaking so much that some tea dribbles into my lap. Of course, Tobias notices.

"Mum, watch what you're doing."

I can't find the wherewithal to answer.

"Mum, you're dripping tea all down your trousers." He grabs the half-full mug from my hand.

"What's happened to your wrist?" He puts down his own tea and squats in front of me. "Your whole hand is purple. All the way to your fingertips." The angry creases disappear from his face. "What happened? Why didn't you say anything?"

"It's all right. I'll be all right."

But I can't help wincing when he touches my wrist. He supports my hand with his, gently, as if he's lifting a bird that's crashed into a window pane. "How did this happen?" The last few grains of anger are still rattling around his throat. "Was it that punch?" His pinkie gives the purplish-red patch a cautious prod.

"Ow-ow-ow," I gasp. "Just leave it, will you."

"Try to move your fingers." I want to pull my hand back but Tobias won't let go.

"Mum, you really need to see a doctor about this." He looks up at Nadine. "We'll need to get this x-rayed, don't you reckon?"

## 20

I wind up with a big plaster mitt that reaches half-way to my elbow.

"All this fuss about nothing."

"Mum. You broke your wrist."

"Don't you start. It was only a bone in my thumb."

With one hand encased in concrete, steering my walker is trickier than ever. Never mind, I'm almost home. Despite the summer heat, I keep my coat on to stave off questions from the neighbours.

First, we had to drop Nadine at the station, so she could head home. Tobias got out of the car with her and they strolled off and stood at a distance. They talked for a while, faces close together, then Nadine gave Tobias a lingering goodbye kiss. I looked away.

Back behind the wheel, all Tobias said was "Nadine is waving." I could see her at a distance, fluttering her fingers. I stuck my good hand in the air in reply.

Then Tobias drove me to the doctor's, who referred me straight to the hospital for an X-ray. We spent all afternoon sitting side by side in waiting rooms but I'd be surprised if anyone thought we were together.

"Right then," Tobias sighs. He reaches into his bag and pulls out a leaflet on fractures and the card with the date of my check-up. He puts them down on the stainless-steel kitchen counter and runs a fingernail across the little bumps in the metal. "Oh yes, almost forgot." He fishes two boxes of painkillers from the bottom of his bag. "I'll leave these in the bathroom."

"You do that, son."

The two dining room chairs are still standing by the window opposite my armchair, just as we left them when we hurried out after this morning's shouting match. As if they're waiting for us to take our seats and pick up where we left off.

"Do you want something to drink?"

Toby shakes his head and turns towards the door.

"Not even a glass of cola?"

"I've had enough to drink today. I'd like to get home to Nadine."

"Of course."

I don't know how we're supposed to say goodbye after a day like this.

"Shouldn't you go to the toilet first? It can be a long drive in the rush hour."

"Mum, I'm forty-eight years old." A chirrup from his coat. Tobias looks at the screen and smiles. A message from Nadine, no doubt. A tap or two, then he slides the phone into his trouser pocket.

"I'll be off then, Mum."

"Okay, love. See you soon."

"Oh yes, I'll be in the neighbourhood next week. Taking the last of the junk to the dump."

"That'll be the house empty then?"

"All cleared out. At last."

A nod is the best I can do.

"And after that I can drive over and hand in the keys

at the housing association. No need for you to come along, is there?"

"What exactly does it involve?" I don't really mind what Tobias says, as long as he keeps talking and doesn't leave. "We could go together," I suggest.

"Best leave it to me. It's only a formality."

"Ah, I see. In that case ..."

"And then the whole rigmarole will be behind me." Tobias presses creases into his cheeks and massages the corners of his eyes.

"Will you pop over once you've handed in the keys?"

"Uh ... could do."

"See how you go. Don't feel obliged."

He glances at the little clock on the microwave. "Time to hit the road, Mum." He gives me a quick kiss.

"Give Nadine my love, won't you?"

"Sure will."

"Don't forget now."

"I won't." His hand reaches for the door handle.

"When all this is over, I imagine I'll be seeing a bit less of you."

"How come?" he asks.

"Stands to reason." I flutter my hand so he knows I'm not making a fuss, that I don't want to hold him up. "You know, once the house is taken care of, you'll have less occasion to drive out this way. And soon you'll have a family of your own to keep you occupied."

"Oh," Tobias says. "I ... uh ..."

"Never mind. I don't mean anything by it."

Tobias is halfway out the door, bag slung over his

shoulder. “Okay then. Bye now.” Phone in hand, thoughts already somewhere else.

“I’m sorry, Toby.” I wish I could put my arms around him. “I ...”

“It’s okay, Mum.” He backs away, one step then another, looks up from his phone. “We’ll talk it through another time.”

“You hurry off now. I’ll keep my fingers crossed for the traffic.”

## 21

It must have been mid-September.

Otto had been on holiday somewhere in the south of France and it had been nearly three weeks since we'd seen each other. The first Saturday after his return, I had to work well into the afternoon. Otto was standing by his car waiting for me, sporting a fresh haircut and a coat I had never seen him wear. In the course of that other life, his skin had turned a summer shade of brown. It changed how he looked, his hands especially. I touched his hair, ruffled it a little around the edges. And I couldn't stop myself kissing him, though that was something we never did in public. His kiss was little more than a peck to round things off and nudge me towards my side of the car. "We have the whole night ahead of us."

I had resolved to bring it up at last. Otto was already in the driver's seat, engine running, as I climbed in beside him.

The roads were busy.

It was as if we had to tune in to each other again, a feeling that harked back to our very first trips in the car, though we held hands as he drove and changed gears together. When the traffic allowed, Otto stole glances in my direction. We drove over the Maas bridge. It was late afternoon and the rays of the setting sun angled low across the water, a light that belonged in paintings.

"Would you look at that," he said. "Magnificent."

"What is?"

"The river, the light." Otto chuckled. "The sun is showing off."

"Showing off?"

"Trying to impress you. Insisting you look at him too, not just at me."

We turned off in the direction of the dyke, where the barn swallows were waiting for us again. The last chicks of the season had been chased from the nest for flying lessons and were perched on outhouse roofs and power cables awaiting their turn to fly.

"Can we stop here for a bit?" I said.

"Why?"

"Just for a look."

Otto steered us halfway onto the grassy verge and turned off the engine. The September sun was setting the Maas ablaze and the old beech trees around the city were turning a hesitant yellow. Crows circled the steeple. I still found it hard to believe that all this went on without us being there to see it.

"Are you crying?" Otto asked, after we had been sitting for a while. He sounded shocked.

"No." I heard the wobble in my voice. Tears had wet my cheeks without me noticing.

"What is it?"

"Nothing."

"And yet you're crying?"

"I want to go on seeing the world the way we see it together."

"Oh, Elfie, come now." He wiped my cheek with the

back of his hand. "I want that too." And he meant it. Otto pressed my head to his shoulder. His right hand lingered on my thigh.

"Otto?"

"Hmm?"

"I'm expecting."

Otto jolted away from me. "What did you say?"

"At least, I think I am," I added, desperate to soften the blow. "Maybe. I think I may be expecting." I reached out to stroke his face, but he recoiled. "Otto? Please?"

He opened his mouth and closed it.

"I don't know for certain," I kept on. "It might be ..." This room for doubt seemed to snap him back to his senses.

"Have you seen a doctor?"

"No, it's ... My period is late."

"Only this month?"

"It's not very regular. I've never kept track. I've never had to."

"When was the last time?"

"Three months ago, I think. Maybe two."

"And *now* you tell me?"

"You were on holiday." I didn't see why I should shoulder the blame for this. "What was I supposed to do? Turn up on your doorstep? I don't even know where you live."

"How do you know it's mine?"

"What?"

"You know that Brigitte and I ..." I must have looked at him with such venom that he didn't dare finish his sentence. "We were careful, weren't we?" he went on. "And this last while we were extra careful. You used the pessary, didn't you?" He sounded like he was scanning the small print on an insurance policy. He looked at my waist under my autumn coat. There was nothing much to see. "And you haven't ...?"

"What?"

"Well, you know. Have you only been with me?"

"What do you take me for?" I barked the words, had to fight the urge to hurt him.

"Easy now," he said, as much to himself as to me. "We don't know anything at this stage. It could well be ... if you're irregular, like you said." He put his palms to his forehead, dragged them over his eyes and down his cheeks. "Easy now."

I had hardly expected him to be over the moon, but perhaps I'd held out a little hope.

"You can't get pregnant just like that."

"That's what Gemma said."

"Gemma?"

"No one. I ... a friend ... from work."

"You mean to say you've told other people about us?"

"I had to tell someone. And anyway, she reassured me."

"How long have you known?"

"N-not that long," I stammered. "A few weeks at most."

Without another word, Otto turned the key in the ignition.

"What are you doing?"

The engine screamed.

"Where are we going?"

The car lurched into top speed, every gearchange mistimed. "To find a doctor."

"Now? Do you know someone?"

"There must be at least one doctor in this village."

A resoluteness had come over him, as if he'd had a contingency plan tucked away all along and the time had come to put it into action.

"But we don't know them."

"That's exactly what we need: a doctor we don't know." A car heading our way flashed its headlights. Otto turned his on.

"Can't we talk first? Please?" Otto appeared to be oblivious. "Why can't we go tomorrow? Or Monday?" He had shrunk into a man no bigger than his body. I was no longer sure I was actually there in the car beside him. Hunched at the wheel, he sped through the streets, tensely scanning every housefront. How he expected to find a doctor like that, I had no idea. He took the corners at full speed and slammed on the brakes to accost a cyclist.

"We're looking for a doctor," Otto shouted, winding down the window. The cyclist pointed the way, two streets along. He even knew the house number.

Almost every window in the doctor's house was a rectangle of light. We hurried up the garden path as if trying to make up for lost time. Otto was practically propelling me forward. I was a daughter who had committed some heinous act, a fire that had to be put out.

"Otto, please."

He rang the doorbell. The sound seemed to drill into the quiet inside. I started to feel sick. A light snapped on and through the frosted glass we watched a silhouette approach.

"Good evening." The girl at the door couldn't have been a day over twelve.

"We need to see the doctor," Otto said.

"He's not here at the moment." We must have looked so lost and panicked that she let us in without any further questions. "You can wait here." The girl gestured to two chairs next to the hat stand and addressed us in grown-up sentences learned by rote. "The doctor is on his rounds. He will be back presently." She was too timid to look us in the eye. "Is it serious?"

"Excuse me?"

"Are you in need of urgent medical attention?"

I shook my head. Otto nodded.

"Oh." Her eyes darted from my face to his and back. "Should I hang the lantern or not?" she said in a tone that matched her age.

"Lantern?" Otto asked.

"If the doctor is on his rounds and sees a lantern at the gate, he knows there's an emergency and he will return immediately."

"No, that won't be necessary," Otto said. "We can wait."

Before slipping back into the living room, she unthinkingly switched off the hall light. We heard a "shhh," presumably to quieten the younger children. One by one, the doors that opened onto the hall were closed from the other side. The smell of marrowbone and stewed vegetables hung in the air. The kitchen door was last to close, leaving us in twilight blue, perched on our wooden chairs. Otto cleared his throat. His coat made a noise whenever he moved, his shoe tapped nervously against the chair leg. For a moment, I thought he might pull me close and whisper that this was a mistake, an act of panic. That my news had caught him unawares. I pictured us sneaking out of the doctor's house hand in hand, without telling a soul.

"It'll be all right," Otto said in a low voice. "You don't have to be afraid."

"Of what?"

"That I'll leave you to deal with this alone."

That had never occurred to me as something to be afraid of. "But we're together, aren't we?"

Otto jiggled his leg, went to stand up, then sat back down. "I will try to help you," he said.

The doctor came in through the front door, switched the light on, wiped his feet, and walked past us into his office. A second later, he popped his head round the door and motioned for us to enter. Otto steered me inside. The room was cold and a bookshelf on the wall was filled with identical leather-bound volumes. There were knee joints mounted on a stand and a skull with a lid you could open. An unidentifiable organ was suspended in a glass jar filled with green liquid.

"Death is no respecter of dinnertime," the doctor mused. "When they go, they drop like flies." His thoughts were with the dying, his stomach crying out for soup. "What brings you to my practice?" he asked Otto, glancing at his watch. "At this hour on a Saturday evening." He still had his coat on and his bag was on his desk.

Otto cut me off at the pass. "She thinks she might be in the family way. And we would very much like ..."

The doctor turned from Otto to me with a quick nod of the head. "Congratulations."

"Could we ask you to take a listen?" Otto asked.

"Has your wife experienced any sharp pain?" The doctor's face clouded over, more tired than concerned. "Has there been any bleeding?"

Otto looked to the side, at me.

"Not really," I answered. Otto turned back to see what effect my answer had had on the doctor. It felt unreal to be answering these questions out loud, the questions of a complete stranger.

"And yet you are concerned?" He looked at me properly for the first time. "If this can't wait until Monday morning, I assume there must be some problem?"

The doctor's hands were spread flat on his grand desk. I gazed at the fingers that had just touched a dead body.

"How far along are you?"

"Could I ask you to examine her?" Otto pleaded, taking his wallet from his inside pocket. "Please, doctor. This is very important to us."

The doctor shifted a paperweight on his desk and looked at the sheet of paper underneath, as if Otto's wallet had never appeared. "Fair enough. It can't hurt to check that all's well." He waved a hand towards the examination table behind a folding screen.

Otto was ushered back into the hall. The doctor took off his coat and I was told to expose my bare belly. Once we were alone in the room, he did not say another word. His deathly cold fingers pressed my abdomen and along the waistband of my skirt. My hip bones used to stick out, but the doctor couldn't have known that.

From his bag he took a small metal funnel, so cold it gave me goosebumps. He listened in on the sounds coming from beneath my belly button, sounds I had never heard myself. He did all this without once looking at me, though I could feel his breath on my skin. I looked down at the back of his head, as if that might tell me what he was hearing. He placed his little funnel on a different spot, listened again, then nodded. "Nothing out of the ordinary," he mumbled, more to himself than to me. "Satisfactory, I'd say." He walked away and I wondered what instrument would be next, but instead he turned on the tap and washed his hands in a small basin. Otto was let back in while I made myself decent. "And?" I heard him ask before he had even entered the room. But he was made to wait until the door was closed and the doctor was back at his desk.

"On the face of things, there is nothing unusual. Provided there are no other warning signs to speak of, I see no reason to be concerned."

"Then she's not ...?" Otto asked in amazement. "She isn't ...?"

"She isn't what?"

"She's not expecting a baby?"

"She most certainly is." The doctor looked at me. "I thought you had come to see me because you were worried about the foetus."

"That's right," I said, to fill the silence left by Otto.

"Nothing at all to worry about. The heartbeat is strong and regular." He opened a desk drawer, pulled out a notepad, and penned a few hurried strokes. Date at the top, fee at the bottom.

"Are you sure?" Otto asked.

"My good man," the doctor sighed. "I heard the baby's heartbeat loud and clear." He smiled at me as if this was a little scheme we had cooked up between the two of us while we were alone.

*A heart. A baby's heartbeat.* The words pounded in my head. I wanted to feel my belly but with the two of them looking on, I didn't dare.

"Four months is my best estimate. So, the little one will be with you in the new year." He handed Otto the bill. "Here you are, sir." Otto appeared to be incapable of movement. "My bill." The doctor waved the piece of paper.

Otto took it but made no effort to reach for his wallet.

"If you wouldn't mind." The doctor gestured towards the door. "It's Saturday evening and I would like to join my family for dinner."

"Four months," Otto said at last, with a shake of the head. "Then it's far too ..."

"Far too ...? Far too late?" The doctor drummed his fingers together. "Is that what you were about to say?"

Otto looked at him, glassy-eyed.

"What is your relationship with this young lady? Are you married?" I shot Otto a quick look, unsure what we were supposed to be. Our hesitation was answer enough. "And now you are considering terminating the pregnancy?"

"No. No, of course not." I had no clue where the doctor had got that idea from. But apparently, Otto did.

"You have to help us. Please, isn't there something you can do?"

"Get out." His voice was twice as loud, as if he was shooing away a couple of stray cats. "Out. Now."

The front door slammed behind us and the porch light clicked off. Even walking in his light was too good for us. Back in the car, Otto jammed the key in the ignition but didn't start the engine. "Oh Elfie, this ... this is not on. It's really not on." He just sat there. "He heard a heartbeat." He said it emphatically, as if I was slow on the uptake. "A *heart*beat. You really are expecting. Four months gone!"

My face was hot and feverish, while my feet seemed to shrink from the cold in my shoes. I was someone with another heart beating inside them. I thought of my mother—her wild eyes, the empty pail. A heartbeat. It doesn't happen just like that.

Tap-tap-tap. At Otto's window. We nearly jumped out of our skin. It was the doctor. "Don't worry, we're leaving." Otto reached for the ignition. The doctor opened the car door. "You didn't get this from me." There was a paper bag in his hand. "I strongly advise against it, but, if you do decide to terminate the pregnancy, the young lady should start this course of penicillin ten days beforehand." Otto took the bag but the doctor did not let go straight away. "I implore you, do not do this."

"Then why help us?"

"Because if I don't, you'll find some quack who will. And there's a life at stake."

"Thank you," I stammered as the car door slammed. I pressed my forehead to the cold window. A dull sliver of moon was hanging high in the darkness. A fish hook that could lift me from the earth. It was a long, long way off.

* * *

"Ah, Mr. and Mrs. Tendelow," the hotel owner said with a smile. "A very good evening to you." He was waiting for us behind the desk in the same grey cable sweater, as if he hadn't moved from the spot in the weeks since our last visit. When I called from the shop after closing time to book the room, he had recognised our name immediately.

"I was beginning to wonder if you were still coming. And you'll be with us for one night?"

Otto nodded so he wouldn't need to answer.

"Breakfast will be served from eight but I won't expect you that early, Mr. and Mrs. Tendelow." His warm smile as he said our name gave me such a surge of hope, I could have thrown my arms around him and buried my face in his bushy beard. Mr. and Mrs. Tendelow. It would all work out. Otto squiggled a signature in the register and took the key that was waiting for us on the counter.

"I've turned down the bed. Same room as your last visit." A sly smile played on his lips. "It only remains for me to wish you a very pleasant night, Mr. and Mrs. Tendelow." He repeated our name with such relish, it wasn't hard to imagine that he was in on our little game. "And if you feel so inclined, I'd be happy to pour you a small nightcap in the lobby."

Though the room was cold, we left the heating off. The only light came from the lamppost outside the window. It felt oddly familiar to be there again. I was afraid Otto would fly into a rage as soon as the door was closed. Why had I waited? Why hadn't I taken care of this myself? Had I forgotten that he was a married man?

Instead, he lay down on the bed, coat and all. I edged onto the mattress, couldn't find the nerve to touch him. "Are you all right?" I asked after a while.

I had no idea whether he had heard me.

"Do you want to go home?"

He left that unanswered too. Cautiously, I lay down beside him. Otto was lying with his face to the wall, almost folded in on himself. It was impossible to hold him.

"I could," he whispered at last.

"What?"

"Go home." He lay silent a while. "Brigitte isn't there."

"Oh."

"She's spending the night at her sister's."

He leaned up to pull the covers over us, then crossed his arms again. I tucked my cold hands under my sweater. I was the same person I had been earlier that day. Yet everything had changed completely, now I knew there was another heart beating inside me. *A heartbeat. A baby's heartbeat. A baby.* I couldn't take my hands from my belly, though I didn't dare press as hard as I had in weeks gone by. It seemed to swell with every breath, and each time, I was afraid it would never shrink again. *A baby, a baby.* Minutes passed as we lay there, perhaps even hours.

"I'll find someone," Otto whispered in the dark. "Elfie?"

"Yes." My voice was unsteady.

"Someone to get rid of it for you."

"Okay," I answered, though I barely knew what I wanted. Or if I had a choice at all.

"There must be someone who does this kind of thing," Otto went on. "My pharmacist friend might know of someone trustworthy." Under the covers his hand found mine. "I can drive you to Amsterdam next week if need be." He said it in such a way that a whispered "thank you" was the only answer.

"Elfie?" He was almost pleading. "It's what you want too, isn't it?"

"Yes, it is." All these weeks it had been abstract, feeling my insides from the outside, searching for symptoms of something incurable, something fatal. But there was no illness. All this time, there had been a baby. A tiny heart, beating along with my own. As I lay there, it hit me that I was going to lose this baby, and Otto too. "This baby," I said out of nowhere. I had to let the words out. "Our baby, Otto."

I heard him gasp, as if his head had been held underwater. But even on dry land he seemed to be choking. "Oh God ... We tried for so long ..." *We* was back to being him and her. She was with us in the room again, though of course she had been there all along. "And now ... with you." Otto began to cry, sobs that came from deep within. He fended off my attempts to comfort him. Then his trembling hand fought its way to my belly and followed the contours of my sweater without really touching. "And you, inside you ..." I lifted the sweater but Otto pulled back from my bare skin, as if touching me would somehow make things worse. "There, inside you. A baby ..."

I longed for him to say something more. To start a sentence with "you and I." For "you and I" to become "we." For the baby to be "our baby."

The night passed and the words didn't come.

# 22

Jamie is back. I didn't hear the door but I can sense him moving around the room. He lets in a strip of morning sun.

"Hello there, lad." I cast around for my glasses.

"Good morning."

While I surface, he gets everything ready in the bathroom. As for the punch, I don't know where to start. I take a gulp of water from the glass by my bed. "Long time, no see." Day after day, I hoped it would be Jamie. But now he's here, the silent ministrations of the Polish lady don't seem so bad after all.

"Did you sleep well?"

"I slept."

"Okey-doke," Jamie says, standing two steps from the bed.

"Okey-doke," I answer, and the silence seems to stretch. It's hard to look him in the eye, so I pretend I'm still waking up.

"Ready for another rumble in the jungle?"

It takes a while to land. Then the relief washes over me and I giggle so hard it makes me wee.

"Try following up with a left hook this time."

"I'll give it a go."

He raps a knuckle on my concrete mitt. "Does it still hurt?"

"No, no. And you?"

"The pain was gone by the time I closed the door behind me. You're not the only one around here who lashes out from time to time."

"It was an accident," I tell him. "I wanted to grab something." He leaves that for what it is.

Once he has undressed me, Jamie pulls the waterproof glove over my plaster. The rubber clenches around my upper arm. "Can I sign it later?"

"Don't you dare."

He lets the water run over his wrist until it reaches the right temperature. His face and neck are tanned, shining. I see his neck muscles tense up.

"Not too warm?" He sprays my feet, carefully.

"Just right."

He hands me the shower head and picks up the bottle of shower cream standing by the basin.

"Have you been away on holiday?"

"No, why?"

"You've got a fine tan on you."

Jamie looks down at his arms. "Just been hanging around the beaches down by the Waal. Taking it easy with a few friends. Walk for a bit and you have the whole place to yourself."

I chuckle.

Jamie lets the shower cream work up a foam on the flannel. "What's so funny?"

"Nothing, I ..." I keep my memories to myself and ask quickly, "Can you get sunburned under your tattoos?"

Once he's finished washing, he lets me catch my breath on the chair in the shower. Foam has collected around the plughole and the mirror has steamed up.

"Let's get these nice and dry." Jamie takes a corner of the towel and has a good rub between my toes. I look down at my freshly clipped toenails.

"Could I ask you to help me with something?"

Down on one knee, looking up at me, it's as if he's about to propose.

"Why the laugh?" he says.

"Nothing, nothing. Never mind."

"You wanted me to help you out?"

"Could you look something up on the internet for me?"

"Now?"

"If you have a moment."

"I'm not really supposed to spend time on that kind of thing."

"I'm trying to find someone from back in the day."

Jamie dries the fold beside my little toe. "A lover, I bet."

"You might say that, yes."

"Seriously? A lover?"

I shrug, just the one shoulder. "It was a very long time ago."

Jamie slips the rubber glove from my arm in one smooth motion. "If we get a move on, I can spare a few minutes."

I thread my scrawny arms through my bra straps and bend over quickly so he can fasten the clips between my shoulder blades.

"Okey-doke ..." Jamie tugs an undershirt over my outstretched arms. Pulls support stockings over my stiff, damp feet. A quick tussle and my trousers are on too. My blouse is buttoned crooked, but I can give that another go myself later on. "Right then." I stand in front of the mirror and Jamie manhandles my hair into some kind of shape. "We've broken the house record for dressing."

Huffing and puffing, I nod in agreement.

I shuffle to the chair which I hang my clothes over at night, while Jamie sits with one buttock on the corner of my mattress.

"His name is Otto."

"Otto what?" His finger swipes the screen.

"Drehmann. With an *h* and double *n*."

"What else do you know about him?"

"My son found a photo. Just the one. From a university in America. He used to live locally." It's embarrassing how little I know about Otto.

"Does he have any children?"

"What's that got to do with anything?" I'm startled by my own indignation.

"Sorry, I ..." Jamie raises his eyebrows at me. "It's just that if you knew their names, I could look them up on social media. Looks like our Otto isn't on Facebook in any case."

"I don't think so."

"Don't think what?"

"You asked if he has children. I don't think he does."

Jamie crouches by my chair, so I can peer over his shoulder. Everything whizzes past, too quickly for me to focus on the words. He tilts his screen and shows me a series of Otto Drehmanns. "Could this be him?" He holds his phone up to my face.

"Hardly!" It's a black-and-white portrait of a German soldier from the First World War. "How old do you think I am?"

Undaunted, he continues his search. "You don't have a date of birth, by any chance?"

"Back then, he was eleven years older than me." I don't even know something as basic as his birthday.

"So, he'll still be eleven years older?"

"That makes him ninety-two." I have visions of Jamie turning up Otto's obituary on a website for moth enthusiasts, after all these years spent thinking I might bump into him one day.

"What about this guy?" It's the same grainy, sepia image Tobias conjured up for me on his iPad.

"Yes, that's him."

"Really?" Jamie beams. "Here." He hands me his phone, so pleased with himself that I can't bring myself to tell him I've seen this photo already. Otto with a little beard, a detail I hadn't even registered last time. It suits him. Glasses that were the height of fashion back in the eighties. A smart tie, that same long nose. It dawns on me that, at ninety-two, he won't look anything like this anymore.

"Your Otto has kept a low profile online. No signs of life whatsoever."

"But there's nothing to say that he's passed on?"

Jamie shakes his head as he gets to his feet. "I have to run, Ellie. The other ladies will be getting restless." He winks. "Waiting in their beds with the curtains closed." Jamie holds out a hand for his phone. "I really have to go now," he says softly, but urgently. "They've already got me down as a slowcoach."

As Jamie takes back his phone, I try to commit Otto's face to memory.

"Are you any good with computers?"

"Not especially."

"That's a pity."

"Louis was. He did all sorts on the internet."

"There's a computer in the restaurant. Perhaps there you'll have more time to poke around. And there's a printer, if you want to print out the photo."

The cheery calm of morning has descended on the restaurant. With breakfast behind them, the residents are already looking for a snack to tide them over till lunchtime. A couple of chaps parked by the aquarium are nodding off, though they've only been up for an hour or two. One table over, a gaggle of women natter away, all dolled up for an unexpected caller or their daily stroll around the shopping centre.

"Good morning, Mrs. Buitink-Tendelow." I feel as if someone's caught me staring, but it's only the lass at reception. "How are you?"

"Fine, thanks."

"You're looking tip-top again today."

"Hmmm." I give her a dismissive wave. At this age, the only things worth complimenting are the clothes we've been helped into or what the hairdresser has struggled to make of our hair.

"Could you point me in the direction of the computer?"

"Over there in the corner. Behind the plants."

I'm more restless than I've been in half a lifetime. The backs of my knees are itchy and I have a folded hankie in my good hand to dab away the sweat. I park my walker, put the brake on, and plonk myself down at the desk. From here I can follow the conversation at the ladies' table word for word, but no one pays me any notice. The computer screen springs to life as soon as I touch the mouse. With my plaster cast, I have all kinds of trouble taming the little arrow on the screen but eventually I manage to click my way to the internet. The cursor flashes impatiently in the search bar. Letter by letter his name appears on the screen. When I'm sure it's all present and correct, I press enter.

The Ottos that Jamie showed me file past. There's that soldier from the First World War again. "Ah, here you are!" Otto's face in the photo is already starting to feel familiar. That same hint of a joke on his lips—it's almost as if he's been waiting for me. Above his picture, the words *University of Pittsburgh* and below it a few titles in English, articles by the look of them. I can read the words but working out what they mean is another matter. I go back and search for an American telephone directory, but there doesn't seem to be one. I type, click and, when the words disappear without warning, I start all over again. I combine his name with Pittsburgh. *No results*. On the off chance, I try our local directory, but the name Drehmann doesn't appear in Nijmegen at all, never mind Otto Drehmann. "Don't you want to be found?" It dawns on me I've said the words out loud and I look over my shoulder, but no one has heard me. My concrete wrist is heavy and tired, the fingers of my other hand are becoming painful and slow.

All the while, Otto smiles back at me. I type my own name into the search bar to see if Otto could find me if ever he wanted to. *No results*. I have better luck with the telephone directory. *Mr. and Mrs. Buitink-Tendelow and family*. That's a surprise. I always thought all us Tendelow girls had disappeared behind our husbands' surnames. But the address is our old one. Tobias will need to remedy that as soon as possible. I want to return to Otto's photo, but I seem to have clicked the page away. I try the name Brigitte but that gives me a bunch of businesses, nail studios mostly. I type in *moths*. And then *spotting moths*. That generates a slew of random results, and soon I'm lost completely. *Spotting moths with Otto Drehmann. Does Otto Drehmann have children?*

"Where on earth are you?" I ask him.

"Excuse me. It's my turn." There's a man behind me, standing much too close.

"Leave me alone." I try to block his view of the screen with my good hand.

"But this is my time slot."

"What time slot?" He's more like a beak of a nose with a body attached.

"You have to book a time slot to use the computer."

"And where does it say that?"

"There." He nods at a sheet of paper on the wall. "I've already given you ten minutes of my time." His eyes are glued to the screen. "You were so absorbed, I thought, I'll let the little lady get on with it. Are you new here?"

"I'm nearly finished."

"Yes, but in fifteen minutes the next in line will be breathing down my neck."

"What do *you* need to look up in such a hurry?"

He looks at me, dumbfounded. "Is that any of your business?"

"I-I mean," I stammer. "It's my first time and I ..."

"There's a slot free tomorrow morning." He shows me the sheet, an overview of the week divided into little boxes. The computer is almost always booked. I get up from the chair and take the pen he holds out to me. But with my good hand in plaster I can barely write my name.

"Let me help." He takes the pen and nudges up beside me, his coffee breath wheezing in his throat. His glasses have slid down that big, bony nose of his. He winds his neck in to read his own writing and I spot a patch of stray bristles under his chin. I always gave Louis a quick once-over after he'd used the shaver.

"What's your name?" He has already written *Mrs.*

"Buitink. Tendelow as was."

"Ah, you're a Tendelow, are you?" A question I haven't heard in years. "Could you be one of the Tendelows who used to live round our way? I grew up on Willemsweg. Lammert Peters is the name." He looks at me all bright-eyed, but I can't see the boy I'm supposed to recognise in this face. "Everyone used to call me Lammie."

"Could be," I say. "We lived on that side of the railway tracks too."

"Haven't heard the name Tendelow in a long time."

"I'm not surprised."

"Why's that?"

"I have three sisters. No boys to pass on the name."

"I danced with a Corrie Tendelow once. Were you related?"

"Corrie was our eldest."

"Ah, Corrie Tendelow. Oh yes. I had an eye on her all right ..." He shakes his head and wrinkles his nose, which plays all kinds of havoc with his face. "Only she wanted nothing to do with me. Didn't she emigrate to Canada in the end?"

"Mm-hmm."

"And what was your name again?"

Why did I have to go and mention my maiden name?

"Frieda."

"Frie-da?" He repeats it to himself. Suddenly, I'm afraid of what he might remember. That after all these years something he heard from someone who heard it from someone else might pop into his brain. He gives a slow shake of the head and chuckles. "Corrie Tendelow's little sister." He holds out his hand but I'm in no mood for formal introductions, so he lowers it again.

"As I said, I'm Lammert Peters. But you can still call me Lammie."

"I'll stick to Mr Peters, if it's all the same to you."

"Suit yourself."

"See you around."

"You will indeed."

"What's that supposed to mean?"

"It's not as if we can avoid each other long in this place." The chair sighs as he sits himself down at the desk. I turn my walker around and release the brakes.

"Otto Drehmann?" he asks loudly.

I get such a fright that it stings in my chest.

"Guilty conscience?" Lammert Peters leans back and folds his arms.

"What?" I have to fight the urge to wipe the smirk off his face. "How dare you ..."

All at once, he's a crestfallen little boy. "I couldn't help it. You left your screen open."

I yank the mouse from his hand but I can't stop the little arrow whizzing around. "Easy does it," he says. I slam the mouse on the mat. "Easy now. Let me."

"I want it gone. Now! All of it!"

"No need to shout. I'm trying to help."

Clickety-click-click. A series of screens and menus flash past.

"What's all that?"

"Shh! I know what I'm doing." Dimples appear in his cheeks. "I sometimes like to take a peek at what my predecessors have been looking up." He gives a little hiccup of delight. "No one knows I can see the lot. Well, would you look at this ..." he says. "We should probably delete this one too."

"What does it say?"

He leans over to me and whispers, "Where can I buy suicide pills?"

"Really?"

His fat finger leaves a smudge on the screen. "Someone looked that up at twelve minutes past three yesterday afternoon." He leans over and peers at the calendar with the time slots.

"You should keep that nose of yours out of other people's business."

"Where's the harm?" The words *moths* and *Otto Drehmann* appear in big black letters on the screen.

"Please?" I ask softly.

"What?" Lammert looks up at me.

"Please could you get rid of everything I looked up?" He can see how upset I am and that seems to do the trick.

"Of course," he answers meekly. "Of course, I will. Look." The list of search items starts to shrink. "Here's another Otto Drehmann," he mumbles and points the arrow at it. "Gone." His finger bangs away at the keyboard while he reads everything that pops up on screen out loud. Those childish queries of mine coming from his mouth have me wincing with shame.

*Are you still alive Otto Drehmann?* In black and white on a computer screen, read out for everyone to hear.

"That was the last one," he says. Clickety-click. "Happy now? Every last Otto gone for good."

# 23

He was leaning against the Simca, staring holes in the ground. I caught sight of him across the street. He looked up, startled, then shook his head gently, as if he was seeing something he couldn't quite believe. Otto hadn't picked me up from work for days, yet there he was again. I had to bite my lip to stop myself from crying. He shrugged and held out his pale palms, as if to tell me he had come in peace, but with nothing to offer. Between one car and the next, I ran to him.

It was only inside the car that we embraced. "Oh, Elfie ..." he whispered. "My poor darling Elfie." He started the engine and turned the car around. We drove for a while, heading out of town. Not into the polder but over the hill, winding down the other side until we came to a stop at a stretch of woodland. "Shall we take a little walk?"

"If you like," I said.

Otto took the key from the ignition, and we both just sat there. I placed my hand on his. He clasped his fingers around mine.

"Have you given it some thought?" he asked, gazing out through the windscreen. The words came more easily if we didn't look at each other.

"I've thought of nothing else."

"Same here." Otto sniffed. "Have you already started?"

"Started what?"

"The course of penicillin the doctor gave us."

"Uh ... no."

"Maybe you should. He said to start ten days in advance." Otto turned his attention to the view through his side window. A cart track wound up the slope and disappeared into the mist among the trees. We could have reached those trees by now. Hand in hand, perhaps. A hilltop embrace before wandering back to the car. "I've made a few inquiries. I hope to have a name by tomorrow ... After that, we might have to act swiftly."

A flock of geese flew over, a sign pointing southwards, an arrow without a tail.

"We can't wait much longer."

"I'm not sure ..."

Otto didn't ask what I wasn't sure of. The silence held, spread in all directions.

"I might want to keep it."

I expected Otto to shout at me. To remind me that he was married and that I stood to lose everything. To ask if I understood what I was letting myself in for. That this was madness. Senseless, reckless talk. It would be a disgrace in the eyes of the world. And what about my parents? Had I thought about the damage I would inflict?

"Or maybe ..." I began, but rather than listen, Otto started the car.

"Fine." It barely carried beyond his lips.

"Fine?"

He left it at that.

We drove back into town without a word as the lampposts by the side of the road lit up one by one.

He stopped round the corner from my parents' house and kept the engine running. Just before I got out, he said, "I will help you."

"Help me?"

"With your baby."

My baby? Our baby.

Otto turned the corner at the end of the street and was gone. I stood on the pavement in front of the house, the curtains at every window drawn tight. The drizzle was so fine it was almost mist. I stood and I stood, unable to take the next step, to set the world in motion. *I will help you with your baby.* Two thumbs squeezing the hollow at the base of my throat.

"Elfrieda?"

My mother, framed in light at the front door. "What are you doing out there in the cold? And what kept you?" With one hand she clasped her cardigan to her neck. "Come inside! Your dinner's getting cold."

I had no appetite, but my plate had already been filled with potatoes, cauliflower, and a beef patty. My hand lifted the fork to my mouth, again and again. I chewed, I swallowed, took another mouthful.

"Working late again?" my father asked.

"Mmm," I answered. "Gemma took a turn this afternoon."

I could feel my mother's eyes on me, but she said nothing. When the dishes were washed, dried, and put away, I said I was out of sorts and climbed the stairs to my bedroom.

Evening dragged me into night, sleep came at last and delivered me to morning. My pale belly looked much the same as it had the day before. The rap of my mother's knuckles on the door got me out of bed. "Elfrieda!"

My feet carried me to the bus stop. My hand groped in my pocket for the key to the florist's. The clock ticked towards lunchtime, nudged me through the afternoon and into twilight. The parking space across the road remained empty, as Otto had told me it would. My feet took me back to the bus stop, the bus took me home. Upstairs, I searched my suitcase for the brown paper bag with the penicillin. It wasn't there. I didn't dare ask my mother if she had seen it.

By then, the evening was already half gone.

# 24

Four rings before he finally picks up.

"Hello, Mum."

"Toby?"

"Yes?"

"Mum here."

"Yes, I could see that." I hear straight off that he's being short with me after all the commotion last time.

"Not interrupting, am I?"

"No, I've got a minute. How's your hand?"

"I need you to do something for me."

No answer.

"You know how you said you would give everyone my new address?"

"Oh, Mum. There's nothing to worry about." It's exactly the tone of voice Louis used to put on when my mood didn't suit him, so sweet it sets my teeth on edge. "It's been sorted."

"Well, it's not *all* been sorted."

"Mum, Nadine spent a whole afternoon last week letting everyone know your change of address."

"And that was very good of her. But the internet still gives our old address. Look me up and that's all you get."

"Your old address on the internet? Where?"

"In the telephone directory."

"Oh. Well, it takes them a while to process this kind of thing."

"That's as may be, but in the meantime, no one can find me."

"It'll all be taken care of." It's like talking to a help-desk. "You've just sent thank-you cards with your new address to everyone who got in touch about Dad. And all your post will be forwarded for the first month."

"It's not the post I'm worried about."

"Then what *are* you worried about?"

"Suppose someone comes looking for me. And they go to our old address. They'll be faced with an empty house and think I'm dead."

"Tell me, Mum. Who do you think is about to come looking for you?"

"Someone."

"Someone?"

"Someone from a long time ago."

"Mum, look ... I really need to go now."

# 25

Pruims the baker was an odd shape. Everything about him seemed to sag. A thin strip of hair encircled his shiny scalp and the slump of his cheeks left two dents in his face. From the neck down he grew steadily wider, until his waistband pulled him up short and stopped his rolls of fat from rolling any further. Yet his baggy trousers concealed a pair of skinny legs, which only saw the light on hot summer days.

It was my turn, but Pruims turned to Mrs. Oberjé first, slipping me a wink as she shuffled up to the counter. "Good morning, Mrs. Oberjé. A small white loaf and two currant buns?"

"I think I'll have a ..." She always inserted a pause as if she might order something else. "Yes, a small white loaf. And give me two currant buns while you're at it."

Another wink fluttered in my direction. I had no desire to be a one-woman audience for the baker's little skit and turned to look out the window.

"So-o-o," Pruims said to me, rubbing his hands, once Mrs. Oberjé had shuffled off. "Feeling fine, are we?"

I nodded and thanked him for asking. "Two brown loaves and ten slices of rye, please." He didn't move a muscle.

"And?" he asked.

"Pardon?"

"I asked if you were feeling fine."

"Absolutely. Right as rain." I pointed at the shelves behind him. "Two brown loaves, sliced please, and ten slices of rye bread." He lowered his eyes to my waist.

"Is anything the matter?" I asked.

"No. Nothing at all." He turned at last and began running the loaves through the slicer and into the bags. I looked down. There was no bulge visible beneath my sweater. He told me the price and I rummaged among the coins in my purse.

"That *is* good news."

"What?"

"That you're feeling so fine."

I couldn't give him the right money so I had to wait and watch wasps drilling into the iced tarts and cream cakes. Pruims took his time at the cash drawer, and looked to be counting out my change coin by coin. "Hmm."

Suddenly the door behind him flew open. I don't know which of us was more startled. His wife backed into the shop with a full bread trolley in tow. "Morning," she said, without looking around.

"Good morning," I said. Only then did she notice it was me. "Oh," she said, exchanged a glance with her husband, and vanished back into the storeroom.

"Ten cents makes fifty," the baker said, loud enough to be heard on the other side of the door. "And two quarters makes one." He held his hand high so that I had to reach for my change. A shiny guilder coin lay on his palm. "Our little secret," he whispered. "I'm sure you can use the extra. You know, with the way things are."

Walking away as the shop door closed behind me, I tried to stay calm, but I kept breaking into a trot. How could he possibly know?

# 26

My parents found out. Of course they did.

My mother's agonies spewed out of her. And when she discovered Otto was married, the fury unleashed was enough to crack every window and wall. My father sat silent and unblinking, teeth grinding as he contemplated the grain in the dark wood of the dining table.

"Three daughters I've raised. Three!" Her wail hardened to a scream. "Got them all to the altar without a hint of scandal and now you do this to me." Her finger jabbed my chest, jabbed it hard. "Well?" she shrieked, the hair in her neck spiked with sweat. "What do you have to say for yourself?"

I had no idea what to say. She slapped me full in the face, then stared long and hard to see if I felt her pain. "Answer your mother!"

"I didn't mean for this to happen," I blurted out.

"Didn't mean to, didn't mean to. I should bloody well hope not! You're nothing but a common whore."

"You'll stay with your sister Emma." My father spoke.

"Fine," I said, not even pausing for breath. This was something to cling to, a shield from my mother's searing rage.

"I asked you straight, that day in the bathroom. And you looked me in the eye and you lied."

"Call our Emma," my father commanded. "Tell her

we're coming to Winterswijk on Saturday. With Elfrieda." I was glad he was finally speaking, though every word was weighed by the ounce.

"And what then?" I asked, as calmly as I could. "What am I supposed to do there?" I edged round the table to enter his field of vision. "Pa?"

"You'll serve out your term."

"My term?"

"Your sister has a good farming family. Who knows? They may be willing to take yours too."

"Exactly," my mother chimed in. "And you can come back here without the child and pick up where you left off."

No one expected me to say anything.

"I'm keeping the baby," I said. They both gawped at me. Perhaps it was the sheer impossibility of me daring to contradict them. To this day, I can see the expression on my father's face.

"Out of the question," my mother snapped. "Now get out of my sight!" I let her chase me up the stairs as if I was an unruly toddler. I shut myself in my room.

Through the floorboards, I could hear her raging on.

Even after my father left, she continued to bawl her side of the argument. From the window, I watched him walk down the street and disappear round the corner. I may have said I was keeping the baby, but once I was alone, the thought became a noose around my neck. And as soon as someone tried to take the baby from me, all I could do was hold on tighter.

Later that evening, my father knocked at my door. "Elfrieda?"

"Yes?"

It felt like some strange misunderstanding. I couldn't remember the last time he had set foot in my room. The handle turned and I sat up straight on my bed. "Listen, Elfrieda." He stepped inside and closed the door behind him, still wearing his overcoat. A guest so intent on delivering his message that he passed up the chance to sit down.

With a few brisk scratches behind his ear, he began, "I've been to see Johan's parents. Because you ..." At a loss for words, he gestured towards my belly. "Because you want to keep it."

I was so moved by the fact he had actually listened to me, I could have leapt off the bed and hugged him. I wanted to whisper in his ear that I wasn't sure at all. That I was terrified, choking on my fear.

"Johan will be home from the barracks at the weekend." He made it sound like a stroke of good luck. "His father is prepared to sit down and discuss it with him." His hand was already floating towards the door handle.

"Discuss what?"

"He is not engaged either. I've yet to tell his father about your ..." His thumb and forefinger traced the tight line of his lips. "We can only pray that he's willing to go along with it when you break the news to him."

"Go along with it?" My voice was unsteady.

"That he is prepared to wed you under the circumstances. And raise the child as his own."

"Never!"

My father didn't seem to understand that I was capable of contradicting him.

"I'd sooner make an angel of it."

"You'd sooner what?" my father roared. "Wash your mouth out!"

"I'm not going to marry this Johan."

"You will go there as agreed on Friday evening," he commanded. "Or this is no longer your home."

"But ..."

"Do you understand me?"

My father was so angry that I had no choice but to nod. Before he had even closed the door, I turned off the light. Hunkered down in my bed with all my clothes on, I swore to myself that I would never-never-never let this happen.

## 27

I came home from work to find the living room curtains drawn. I opened the front door and hung my coat on the stand. The house was quiet—not even the smell of dinner on the go. Since my refusal to call at the home of Johan's parents, conversation had come to a standstill.

The living room light was on. Ma and Pa were sitting at the table but not on their usual chairs. Their hands were clasped in prayer. Only then did I notice Father Gremhaars in Pa's place. My stomach clenched.

"Elfrieda," he said, in a mild but earnest tone, motioning for me to take a seat. "You'll understand what brings me here." We were guests in our own home. My mother did not look up from her hands as I passed her. My father shot me a look from beneath his brow.

"I am here in light of the situation. Your parents have asked me to intercede." He paused for a sip of tea. There was no steam rising from the cup. They must have been waiting a while. "I have been in touch with Oosterbeek. Our experiences there have been positive. And they have informed us that you are welcome."

"Oosterbeek?"

"The Paula Foundation," the priest whispered, as if he was sharing an intimacy. "A place for girls in your predicament."

"Why?"

"Elfrieda," my mother burst out, her eyes burning.

"Let her ask all the questions she wants," the priest said reassuringly.

"You will go there," my father said firmly. "In a few weeks there will be no denying that belly of yours."

Ma chipped in with her standard lament. "Three upstanding girls delivered to the altar and this is what I get from my youngest."

"Oosterbeek is a fine solution, Father." Pa nodded at the priest. The three of them seemed to be having separate conversations. I looked around the table and the priest continued patiently, as if there had been no interruptions. "The Paula Foundation takes in young women so that they can see out their pregnancy."

"And then?"

The priest pursed his lips. "Then you will stay with the Little Sisters of Saint Joseph ..." He held up his hands as if to indicate two walls, then brought his palms together.

"And what will happen to my baby?"

"Elfrieda!" my mother barked, but the priest went on talking.

"The Little Sisters of Saint Joseph will bestow their loving care on the child until its true parents come to take it home."

"Its true parents?"

"You can rest assured that the sisters know of good Catholic couples who can give this child of God the one true love it needs." He made it sound like the baby had appeared in my belly by mistake and really belonged to someone else. Stolen property that would be lovingly restored in a few months' time. "And should you marry before that time, you and your husband will be given the opportunity to adopt the child."

"A married man," Ma groaned. "You'd think he'd have known better. A wife of his own and then taking advantage of our Elfrieda like this." By which she meant the man was more to blame than I was. It occurred to me that she was begging forgiveness on my behalf. Everything my mother fired across the table was met with a nod from Father Gremhaars, not a nod of agreement, but simply a sign that she had been heard. He turned back to me. "They will be the only parents the child will ever know." He placed his soft hand on mine. "All you have to do is bring it into this world and forget."

I pulled my hand out from under his.

After Pa had followed him out to the hall and helped him into his coat, Father Gremhaars appeared briefly in the doorway and gave me and my mother a curt nod between us. The two men shared a long farewell handshake, the priest looking deep into my father's eyes.

"Thank you, Father. Thank you," Pa mumbled. "We will never forget your help."

This is no longer your home.

I hadn't said a word but perhaps my silence was enough to cement my father's resolve.

"You will do as the priest says. You will give up the child. That's all there is to it."

"Fine," I said.

"What do you mean, fine?"

"I'll leave first thing tomorrow."

"No," my father said.

"What?"

"You will leave now."

"Oh, sweet Jesus," my mother whimpered.

"That's enough from you," he snapped.

"We can't just send the girl away ..." But she did nothing to stop it. With a face like a dripping candle, she stomped up the stairs and locked herself in the bathroom.

"Won't you at least go to your sister's?" Once we were alone in the kitchen, my father's voice softened. It was almost pleading. "You've no other choice, Frieda." He had never called me that before. A furtive tear slid down the side of his nose. He pinched the fold between his eyes, perhaps to punish himself for admitting to this much feeling.

# 28

Otto had promised to wait for me around the corner in his car. I went up the stone steps to the front door. A sign in one of the tall windows said ROOM TO RENT.

The house stood on the corner of two nondescript streets but to me it looked like a castle, albeit a small one that rented rooms to single ladies. Otto had already made inquiries.

I had managed to secure two nights' respite from my parents, but after the second night I got up to find the front door key missing from the ring in my coat pocket.

"Elfrieda, please." I jumped at the sound of her voice, which came from the unlit kitchen. "Let us help you." Ma hadn't said a word to me since the priest's visit. "We only want what's best for you, Elfrieda."

"Then let me stay."

She had no answer to that.

There was nothing else for it. I went upstairs to pack my big holiday suitcase. My mother didn't stop me. And by the time I stepped out of the front door, there was no one home to say goodbye to. A shaky state of relief came over me.

Beside the castle door was a copper bell with a string you could pull. I had to tug for all I was worth before I heard it ring inside.

"Good afternoon." A slender Indonesian woman opened the door a fraction and eyed me up and down without the least embarrassment.

"I understand you have a room to rent," I said brightly. My hair, my nails, the buttons on my coat, my shoes. I felt the urge to check every part of me her eyes lit upon.

"You would appear to be in urgent need."

"What makes you say that?"

She nodded at my suitcase.

"Yes ... well, I ..." The door swung open.

"Come in for a moment." The hall was laid with marble and the floor beyond was like a chessboard of yellow and black tiles. The whole situation felt dreamlike. I had only ever lived with my parents. I wanted my mother to see me there, to understand that I didn't need them at all. I was going to live in this castle of a house and manage all by myself.

"All of the other ladies are out at work, so it's quiet during the day." Behind every door lived an unmarried woman my age and soon I would get to know them all. So many friends to be made. "There's a kitchen in the basement which you are permitted to use." The stairs were carpeted in the same deep red as the hotel where I had stayed with Otto. "The recently vacated room is on the first floor." Seen from behind, the woman had the appearance of a child, but her face was as old as a grandmother's. Unsteady on her feet, she zigzagged moth-like through the hall, from table to doorpost to bannister, always within reach of something to hold on to. "The rent is thirty guilders a month. Payment in advance."

"That's what I thought, yes." Otto had even given me an envelope, though it was a sum I could pay myself without too much trouble. An unexpected clarity came over me. I felt like someone who belonged completely to herself.

"What do you do for a living?" the woman asked as she climbed the stairs ahead of me.

"I work at a florist's."

"Are you engaged?"

"No, I'm not."

"No gentleman callers, mind."

The lack of an answer caused her to halt on the stairs and look down at me over her shoulder.

"That goes without saying," I said.

"Family visits are permitted until nine in the evening. All of our ladies have to be up early for work." She climbed the last of the stairs and stepped onto a dim landing, where most of the light came peeping through the keyholes. There were three doors. No sound but our breathing and the chink of her keys. "Now, here we have ..." A fumble at the lock and the door swung open. The sun seemed to reside in the room beyond. The windows were tall and wide, with small stained-glass panes at the top.

She motioned to me to look inside while she stayed out on the landing. The floorboards creaked and all the warmth in the room seemed to go to my head. I loosened my scarf and unbuttoned my coat. The room overlooked the bustle of the street below and the houses opposite. "It's like *Rear Window*," I chuckled.

"What did you say?"

"Oh, I'm sorry. It's a film. With James Stewart."

She barely nodded, lips creased in the same thin line. A bed had already been made up for me. There was a bedside cabinet and a table with two chairs. Without me knowing, a new life had been furnished for me in this place, ready for me to step into. There were nails to hang pictures on. An empty shelf with space for all the books I would buy. And the LPs that Otto would give me as gifts. Next to the bed there was room enough for a cradle. The thought made me smile. In that moment, I felt like I could take on the world. "What a wonderful room," I said.

All the while, the landlady was craning her neck. She tracked my every movement with an expression that said she half expected me to pocket the paint when I ran a finger along the window sill. A sill that could accommodate two vases of flowers with ease.

"I would love to rent this room."

Her gaze had returned to my waist. "Are you in the family way?"

"No," I said, trying to sound as surprised as I could. I scratched at my neck and turned my face to the windows and the street beyond. From where I was standing, I could see the roof of Otto's car.

"I thought as much when you walked through the door." She gave me such a fierce stare that her head began to wobble slightly. I mustered an indignant look in return but had to consciously stop my hand from settling on my belly. "I've been taking in lodgers since the war and I can weed your kind out just like that. I do not rent rooms to girls like you." Her tone was unexpectedly friendly, so much so that it frightened me.

"I am not expecting."

"And I have no time for girls who lie. Please leave before you demean yourself even further."

"One month is all I ask. Please! A month will give me time to find somewhere else." But there I was, back out on the darkened landing as the key ground in the lock. The room had already felt like mine, I loved its light. She rattled the door to make sure it was locked, as if everything behind it had to be protected from me.

"I can pay you more, if that's what you want." I traipsed down the stairs behind her. My suitcase bumped against the bannisters, knocked a dent in the plaster on the wall.

"The same rules apply to all the ladies who live here."

"I'll make sure your other lodgers don't notice a thing. I promise."

One more flight and we were back in the hall.

"Please?"

"Rooms for single ladies are a rarity in this city. But lodgings for a young woman in your position are nowhere to be found."

And with that I was out on the stone steps.

"No one will ever know," I tried again. I put my case down, wanted to put my foot in the door, but I didn't dare. "And I can pay you considerably more."

I could sense her weighing up my offer.

"Please?" I pressed my praying hands to my lips. "I have nowhere else to go."

"There's no need to beg. I have a reputation, one I wish to uphold."

"And?" Otto asked.

I shoved my suitcase onto the back seat and got in

the front, beside him. My expression told him all he needed to know. "Drive," I ordered. I could see the landlady looking down on us from one of the tall windows. "Just drive. Get me out of here."

"Where to?"

"How should I know?"

At last he started the engine and we pulled away from the kerb.

The streets were busy and I stared out at the stream of houses we passed. People were coming home from work. A man with a briefcase got out of a car and waved back at two little girls waiting by the window. A few doors along, someone was setting the table. At the corner of St. Annastraat, Otto dithered over whether to turn left or right. "Just drive, will you?" I barked at him. "How hard can it be? Weren't you the one who always knew where to go?" The driver behind us parped his horn. Otto accelerated in a hurry and fumbled with the gears. The engine shrieked. I stared out the window and rubbed my forehead.

After driving for a while, he asked, "What happened?"

"She could see I was pregnant."

"How?"

I shrugged. "Said she could spot my kind a mile off." Otto drove to the polder, to the spot under the weeping willow where we had made love again and again. He switched off the engine and we sat there stiffly side by side.

"And if you ..." Otto seemed to be laying the groundwork for a new plan. It stalled after three words.

"She said no one will rent me a room." I rested my head against the cold window. "I don't know. What are we are supposed to do now?"

Otto said nothing.

"I really don't know anymore ..." I bit the skin by my thumbnail.

"Elfie ..."

"Hmm?"

"This can't go on, Elfie. I've barely slept in weeks. I just don't know anymore. This ... all this ... there's no way through. Even now, there's no hope. You have nothing left and the baby hasn't even been born."

"I have myself, don't I? And I have you."

I tried to take his hand to reassure him, but he wouldn't let me.

"Brigitte can see that I'm worried. I don't know how much longer I can keep this from her."

I could only feel hatred for Brigitte. "Then tell her!"

"Of course not. How can we go on like this? How do you expect to take care of your child? Have you given that any thought at all? I can't spend the rest of my life caring ... for you, the two of you. We can't even find a place for you to stay."

"Something will turn up," I said.

"Elfie, are you really that naïve? Look at what you've already lost. Everyone's turning their back on you."

"It's too late to fix things now." My voice had risen to a scream. "Too late!"

"Elfie, Elfie." His arms reached out to smother my panic. "Hear me out. If only for a minute." The last thing I wanted was for him to hold me.

"Listen." Otto's hands were shaking. He grasped the steering wheel, knuckles white, as if we were driving through a storm. "Perhaps you should consider what the priest, what your parents proposed."

"And marry that boy?"
"No, of course not."
"Then what?"
"The Little Sisters, their foundation."
"You think so?"
"Perhaps you should give birth in the convent." Otto turned his face away and a breath shivered out of him.
"And then?"
"Then you can choose us as adoptive parents."
"Us?" There was hope after all. "You mean we could ...?"
"Listen, Elfie. Please." Again, his hands reached over to soothe me, to stop my emotions flaring. "Perhaps Brigitte and I should take the baby."
"You and Brigitte? Take ..." I couldn't believe what I was hearing. His words, the measured way he said them.
"Adopt," Otto clarified, as if there was some confusion about what he meant by *take*. "She has wanted a child for so long and ... well, perhaps I can persuade her."
"Am I supposed to hand over my child to your wife?" I said it so softly, I could hardly hear myself speak. "Is that what you're saying?"
"This is my child, too," Otto said. "Brigitte would never have to know."
"Know what?"
"That I am the father. And you ... you're still so young."
I said nothing. Breath came in empty gulps. I seemed to be looking at him through reverse binoculars, a

complete stranger, a man backing off into the distance.

"Brigitte and I can give the baby a safe home." I suddenly felt so much younger. Otto had become an uncle intent on helping me out of this impetuous mess I had got myself into.

"No ..." I had to say something, for fear I might consent without meaning to. For fear there was already no way back, that my baby was already someone else's. "How could you think—"

"Elfie, Elfie." Otto wanted me to hear him out. "I've made some inquiries. The mother has to approve the parents she gives her baby to. Which means that you ... you could choose Brigitte and me." His words stumbled over each other. "And then you and I could work something out. A way for you to keep seeing the child. With us, you can be sure it will have a loving home."

I found myself staring at his mouth, a way to be sure that he was actually saying these words, unfolding this plan he had come up with days, maybe weeks ago. He had even made inquiries. Perhaps it was the considered nature of his proposal that shook me the most.

"The way things are going, Elfie. This can't end well. Everyone who knows wants nothing to do with you. And what do you think will happen once the baby is born? Child protection could take it from you. Refuse to cooperate, and they could lock you away in some institution or other." Otto's mouth was a sputtering volcano. "Only Brigitte can never know it's ours, that I am the father." He looked deep into my eyes, as if the time had come for me to promise him everything. "She can never know, never. Do you understand?"

I tugged furiously at my blouse so that he could see my bare belly bulging over the waistband of my skirt. "Shall I hand it over now? Here, take it." I slapped the tight skin. "And then you can spend the rest of your life denying your own child."

"It will be loved, I promise you. From the bottom of my heart, I promise."

"How can you even come out with such nonsense?"

"I can't keep this up, Elfie. I can't care for two families at once, now can I?"

"Oh, no? Can't you?" At first it was words I threw in his face, but when he cowered from me, I had no choice but to hit him. On his back, his shoulders. "Get lost! Get away from me!" He just sat there. "This is our child, Otto!" I put my mouth to his ear and roared. "Yours and mine!"

"Then what do you want?"

"If you want this child so much, then marry me. Marry me!"

Our eyes met. "That's not going to happen, Elfie. There's no way. It's not just my marriage, it's my position at the university. I could never set foot in church again."

"Church? After all this, it's church you're worried about?"

"I'm only trying to think what's best for everyone."

"And the best you can do is this insane adoption? A life spent lying that your child is not your own!"

"You knew from the start I was married."

"What's that got to do with it? Being married didn't seem to be much of a problem when you were making love to me."

"I love you. Honestly, I do." His tone was one of appeasement. "I meant it then and I mean it now. Thanks to you I've discovered who I am. I would change the world for you if I could. But I can't."

I tried to pull him closer, pull his mouth closer to mine. "Then marry me."

"Elfie, please." Otto fended me off, as if I was humiliating myself and he couldn't bear to watch.

"Marry me, Otto. I'll give you all the time you need to make that happen. I'll wait for you."

Otto didn't answer and my fingers found the handle on the door. With all my strength, I threw it open and dragged my case from the back seat.

"What are you doing?"

"Perhaps it's best if your wife knows about us."

Panicked, Otto made a grab for me over the passenger seat.

"Tell her everything. If you've discovered who you are through me, then let her see who you've become. Perhaps she'll want to leave you and that will resolve everything. Or shall I tell her for you?"

"Elfie, please ..."

I slammed the door. Otto got out of the car, but I was already striding away from him. He took a step or two, then turned on his heels and got back behind the wheel. Driving alongside me at a crawl, he wound down the passenger window. He begged me to get in, not to part like this, to be reasonable.

"Reasonable? You want me to be reasonable?"

A farmer came cycling stoically towards us, unfazed by the sight of a young woman screaming at a slow-driving car.

"Elfie, get in. Please. Let me take you somewhere."

"And where might that be?"

He had no idea. I stood still and he slammed on the brakes. I leaned in through the passenger window. "Leave me alone," I yelled. "Unless you want a dent in your door!"

It turned out to be my parting shot. Otto drove away.

With every step I took along the dyke, he sped further away from me, until he disappeared beyond the trees, absorbed back into the life he called his own.

Those first few nights, I slept in the storeroom at the florist's, closing up at the end of the day and using my key to return after dark. I lay on a bed of horse blankets with my coat pulled over me. Water from the tap we used to fill the flower buckets was enough for a quick wash. I ate at the American Lunchroom, at a little table by the window. All things considered, it was a luxury I couldn't afford, but I ate as slowly as I could so that the radiator could warm me through. As I whiled away the hours, the sky turned dark, until it felt like I was sitting in a lit shop window. I hoped that someone might recognise me, tell my parents where they had seen me and comment that I must be doing all right for myself. Or that Otto would get out of his car one evening, perhaps on his way to the pictures, and see me sitting there. Ever since our blazing row, he was nowhere to be found. It was as if he had driven off and ceased to exist.

In the preceding months, it had begun to feel like I ceased to exist as soon as he left my side. Even during those Otto-less days, I saw myself as an abandoned lover. But could I still call myself a lover when I was no longer sure he loved me?

## 29

"Drehmann, you say?" Down the line I can hear fingers banging away at a keyboard.

"With two *n*'s."

"One moment please." They put me on hold.

No matter how I tossed and turned last night, I couldn't lie still for long without my joints complaining, so I clambered out of bed and made myself some cinnamon milk. Standing at the window, mug in hand, I started thinking of the time that Otto and I drove over the dyke along the Maas. Swallows swooping like stunt flyers, the rustle of poplars through the open window. We turned off down a road that led past a cemetery, and Otto said, "That's where my parents are buried."

The cemetery.

There and then, in the dead of night, I was seized with a sense of urgency. It was all I could do not to stare at my radio alarm, willing the numbers to change and morning to come.

"Mrs. Buitink? Are you still there?"

"I most certainly am."

"Are you sure Mr. and Mrs. Drehmann are buried here?"

"I believe so. At least, that was the case in the 1960s."

"Oh ... as long ago as that. That might explain it. Do you have another moment for me?" Before I can answer, I'm on hold again. That little scrap of cactus looks like it might be taking root. I have to stop myself pulling it out of the soil to check.

"Mrs. Buitink?" Rattling from the other end of the line. "It's me again."

"And?"

"I've been able to trace the grave of Mr. and Mrs. Drehmann. But I'm afraid the plot was cleared back in the 1990s."

"Oh."

"I'm sorry. I'm afraid there's nothing else I can do for you."

"Do you have any contact details? An address for the family, perhaps?"

"No, I'm sorry."

"But someone must have paid for the upkeep?"

"Most likely, a sum was paid at the time of the burial and, when that ran out in 1994, no one contacted us about continuing payment. And the cemetery wasn't able to trace any surviving family members. In cases like these, they always do their best."

# 30

I'm standing with my coat on, about to go to the supermarket—small brown loaf, carton of milk, maybe a packet of biscuits too, depending what's on special offer—when there's a knock at the door.

"Hey," Tobias says. "Just got home or heading out?"

"Off to get a few groceries, but that can wait. No Nadine today?"

"She's at work."

It occurs to me that he might have told me he was coming and it's slipped my mind. But if I ask, they'll start thinking I'm losing the plot again.

"I had a feeling you might come over," I smile.

"Did you now?" Tobias pulls up a chair at the table and plumps himself down. "I came by to give you this." He slides something towards me across the tablecloth. "A keepsake."

"My key ring." Without the familiar clutch of house keys attached, it takes me a moment to recognise the brown leather fob. "Of course, the handover was today. Is the place empty now?"

"Stripped bare. Keys gone. Done and dusted."

I have trouble imagining the house bereft of all our things, without our life inside it.

Tobias gets to his feet and motions towards the fridge for a can of cola from the crisper drawer.

"Of course. Help yourself, son."

"Now it's all in the hands of the new tenants." The can clicks and fizzes. Tobias sucks up the escaping froth and folds back the ring pull. His hair's different since Nadine came on the scene, shaved up the sides and back. It makes him look younger, though the splash of grey at his temples is steadily expanding. I'm probably the only one who sees that this is not a man, but an overgrown little boy.

"Do you know who the new tenants are?"

"Not the foggiest." He takes a big slurp of cola, suppresses a burp. "It'll be empty for a while in any case."

"Not too long, I hope."

"Could be months. The housing association is planning to renovate the place, but the builders are on holiday." Another suppressed hiss-burp. "After them insisting that I plaster over every last hole. Complete waste of time."

"Did Nadine get round to making that change?"

"Change?"

"In the telephone directory."

"Not that again ..."

"It's important to me and not much trouble for you."

"I thought I'd explained this to you on the phone."

"There's no need to be so testy about it."

"I'm not being testy."

"All I asked was whether Nadine had got round to it."

"Mum, would you please just let it go." Tobias goes to take another swig from the can but lowers his arm halfway. "You really are ..." He doesn't say what I am.

"If Nadine were to let me know how—" I venture with a smile.

"Mum!"

"Then I could do it myself."

"It's done. All of it! I came all the way over here to tell you it's done. And here you go again, picking over every last detail. Wanting this, that, and the other." Swamped by his anger, I'm barely able to get a word in. "The cabinet in the hall. The telephone directory. That fucking cactus drying up. Ever since Dad died, I've been at it non-stop: sorting out the cremation, getting you priority status for this room, getting you moved in, and meanwhile I'm over there clearing out your entire house." His voice slows. "And now that's behind us at last, not so much as a thank you. All you can do is ask"—he takes a deep breath to rein himself in, then erupts louder than ever—"if Nadine has sorted out that one fucking change of address."

"But it's important to me."

"You, you, you!" Tobias jabs his finger at me three times. "It's all about you. You never ask how we're doing. Never! Not me, not Nadine. We come over to share the ultrasound and you bawl us out for over-reacting. Can't you just be happy for us, like a normal mother? You don't seem to give a shit about becoming a grandparent. Yet for Dad it was the greatest gift he could have wished for. And now Dad is dead. Dead ... just like that. And he isn't just your husband, he's my father, and my daughter's grandfather." Tobias is tripping over his words, the way he used to as a kid when frustration got the better of him. "It was always you everyone was concerned about, afraid you'd be the first to go. And then out of nowhere Dad is gone. And I never had a chance to say ... At least Dad knew how to show someone he loved them."

I get to my feet to put my arms around Tobias in the hope it might calm him down, but he keeps me at a distance.

"Sometimes I wonder if you miss him at all. You never talk about him."

"That is ... that's not true, Toby."

"Oh no?" He looks around the room. Thank goodness the top window is closed or the whole place would have heard him blowing his top.

"Then where's Dad's photo?" His eyes dart from the empty walls to the window sill to the bedside cabinet and then look straight at me. "Well?"

"That's because ... just for now, I ..."

"You see?"

"I didn't like where he was hanging." My hearing aids start whining. "Perhaps next time you can bring a drill with you?"

"That's enough, Mum." Tobias crushes the can in his fist. "It's always been up to me to find excuses for your behaviour. Well not anymore."

"Nobody asked you to."

"Asked me to what?" Tobias's eyes widen. I need to say something quick before he explodes again.

"I never asked you to excuse anything I did."

"No, Dad was the one who always had to smooth things over and keep the peace. He used to say the weather was easier to forecast than your moods."

"Oh, that was just one of your dad's little jokes."

"And now he's not around for you to walk all over, you're starting on me. Well, I'm not going to stand for it."

"There's no need to make such a fuss. It's all one to me if the telephone directory hasn't been updated. I really don't mind doing it myself. You two have already done so much."

"That's it, I'm leaving."

"What?"

"Sort your own life out."

"Toby, come on. There's no need to go like this." But Tobias is gone. Off down the hall. No slamming door, but only because it's fitted with one of those closer thingies.

I sit down at the table, hands shaking, sweat itching under the plaster cast. I wait for Tobias to come back. He always used to after I gave him a telling off. My anger was a magnet that drew him to me, sticking close until it died down, until I ruffled his hair and took him on my lap.

But Tobias doesn't come back. His absence has punched a hole in the room. I don't dare take a look in the hall in case the neighbours heard the racket and are stationed at their half-opened doors waiting for me to appear.

I sit at the table until the big hand reaches quarter-to, then the hour. I want to call Tobias but I don't, knowing it would only stoke his anger. I open the sideboard drawer and Louis looks up at me from his frame. "Sorry," I whisper. "But what can I do now? What can I do? I'm scared Toby might ... I'm scared."

Louis doesn't answer, doesn't hold me close. He would have, once. But Louis is as dead as his photograph.

# 31

It was at a birthday party, I don't remember whose. This was a few months after the birth, and I had been sleepwalking from one day to the next. Noises were louder, life itself was muted. We were smoking, listening to records. There were bottles of red wine in wicker baskets. I drank a lot so I wouldn't have to say much. Then a pal from college buttonholed me.

"Frieda, Frieda. I want you to meet somebody."

"Who?"

"Remember that sweet guy I was telling you about?"

I shook my head.

"Well, here he is." She reached into the hall and yanked in a boyish young man with red hair. Not my type, I saw that right away. He was trying to grow a moustache, no doubt as a cover for his shyness.

"Hi," I said, over his shoulder, scanning the room for another conversation to latch on to.

"At least introduce yourself," my friend said indignantly. I held out my hand and he held out his. Definitely not my type. I braced myself for a damp handshake. But no, his hands were smooth and dry.

"Frie," I said.

"Louis." He gave a little chuckle.

"What's so funny?"

"Our names rhyme."

As the years went by, this became the story. How unimpressed I was with him at first, while he insisted he knew that I was the one from the moment he saw me. It took three more encounters to open my eyes. In the end, I felt everything for Louis, I even fell in love with him. Perhaps the only thing I missed was that sense of newness. I never really felt new with Louis, not the way I had with Otto. But that was hardly Louis's fault.

We messed about a bit when we started seeing each other but, at my insistence, we waited until our wedding night to make love. In those first weeks after the wedding, Louis was mainly concerned about where to put his hands. He kept asking me if he was doing it right and, before we started, he would spend a good five minutes on the toilet. It took him months to gain more confidence between the sheets, not to be in such a rush. But after a while he got used to us being so close physically. I think it was only then that he actually dared to look at me.

The Monday after we got married, I stopped working a second time. We moved into a brand-new house in the district of Hatert, where we would live out the rest of our married life. A neat little box of a place. The saplings out front were dwarfed by the people who walked by on the freshly laid pavements. After horticultural college, I had found a job at a tree nursery in Bemmel and still had vague ideas of studying to do something else. In reality, I was too old, too female and, as was the way of things, I would soon be too much of a mother. As a matter of course, we tried for a child in the years after we were wed. But nothing happened.

I didn't know how to tell Louis that our inability to conceive was probably down to him. After holding out for a while, I agreed to a medical examination and, to my surprise, they discovered my tubes were blocked. I was admitted to hospital, where I underwent a minor procedure.

When the doctors gave the go-ahead for us to have sex again, the glad tidings arrived within two months. I didn't realise I was expecting until, for no apparent reason, my thoughts kept drifting back to that summer with Otto. My breasts became more sensitive, as if they were being touched for the first time. When I started to show, panic took hold. I had episodes that became more frequent as the birth came closer, but I don't think anyone noticed. Not even Louis. With hindsight, I think I was too scared to be pregnant.

It was Louis who came up with the name if it was a boy. I liked Tobias instantly, mainly because it didn't remind me of anyone. As for the birth itself, I mostly remember how angry I was. Afraid, too, that everyone would abandon me. Even though it was a home birth and Louis came as soon as he was called.

"You have to trust yourself to let go," the midwife said. "Just relax."

"I'm trying!"

"Then try a little harder."

I didn't know how.

"Please, Frieda, you have to release that tension. It's never going to come like this." It was only when she went into the hall to ask Louis if he could drive me to hospital that Tobias forced his way out. After nearly a day and a half of labour, our son came into the world.

"Hey, little fella," I crooned to him. "My sweet little fella." His small body, so real, wet, and warm. There was something ferrous in the air, I couldn't get enough of the smell of him. My legs trembled violently. Shockwaves rose inside me and ebbed away.

Calm filled the room.

Tobias was here.

And he stayed.

Each day anew.

"It's a boy!" Louis was crying as he cut the cord. "A son." Only then did I let my tears flow, as if someone had to show me the emotions before I could feel them for myself. In those first hours, Tobias's eyes were black as coal, more animal than human. His body was covered in a haze of little blond hairs, a waxy cream in every crease, the addictive smell of his little head.

Within days, my parents came to visit. Our contact in the preceding years had been sparse. I had never really gone back to being their daughter. My father shook Louis by the hand and congratulated him. I received three awkward kisses from my mother.

"Congratulations on the little one," my father said, sitting down on the chair by the head of my bed.

"Thanks, Pa."

I looked on in a daze as my mother lifted Tobias from his cradle. "Careful, Ma."

"I've had four of my own, so don't you fuss. I know what I'm doing," my mother said, winking at Louis.

"Look at that fine little head on his shoulders," she said to my father. "Louis's profile to a tee."

"He's a healthy specimen all right," my father beamed and slapped Louis on the shoulder. "Well done, man. You've fathered a son. More than I ever did."

When Tobias began to croak in protest, instead of handing him to me, my mother stuck her pinkie between his lips. "This is how to do it," she instructed, pressing her finger to the roof of his mouth. "Hushes them up in no time." I could feel a prickling sensation in my breasts. My mother danced Tobias across the room as if he were hers, and even disappeared out onto the landing with him. The maternity help came in with coffee and cake.

"Give him here, Ma."

"You eat your cake first."

I dug my fingernails into my palms. "I'm in no mood for cake. Give Tobias to me." All that day, he smelled of my mother's perfume.

Those first few nights, Tobias's breath rattled. It was as if an old man was dying right next to our bed. I couldn't give in to sleep, afraid I would miss a vital sign that something was wrong. To my relief, Louis made light of it all. And after a while, so did I.

Louis held Tobias to his chest and walked round and round the room with him at night. He took him into bed with us. "I love you," I said, and was saddened by the surprise in his eyes when he looked at me. "I love you too," he replied.

Tobias was a good drinker. "The cat that got the cream," said the help. Tanya was her name. A sweet girl, though she skimped on the chores. All she really did was serve up coffee and cake to our visitors and tell them, "Her milk started flowing straight away. As if she had never done anything else."

Bunches of flowers arrived. Envelopes containing banknotes were delivered. We even got a telegram or two—one from my sisters in Canada and one from the pharmacy where Louis worked. Everyone who came to visit brought the nicest gifts. I was overwhelmed by how special everyone thought I was. People were so warm to me, so concerned and admiring. No one had ever seen such a beautiful baby. Total strangers would stop me in the street and peer into the pram. Everyone congratulated me on becoming a mother.

* * *

Tobias was a late walker. One of those things you forget with the years, though at the time you worried yourself sick. A late walker and a gentle soul. We'd happily have had a couple more, if they had come our way. But we were happy with what we had. And when I grew too old for another pregnancy, happy was how we stayed.

Louis and I never spoke about the birth. It only ever came up when Tobias asked about his childhood. The night Tobias refused to budge. That became the story: that Tobias didn't want to come out. Louis was the storyteller, all I had to do was nod along. "Yes, that's how it went." Then Louis would tease Tobias, insisting he had always been a mother's boy. "You had the life of Riley in there, sonny boy." And he would tell Tobias how he had kept his poor dad waiting, pacing anxiously up and down the landing. Until at long last the midwife called his name and told him he had a son.

And then, of course, it was time to dig the baby book out of the sideboard to look at the photo Louis took of us that day. Bathed in orange light, a slight haze over the lens—that bloodied, creased-up baby face on my breast and a huge brown nipple that couldn't possibly have been mine.

* * *

Months after the birth, I was walking through Goffert Park with the pram.

Tobias was all bundled up, so it must have been winter. He was over six months old by then. An elderly woman stooped over the pram to admire him. She was no one I knew and I have never met her since.

"What's his name?" she whispered. I let her stroke his sleeping cheek with her bony, wrinkled finger. Tobias's mouth twitched a little.

"Tobias," I answered. We watched him sleeping for a while.

"Is he your first?" she asked, out of the blue. Her question knocked me sideways.

"No." I shook my head, almost imperceptibly. "My second."

She was the only one I ever told.

# 32

"Hello, Elfie."

I practically jumped out of my skin. Without warning, Otto was waiting for me across from the florist's. I expected him to say something, to stammer an apology. Instead he put his arms around me, right there on the street for all to see. "I'm happy to see you again," he nuzzled in my ear.

"Me too."

"Will you come with me?"

"Where?"

"I may have found a room for you."

"Wait a sec." I ran back across the street to fetch my suitcase, hidden in the florist's storeroom. I hadn't heard from him in over a week, but I didn't want to bring that up.

In the car, we sat awkwardly side by side, smiling when our eyes met. It felt wonderful to be there beside him again, though my lower back was aching. At work, I had been able to conceal my condition under a loose-fitting sweater, but after a long day of lifting, crouching, and standing at the counter, my belly felt twice as heavy and seemed to take up more room than ever.

We parked on the market square. Otto carried my

case for me. It was almost like one of our hotel outings, only this time he strode on ahead. Perhaps it was his way of geeing me up. I tried to touch him, to put my arm through his, but he was having none of it. At the tail end of the sloping street lay the lead-grey expanse of the river. Otto motioned in the direction of Pepergas. "This way." And on he went, leaving me straggling.

"Where exactly are we going?"

"Not far now."

I thought he might be taking a kind of detour, to wrongfoot anyone who might be following us. Only two streets lay between us and the Waal. Further along the quay, the gasworks lay sleeping like a dark, hulking beast.

"How did you hear about this place?" I asked.

"Through someone I know."

I wanted to shake something loose, coax something out of him, find a way back to being Mr. and Mrs. Tendelow. I wanted him to hold me, to tell me he had been mulling over what I'd said about marriage.

"You seem to know a lot of people."

"What's that supposed to mean?"

"That you always seem to be making inquiries. Like with those witches in Oosterbeek."

Otto gave me the coldest of stares.

"First there was the pharmacist for the pessary. Then that landlady and her room for rent. And now this ... How do you go about it?"

"Go about what?"

"Finding a room." My voice echoed off the fronts of the houses. "'Elfrieda Tendelow is carrying my child and I'm looking to put a roof over her head.'"

"No," he snapped. Two nuns passed us in the opposite direction and he shot them a pious smile.

"Then what do you say?" I asked, loud enough for the walking habits to hear.

"I tell them I'm helping a niece."

"A niece?"

Otto was already striding ahead.

"What a fine, upstanding fellow you are."

He kept walking.

"Otto?"

He turned to face me. There was bitterness in his eyes and, for all my talk, I didn't want that either.

"What is it you want?" he said. "For me to give up everything too? To leave us both with nothing?"

These streets were strange to me, the people too—condemned to live in condemned buildings that reeked of damp cellars. Otto led me past alleys so narrow and crooked that they seemed to have no end. With barely a street sign in sight, they were more like passageways. The things that went on there happened nowhere.

Now and then, we came across a row of new buildings, then turned a corner to find a sandy wasteland full of parked cars. A bunch of young boys had conquered a pile of debris and were sword fighting with long, pointed bits of wood. Some of the older buildings inhabited a world of their own; unscathed façades that seemed to rise above their surroundings, dark windows glinting arrogantly as if these houses and their occupants had been predestined to withstand aerial bombardments and urban decay. These survivors stood tall amid patches of rubble-strewn land sprouting brown weeds. Above the gaps, horizontal beams saved neighbouring walls from collapse, like a mother keeping two fighting children at arm's length.

"Elfie?"

"Hmm?"

Otto had come to a halt at a narrow passage between two walls. There was a flight of stone steps leading down. A little way along, two shabby girls were playing mother, taking turns to push a Sunlight chest with a plank nailed to it. Every few steps, they stopped to fuss over the pretend baby in their makeshift pram.

"Well remembered," Otto said.

"What?" I thought he was talking about the girls playing mother. But his finger was pointing at the shiny new street sign fixed to the ruined housefront. NONNENPLAATS.

"This way."

"Here?" Beside the stone steps was a cobbled slope for rolling barrels up to the warehouses.

"Is this really the place?" Otto had already trotted halfway down the steps, my suitcase in his hand. The crumbling steps and cobbles led to a long, narrow courtyard that opened onto a cross street further on.

A gang of young lads were rolling a battered metal dustbin up the slope. They all looked like different versions of the same boy, and shot us such dirty looks that we automatically gave them a wider berth. They reached the top and with a "Three, two, one, watch yer back!" they let go and watched the bin rumble down the steps with a sound like hollow thunder. The bigger boys cheered as it steamrollered towards the end of the yard, before they all charged after it, the smallest almost tripping over their own feet as they puffed red-faced at the tail of the swarm. I stopped at a large wooden gate, where a sign read SCHÖNEBERG REMOVALS. "Is this it?" I asked, and looked for a bell to tug on.

"Uh, no ... Over there."

I could hardly believe my eyes. But Otto was serious. The house barely seemed able to hold its own walls together. We were looking up at the back of the building, which still bore the scars of the rooms from the demolished house next door. Here and there, stairs from the flights between floors stuck out of the wall. Cooing rose up from hollows that had once held support beams, the brickwork below streaked with pigeon droppings. The longer I looked, the more I noticed that soot and mould had turned the walls black. Every first floor window was boarded up with planks and old doors. Yet even this hovel showed signs of life: smoke from make-do chimneys curled up past the windows.

"It's only for now," Otto apologised. "I'm afraid you don't have much choice." For a moment, I thought he had brought me here to change my mind, to persuade me to go to the nuns in Oosterbeek after all. But as apology after apology poured out of him, I began to feel guilty. Guilty and afraid of losing him altogether if I made too much trouble.

"Did you arrange to meet someone?"

"They told me we could go straight up. I've paid the first month for you in advance." So, it was settled. This was where I would be living.

We entered through an odd wooden construction,

more a hatch than a door. It opened onto a dark stair-well that led up to a floor where there were no boards covering the windows. Wary eyes followed us from the open doors we passed. Clearly, we looked like people who had come to take something from them. Every room appeared to hold an unlikely number of people. In some I counted seven, eight ... no, wait ... nine children.

"One more flight," Otto said. "Can you manage this?"

"How do you mean?"

"In your condition?"

"Of course."

"I mean in a while. Weeks from now."

"But you told me this was only temporary."

I think we both knew there was nothing temporary about this. Behind another door, in a corner by the stairs, was a kitchen. A woman was standing at the sink, cutting a lump of meat into chunks. Her jet-black hair was tied in a loose bun and she brushed a stray lock from her face with her wrist.

"Mykasintos," she said.

"I'm sorry?" I looked at her blankly.

"Mitra Mykasintos." She pointed at herself.

"Ah ... I'm Elfrieda. You can call me Frieda."

The ferrous scent of blood, thickened with the smell of boiled-out hock, almost made me gag. I pointed over my shoulder at Otto, already halfway up the next flight of stairs. Mrs. Mykasintos gave me a friendly nod.

The top floor was home to another, smaller kitchen, opposite a single closed door. "This must be it." Otto pushed the door open.

"Isn't there a key?"

"Uh ... not that I know of."

A small table and two chairs were waiting for me in silence. There was a wicker seat by the window and a wood stove with a pipe that poked through a broken pane. Against the wall stood the bed that would be mine from then on. You could tell that, until recently, it had been slept in by more than one body. Otto placed my suitcase on the table and turned the taps on in the wash basin. Dry as a bone. All the light switches were dead. "You can use one of my gas lanterns for the time being. I won't be spotting moths for a while. I'll bring it over tomorrow."

I peered out of the window. In a corner of the back yard was a wooden construction with a door. I discovered later that day it was the toilet, and so filthy that I was prepared to hold in my pee for a lifetime rather than use it. Thankfully, Otto soon brought me a bedpan, which I emptied in the gutter that ran along the roof.

Down below, the black-haired woman was walking across the yard. She stopped at the end and tipped the contents of a pan over a low wall. Angry squeals and grunts came from the other side, and an enormous sow got to her feet. The animal was bricked in and unable to turn. Otto came and stood beside me at the window, leaned on the sill. I expected him to mention the nuns again or suggest we might still be able to end the pregnancy. Living here was obviously out of the question. But Otto said nothing.

"At least you can see the river from here," he said at last. "And those buildings over towards the old market are still decent and inhabited." As if the room's location at the edge of this open sore somehow made up for its squalor. "It's just not easy to find something in your situation."

I was fed up of hearing that this was my situation, not ours. I turned my back, knowing that everything I wanted to say could only drive him away for good. I looked in the empty wardrobe and decided to keep my things in my suitcase. I moved a chair out of the way and finally lowered myself onto the lumpy mattress. Otto didn't come and sit next to me, not even when I budged up to make room.

"Do you want to see?" Before he could answer, I pulled up my sweater. The skin of my belly was pale, almost translucent in the twilit room.

Otto stared but said nothing. Sitting there like that, I suddenly had no idea why I had felt the urge to show him, and I pulled my sweater down again. My navel wasn't exactly sticking out, but it was no longer a dimple. As if, after months of enforced discretion, my belly had finally decided to emerge in all its glory. I still couldn't quite believe that there was an actual person growing inside me.

"Right then." Otto took a good look around the room. He had closed himself off, arms crossed, coat buttoned to the collar. It was hard to tell if he was keeping me out or holding himself in. From the instant we knew I was pregnant, our lovemaking had stopped. Every kiss he withheld was an attempt to repay a debt he owed. Doing penance, until even the conception became immaculate, as if all we had done that spring was take an innocent stroll by the river. This was his redemption. He would become a decent man again. A man who had no part in this swollen belly of mine.

"I have to go now," Otto said.

I got up from the bed.

"I'll be back tomorrow. Can I bring you anything?"

"Thanks," I said. "I'll be fine."

I went up to him, placed my hand on his neck and lowered his forehead to mine. We stood like that a while, in the middle of the room. His eyes were closed. The floorboards beneath our feet creaked at the slightest movement. At last, Otto took my face in his cold hands and kissed me for the first time in weeks.

My room grew dark long before night fell.

With Otto gone, I sat down on the corner of the bed and did not get up again. I could feel the draught from the window on my flushed cheeks. Down below, boys fed rubble and stones to the bricked-in sow until the walls trembled with her rage. A truck rattled into the yard and parked behind the gate of the removal company. Cackling voices spilled from a pub down the street. In the space of an hour, I had gone from being someone who did not belong here to someone who lived in this room. I pictured my mother clearing the table in a kitchen not that far away. But I knew she could never find me in a house which might not even have an address, in a room furnished with worn-out things that seemed to belong to no one.

Otto had slipped some food into my case. With my coat on, I spooned baked beans into my mouth, straight from the tin, and chewed on some bread I had saved from lunchtime.

There was a knock at the door. I jumped. "Otto?"

No answer.

I hoped he had come back with the lantern. "Otto?" I asked again. The door inched open to reveal a man with thick, black hair, his face glowing orange in the light of the lamp he was holding. He stood there, silent, just as the black-haired woman in the kitchen had done. "Mysinos?" I asked.

"Mykasintos," he corrected me. "Here." He handed me what looked like a few strands from a wicker chair.

"Uhm ..." I had no idea what to do with this gift. "Thank you."

Mr. Mykasintos pointed at my stove, then crossed his arms and rubbed them with his hands.

"Ah ... for the stove?"

He gestured for me to wait. I listened as he thudded down the creaking stairs, uttered Greek incantations to his wife, and thudded back up again. In his hands, he held a few scrunched-up balls of newspaper.

"Farida." He shook a box of matches and handed it to me. "Farida."

It took me days to realise he was saying my name.

# 33

"Please. At least let me work in the storeroom. I can take orders over the phone, do the paperwork. I can even clean the shop in the evenings." Vlessing waited for my words to run out.

"And ..." he said, calmly continuing his side of the conversation. "How long were you planning to keep up this pretence?"

I was plonked on an upturned bucket, Vlessing towering over me. This had been a long time coming, but even so, I was taken aback when he summoned me into the storeroom. For weeks, I had done all I could to put it off: wearing baggy clothes, working harder, lifting more than I should. Insisting I only kept my coat on because I felt the cold.

"Well, Frieda? Answer me!"

"I-I'll work as hard as I ever did. You won't know the difference."

"And what about the good name of this establishment? A name we have worked hard to maintain, for four generations? In all those years, it has never been sullied by the likes of this."

"I'm sorry. I wanted to tell you."

"Well, it's too late now."

"But ..." I tried to stand up, but with the bucket being so low, I lurched to one side. The doughnut looked down from on high, standing much too close. A sign that I should be ashamed of the space I was taking up and that he wasn't going to give an inch to accommodate me and my swollen belly. This was my fault, after all. I was forced to squeeze past him and catch a whiff of his stagnant breath.

"How long were you planning to make fools of us?"

"Make fools of you? How can you say that?"

"Coming to work, day in, day out, as if all was right with the world," he intoned. "While you ... an unmarried woman ... with God only knows who ..." He spoke in fragments, glossing over the indecencies.

"Please? I need the money. The customers won't even know I'm here." I pressed my palms together and raised my fingertips to my chin. "I'll stay in the storeroom all day, I promise. No one will see me. Let me take care of the funeral wreaths and the wedding bouquets. I'll come in before it gets light and go home after dark. The days are already getting shorter."

Mr. Vlessing gave a long, deep sigh.

"And I'll be happy to work for less," I continued. "Just tell me what you're willing to pay."

"Frieda!" He pulled me up short. "The entire parish buy their flowers here. Sooner or later someone will spot you. If they haven't already." He glared at my belly without the least embarrassment.

"And you know what hurts the most, Frieda?"

I shook my head.

"Children come into this shop. Children! Imagine them being confronted with that ... that belly of yours." He said it as if it was the most revolting sight he could imagine.

"I'll wear looser clothes, I'll—"

"That's enough! You've sunk low enough. The worst thing is that I trusted you. I took you to be a decent young woman. I see now how wrong I was ... This was you all along. I should have listened."

"Listened?"

"I'd have sworn on my life that it was idle gossip."

"Listened to what?"

"Women can sense these things."

"What women?"

"You can go now, Frieda." There was no more room for manoeuvre.

"But what about my pay?"

"You had your pay packet last Saturday."

"Today is Wednesday." My voice was trembling. "Surely I'm entitled to my pay for the days I've worked since?"

"You're lucky it's me you're dealing with. My wife would have refused to give you another cent." As I was putting on my coat, Vlessing handed me an envelope, then waited for me to place the shop key in the palm of his outstretched hand.

As I walked out through the shop, Gemma was at the counter serving an elderly lady, one of our regular customers. She tore a sheet of brown paper from the roll and didn't look up, not even when I stopped in the middle of the floor and tried to catch her eye. She clipped a length of ribbon and curled it with the blade of the scissors.

"Gemma?" I said quietly, hoping only she would hear. The old woman turned to look and gave me a dry smile. I couldn't tell you her name. Her husband used to buy her a bunch of gerberas every week and after he died, she kept up the tradition. Most of her stories began, "You didn't hear this from me ..."

"Frieda," came the voice from the storeroom. "Out!"

"Gemma?" But Gemma's eyes were fixed on the flowers she was wrapping. She stapled the ribbon to the paper. "Gemma, please?" Another staple, then another and another. The gerbera lady looked on from under her rain bonnet, promoted from mere customer to eyewitness, poised to spread the news of how resolutely Vlessing the florist sent me packing after discovering the secret I had kept from him for months.

"Keep walking, Frieda." He came out of the storeroom and marched towards me, shooing me in the direction of the door. "I want you out of here now."

"Gemma?"

No answer.

"I am so sorry you had to witness such a scene, Mrs. Van der Meer. Please accept these flowers with our compliments." Vlessing took me by the arm and steered me towards the exit like a troublesome child. "Out, now!" One shove and I was on the pavement. "And never darken my door again."

I turned back one last time and caught Gemma's helpless expression. Perhaps she said something, but I was too far away to hear. We never saw each other again.

The emptiness of the afternoon unsettled me. I found myself hoping with all my heart that I would run into my mother. Instead of heading back to my room, I boarded a bus to my parents' house.

"Haven't seen you in a while," said the driver as I got on. "Been out of sorts?" I nodded, bought a ticket, and found myself a seat. As we crossed the railway bridge and drove on through familiar streets, the window became a screen that showed me my life without me in it. Another bend in the road. The zebra crossing. Pruims's bakery flashed past, but I couldn't see my mother among the customers. Suddenly, the driver braked, though no one had rung the bell. Everyone stayed seated. He looked at me in his mirror.

"Wakey-wakey."

"I didn't ring."

"But this is your stop, isn't it?"

"Yes, only ... No, not today."

He raised an apologetic hand and the doors puffed and hissed themselves closed. We passed my parents' house and I thought I glimpsed the outline of someone in the living room. My mother, no doubt. I turned my head and watched the house disappear over my shoulder.

# 34

"Will you be home this Saturday?" It's Tobias on the phone.

"Yes, son," I reply. "I'll be here." We've never been good at making up after a quarrel. Usually the anger evaporates and we wander into a different conversation.

"In that case, I'll drop by late afternoon."

"No particular reason?"

"Uh, no."

"Everything okay with the two of you?"

"Yes, yes."

"Grand. I'll see you Saturday."

It's quiet at the other end of the line, but he doesn't hang up.

"Toby?"

"I'm sorry about the other day."

"Oh," I answer.

"For mouthing off at you like that."

"Oh, don't you worry. I understand. You have your own life to lead and suddenly you've been landed with all this."

"With you?"

"Yes, with your cranky old mother."

"Oh, her ... she's always been cranky," Tobias chuckles. "That's not it. I think we have to find our way again. You and me. Now that it's just the two of us. Without Dad."

He doesn't quite sound like himself.

"But you have Nadine now," I say. "And baby makes three."

"Yes, but there's three of us, too."

"Three of us?"

"You, me, and our daughter. Three generations. I really want her to know who her grandma was ... is, I mean. Who her grandma is." There's a wordless hiss on the line. Birds twitter in the background.

"Do you get what I mean?"

"I want that too, son."

"Good." And before I can add another word, Tobias is saying goodbye.

## 35

Poor soul. He's up on a chair, brandishing Louis's drill. At the mercy of my directions.

"Up a bit, and a touch to the right."

Tobias holds the frame to the wall. "Here?"

"Yes, that's grand." To be honest, I could do without all this. But Tobias has got it into his head that the place needs brightening up, a cosier feel. And that means drilling my walls full of holes. I'm just happy to have him here, filling up the place and babbling away like the overgrown boy he is.

"You know, we may try for another baby after this one."

"Really?"

"Nadine is still young. And an only child is ..." Tobias picks up an orangey holiday snap of the three of us on the esplanade in Vlissingen and holds it above the wedding photo of me and Louis.

"I mean, it's not that I missed out as a boy. But the pregnancy is flying past. And I can see how happy it makes Nadine. And me too. Maybe it means that little bit more now that Dad's gone. Do you know what I mean?"

"Mm-hmm." I concentrate on keeping the hoover nozzle in the right place, just below the cross he's marked on the wall.

"It's convinced me all the more that I want a family of my own." Tobias nods that he's about to start. The drill whines three holes in the concrete.

"Anyway, better wait and see how this one turns out first," he chuckles. "Maybe little thingumabob will be a bawler. That might dampen our enthusiasm."

I run a duster over the fancy silver frame with the photo of me and my sisters squeezed onto a three-seat sofa. I was still a girl, the other three already grown women. It must have been taken before the middle two left for Canada. My parents always had this picture of us hanging above the sideboard, surrounded by photographs of almost all their grandchildren.

"Mum?" Tobias holds up my parents' wedding photo, another one in black-and-white. "This one here?"

I nod and hand him the Rawlplugs.

"What was it like for you when you were pregnant with me?"

"What do you mean?"

"You know, what was it like? What do you remember about it?"

"We told you about that, didn't we? The night you refused to budge."

"Yeah, I know that story, but I meant more like ... How was it when you were actually pregnant? You'd already been married a year or two. Were you worried at all? I mean, there were no scans back then. You didn't even know I was a boy till I was born, right?" A cloudburst of questions raining down on me. I open my mouth to answer, but have to lean against the sideboard to stay upright. "You must remember something? Mum?" He looks down at me.

"Toby."

"What is it?"

"There was another time. Before you." I don't know how else to put it.

"What?" His gaze switches from my left eye to my right and back again.

"Only it didn't survive. That's what they said." I can't bring myself to say the word *baby*, though I could have said it for any other child in the world. "It was born that way, early but not all that early. I had a month to go, maybe two."

"But Mum … how …" Tobias climbs down from the chair and lays the drill carefully on the table.

"You had a stillborn baby?"

I nod.

"Why didn't I know this?" It's not an indignant question. It's more surprise. Compassion too.

"Only my parents knew. And one or two other people back then. No one else, not even my sisters."

"And Dad, of course."

"Louis didn't know either."

Tobias shakes his head to get his thoughts straight. "How come? How could Dad not know?"

"It was before we met."

Tobias turns to the photos hanging on the wall, then turns back to me. "So, who was the father?"

"Otto."

"Otto?"

"The Otto whose name you looked up for me. The one in America." I pick up a random frame from the ones in front of me. "Shall we hang this one a little higher? Or there, above the fridge?"

"Mum …" Tobias sits down on the chair. "You can't

just drop this into the conversation and expect us to carry on."

"Fair enough." I swallow and return the frame to the sideboard.

"Are you sure about this?" Tobias asks, crossing his arms.

"Sure?"

"I mean, could you be getting mixed up? You know, with everything that's been going on. Dad dying, Nadine expecting our baby."

"I'm not mixing anything up. I was pregnant all right. Back then everyone did their best to hush things up, never to mention it. Otto disappeared. I met Louis and a new life began. We married, moved into our house. And after a few years, you came along."

"And you never thought of that baby?"

"Yes ... Yes, of course I did. Only ..." The words are hard to find. "It was far away, somewhere else. I think I must have piled my new life on top of it. But ever since your father died ... For some reason, I can't seem to think of anything else."

"Oh, Mum."

My chin starts wobbling, I have to grit my teeth to make it stop. "Soon I'll be gone too and no one will even know it existed." Tobias gets up to hug me. "Just give me a moment, son."

Briefly, he rests his hand on my shoulder, then wanders over to the sink and comes back with a glass of water. "Here. Have a drink."

We sit for a while, until Tobias comes up with another question.

"Is that why you're looking for this guy Otto?"

"I suppose. He was the closest person to me at the time."

"Were you and he together?"

"He was married to another woman." I nip at my water.

"Did he know you were pregnant?"

"Oh, yes. He helped me when I lost everything. The only help I had."

Tobias stops asking and I don't really know what else to tell him.

"So, I could have had a brother? Or a sister?"

"Uhm ..." All this time, the baby has been mine and mine alone. Hidden somewhere deep inside, a hard kernel of magma. It was Otto's, too, of course. But no one else's, not even a grandchild for my parents. It never occurred to me that my baby could be something to Tobias.

"Y-yes," I stammer. "You're right. You would have had a half-brother. Or a half-sister."

"Which was it? A brother or a sister?"

I say nothing.

"You don't know?"

"No."

"Then what happened to the baby?"

"I don't know, love."

"Oh, Mum." His hand lands on my shoulder again and gives it a rub.

"Do you want some more water?"

I shake my head and hand him the empty glass.

"And you never told Dad any of this?" Tobias tries not to make it sound like an accusation. "Something this important? If Nadine had been through something like this ..." He shrugs. "I mean, it's not something you can keep to yourself."

"Louis never asked."

"But Mum, how would he have known to ask?"

"He couldn't ... it was just ... he had ..." I have no answer for him. There were times when it hurt so much, it seemed insane to me that Louis couldn't feel it through my skin when he held me or pressed me to him when we made love.

Tobias has gone back to fiddling with his screws.

"Toby?"

"Hmm."

"Would you mind putting this one up for me?"

"No, of course not." Tobias takes the frame with the photo of Louis we used at the funeral and holds it high. "Here?"

"That'll do nicely."

He scratches a little cross on the wall.

# 36

Louis and I had a good life together.

As the years went by, he said it more and more often. And I agreed—we had it good. On one occasion, not all that long ago, those words moved me to tears. Louis and I were out walking in the Hatertse Fens. I could still walk more or less unaided then, though I had taken to using a stick. After Louis retired, we would go there on weekdays when it was nice and quiet. Perhaps it was early December rolling around that got me so emotional. With the passing of the years, that month had begun to catch me unawares again. The wonderful light on a crisp winter's day. That particular day, the edges of the lake were frozen and I took a cautious step onto the ice. The water was shallow, the sandy bottom just centimetres beneath the surface. "Come on," I said, "it's thick enough for the pair of us."

"No, thank you very much." Louis walked ahead to our bench under the slanting birch. "These are the only shoes I have with me." He took a thermos from the backpack, followed by two plastic cups and our lunchbox of sandwiches.

Tufts of frosted grass peeked above the surface, there were bubbles in the water below. The ice was wet in places and creaked along the edges.

"Aw, be a sport!" I tried to entice him over. "Where's the harm in wet shoes? It's not as if the car park is miles away."

"Watch yourself," Louis said, and I could tell he was getting agitated. "If you fall, you'll break a hip."

"How often do we get the chance these days?" For the hell of it, I shuffled a little further out onto the ice.

"And who's going to have to pick you up and drive you to hospital?"

"If we both fall, we can ring for matching ambulances. Order a cosy hospital room for two. At least there we'll have a TV each."

Louis laughed a little vapour cloud and took a bite of his sandwich. Back on the path, my feet remembered how solid ground feels when you step off smooth, hard ice.

"Here." Louis handed me my coffee.

"Thank you kindly."

He said hello to a passing couple and scratched the head of their dallying dog, before sending him on in search of his owners. "Maybe I should get my skates sharpened, in time for the next big freeze."

"You do that." I didn't tell him I'd thrown those old things out years ago when I found mice nesting inside the boots.

"I wonder if I still have it in me."

"Without a doubt." Louis used to skate across the fens, pulling Tobias behind him on a sled. Our little lad, bundled up in his winter togs with his favourite woolly hat, the yellow one Granny Crossword had crocheted for him. Even when it got too small, he insisted on wearing it. The water at the fens was so shallow, I never had to worry that anything might befall Tobias. I liked to skate off on my own, in wide circles, out into corners where few people ventured. In those rare moments, my thoughts led me back to Otto and I would whisper into the wind.

"I have a little boy now," I would tell him as we skated together awhile. "Yes, life's been good to me." And I would point at the yellow hat in the distance. "That's my little lad. That's Tobias."

"Glorious," Louis said, out of nowhere.

We had walked on, arm in arm to keep out the cold. Our feet always managed to fall into the same rhythm. Halfway, we stopped to look at the mist rising from the heath.

"Well?" Louis asked.

"Yes, it's glorious all right."

"Here and now, the world is ours alone." There wasn't so much as a vapour trail in the blue sky above us. I could feel myself welling up and, before Louis could notice, I planted a quick kiss on his lips. Besides, I really did want to kiss him.

"I love you," I said.

Louis wrapped his arms around me and said, "We've had a good life together." As his big hands rubbed my back, he must have sensed something. "Oh, Frieda," he said.

Suddenly there was no stopping them. The tears came flooding out of me, making wet flecks on my coat. Louis produced a crumpled hanky for my runny nose.

"What's the matter, love?"

"I don't know ... I ... It's so long since we skated here, since I was out on the ice."

"I only meant we've had it good together, I didn't mean our lives are over. Is that what you were thinking?" Before I could answer, Louis began joining the dots for me. "We have years ahead of us yet. Who knows what the future holds? We could end up with a grandchild. Maybe even a couple. You never know with Tobias."

Louis took my face in his hands. "Frieda, love. Don't be sad. It just struck me, with the trees and the sun shining low across the water. It made me think how these trees have grown up alongside us. All the times we've walked this path. First with Tobias in the pram, and later when he raced ahead on that little BMX bike we bought him. The way he'd cheer when we said we were stopping at St. Walrick for pancakes. We walked here after both my parents' funerals. And when your father passed away. Remember? So much leads back to this place. And I ... I ..." Louis shrugged. "We've always had it good together, simple as that." He kissed me on both cheeks, on my forehead. "And there are so many good things to come. Believe me, I can feel it." His wide eyes were so full of conviction, I had no choice but to smile. And to nod.

"Yes." I clasped his fingers tight. "I hope so too."

"I know so," he said.

# 37

There was always a child crying somewhere in the house.

Often, on the edge of waking, I was seized by the fear that someone had robbed me of my belly while I slept. Opening my eyes, there was a surge of relief on seeing it wasn't true, but that discovery seemed to pin me to the mattress, and getting out of bed became a struggle.

The first months of pregnancy had been abstract, something I had to believe because there was so little to see. And even when the curve of my belly was undeniable, it still felt as if the baby was somewhere in the depths of the universe, not a few centimetres beneath my skin. It was only years later, when I was expecting Tobias, that I recognised that gentle twitching inside me for what it was.

My nipples changed colour, though I barely noticed at first. The sides of my belly were scored with uneven lines, and there were nights when I woke three times with a desperate need to pee. Though it was seldom more than a dribble, I would still throw back the covers and sit on the cold metal of the bedpan Otto had brought for me. The fierce, salty smell pricked in my nostrils as the night chill bit through my socks and into my toes. In the morning,

I slid open the window and carried the bedpan carefully across the room, trying not to spill the glistening puddle that swilled across the bottom until I could tip it into the gutter that ran along the roof. One morning it had frozen solid, and a plaque of ice clattered from the pan and cracked into yellow shards. I thought of my sister Emma on her farm in Winterswijk and wondered if she might still be willing to take me in.

Otto dropped by frequently but his visits were mostly brief and unannounced. He always kept his coat on. He would bring a tin of ravioli or brown beans, a net of wood for my stove. It was Otto who introduced me to the taste of milk with cinnamon and sugar, and before long I started craving it.

Sometimes I was out when he came and Mrs. Mykasintos would catch me on my way up to the room. "Meesta Owto," she said, and pointed up the stairs. Over her shoulder I could see her children at the table chomping on bread and dripping. "Thank you," I said, and went up to my room to find a paper bag on the table with "From Mr. Tendelow" written on it. A loaf with a few slices missing.

In those weeks, I was sometimes in such a daze that I fell in love with life again, but my mood could just as easily take a sharp turn and plunge me into panic or choking fear.

One day, Mrs. Mykasintos knocked on the door with a small pile of mended baby clothes, and I asked her to come in. "Could you take a look for me?" She stared at my lips. "Look," I repeated, pointing two fingers at her eyes and then at my sides. I pulled up my jumper to show her the marks that ran across my skin, darker now than they had been. I was afraid they were seams that might one day rip open.

She nodded and, though I couldn't understand what she was saying, it sounded reassuring. I ran my fingers over the baby clothes she had given me and that I would soon tuck away at the back of the wardrobe.

I remember it so well because it was the first time I felt the baby kick. I grabbed at my belly. "What was that?" Mrs. Mykasintos smiled and gestured that it was nothing to worry about. A high-pitched voice called her from the landing. It was one of those fleeting moments when I caught myself thinking that I might be able to do this myself. On my own. Perhaps even here, in this room.

In the beginning, I was constantly aware that I did not belong there, that I was different from the people around me. I found bars or cafés where I could use the toilet, a quiet restaurant where I could give my face a quick rinse in the ladies' room. But before long I was refused entry. Most likely because they recognised me and knew I never ordered anything. Either that or they had begun to smell the poverty on me. Café Den Oever put up with me the longest. There the men at the bar would mock the houses we lived in, joke that the only way to fix them up was to burn them to the ground.

More than once, I saw a family that had been thrown out on the street stretch a sheet over a patch of pavement to shelter their belongings. The mother would cook on a paraffin stove with the window ledge for a kitchen counter, while the older girls would walk around bouncing the youngest on their arm. Fingers raked the kids' greasy hair into some kind of shape. Cheeks were wiped clean with a licked thumb. I seldom saw a father.

What amazed me most was that families like these never replied when you spoke to them. No one so much as looked up when I walked past. They lived on the pavement as if they were surrounded by four stone walls that were invisible to the rest of us. The mothers and their daughters swept the pavement as if it were their own living room. Even when their makeshift tents were flattened and cleared away, they found another place to live. Life always went on, for everyone.

As long as a building had not been demolished or burned down, someone would pull the boards from the windows or force a door. Out of nowhere, a man would appear and claim that you owed him rent. Men showed up claiming you owed them all kinds of things. Some of them followed you when you walked on.

On my daily walks, I would peer through the windows of the shops my mother liked to go to. In a shoe shop on Broerstraat, I saw two girls perched on rocking horses. One was a few years older than the other, but their matching dresses and hairstyles made them twins. They gave me a cheery wave and I waved back, though I was sure I had never seen them before in my life. Could there be two hearts beating behind my navel?

For the first time, I began to notice how many pregnant bumps there were under the coats of the women I passed. How mothers absently stretched out a hand to the child beside them, well-kept children who gazed at their shiny new shoes as they walked. I winked at a little boy and he stared at me open-mouthed until I turned the corner. I looked at children as if I was in search of something, traits I might recognise. Until it dawned on me that our son or daughter had yet to come into the world, that there would be no one to recognise in them but me and Otto. I was overcome by the sudden desire to see our baby. But that desire could fade just as quickly and leave me determined to go in search of an angel maker, though deep down I knew it was much too late for that. Besides, where would I find one? How could I ask complete strangers to help me commit what was nothing short of a crime? These were thoughts I could no longer mention to Otto. When he was with me, I didn't dare show that I had my doubts, such terrible doubts.

On Saturday, there was a flea market around St. Stephen's church. It was teeming with visitors who rooted around among the things spread out for sale, plucking sweaters and skirts from mounds of clothing on the cobbles and holding them up to assess at a glance whether they were in a fit state for mending. Traders in felt hats puffed on cigars as they shuffled among rusty piles of hardware.

There were so many things I still needed before the baby came that I couldn't decide what to look for first. My meagre savings were dwindling fast and the last thing I wanted was to beg favours from Otto. I returned to my room without buying anything.

I had to pause on the landing to catch my breath. In my dizziness, the depths of the stairwell rose up to meet me, to drag me down. For a second, all I wanted was to fall into the dark. But hearing footsteps behind me, I clung to the bannister. A door opened.

"Meesta Owto," Mrs. Mykasintos whispered, and pointed up to my room. "Shhh."

I climbed the last flight of stairs and pushed open the door. Otto was lying on the bed, fast asleep. The room was snug, as if he had brought a helping of warmth with him as a gift. His coat was hung over the back of the chair, shoes parked neatly between the legs. I took off my shoes and got into the bed with him. Otto groaned a sort of apology and lifted the blanket so I could snuggle closer. "Elfie." He pulled me to him. "My dear, sweet Elfie." He kissed me and buried his nose in my hair. "I'm so happy to see you again."

The fire he had lit was flickering behind the little mica window of my stove. Only then did I notice the cradle by the door. A wicker basket with a trim of lace and a white canopy above. There was even a teddy bear waiting for our child.

"Do you want to feel?" I asked.

Otto turned onto his back under the covers. "Feel it moving?"

I took his hand and placed it under my sweater.

"Where is it?" he whispered.

"Wait a little."

"Do I need to do something?"

"Just keep your hand where it is."

A little thump came up through my skin. Otto's startled mouth fell open but he didn't pull back his hand. One nudge, quickly followed by another, as if the baby was signalling in Morse, a message we had yet to understand.

# 38

December came and it froze day and night. Everyone wrapped up in their warmest coats and built their fires high in the hope that this winter might take fright and leave us be till spring. The thickness of the smoke that blew through the streets was a kind of thermometer. The less you could see, the deeper the chill.

I didn't need an alarm clock. Every morning I was woken up by the restlessness inside. Gentle stirrings had made way for an insane churning beneath my skin. As if I was being knocked out of shape from the inside to make room in that increasingly cramped belly of mine.

Lying on my back, I would place my hands on the drum of tight skin, thinking I could calm the baby and it might let me doze a little longer. But more often than not, the hammering continued until daylight, and so I got up anyway. Before I could lever myself upright, I had to roll onto my side. My shoes had started to pinch, and bending to pick something up from the floor became a challenge. I couldn't get up after having a pee without kneeling on the floorboards first. I tried putting the bedpan on a chair but that left my feet dangling off the floor. Eventually I had no choice but to trudge downstairs to the wooden shack out in the yard and then drag myself back up to my room again.

One night I felt a gentle pressure inside and got up for another trip to the yard. I groped around in the dark for the box of matches on my bedside table, slid up the glass of Otto's lantern, and lit the flame by touch. As quietly as I could, I made my way downstairs past the Mykasintos' open door and the orange glow of their smouldering stove. I stole through the house without waking a soul. When I planted my bare buttocks on the freezing wooden seat outside, there was a trickle of pee and the pressure inside me faded. I sat a while longer in the moonlight that sliced through the slits between the planks, listening to the grunts and sighs of the bricked-in sow. Nothing came. Shivering as I pulled up my woollen knickers, I took my lantern by the handle and creaked open the door. To keep the worst of the cold off my feet, I wobbled across the yard on tiptoe. It had begun to snow, flakes so small and light that the wind seemed intent on blowing them back into the sky.

Half an hour later, I was back on the toilet. Again, there was nothing more than a trickle. I reached between my legs and touched myself. My vagina was warm and bulged a little, not that different to recent weeks. Perhaps I had come down with some kind of bladder infection. My bowels showed no sign of activity either, so I got my underthings in order and began the climb back to my room.

Sinking down on the bed, I curled around my belly like a hedgehog and prayed for sleep to come.

And it came.

The next morning, traipsing across the yard for the umpteenth time, I felt my belly tighten and was rooted to the spot. A surge of cramp came, held, held, held, then fell away.

Children were playing all around me. A stick-wielding mother was whacking a carpet that hung like a tongue from an open window. It was as if I had been held underwater while life around me carried on as usual. I rattled at the door to the shack. "Wait your turn," a voice within growled, and seconds later a stranger emerged. Bolting the door behind me, I hitched up my skirt and my old petticoat and peeled down my knickers. My insides had calmed down. Perhaps wind had triggered the cramps. Otto had promised to come by that afternoon and I wondered if he knew a doctor who could take a look at me.

I knitted myself into a more peaceful mood that morning. I no longer had to think my way from one stitch to the next and my needles seemed to clack away with a rhythm all their own. Looking back, it seems absurd that this was how I passed the hours that day, though I had nothing to my name. Not even a scrap of wood to burn in the stove. But for some reason, I wasn't afraid. The fear came later. In another life.

That early December day, waves of pain kept surging through me, increasing in frequency. In the lulls that followed, my mind would clear for twenty, perhaps thirty minutes. Enough for me to pick up my knitting and pray the cramp would stay away. But it kept on rising, pulling my belly tighter and tighter. When I lay down, I could barely heave myself upright. Instead I tried to stay on my feet, shuffling from one end of the room to the other. I clung to the doorpost or the tabletop to withstand the searing pain, praying to no one for Otto to appear. I counted the hours until the afternoon's end. I counted the months—seven, maybe eight at a push. "You can't be born yet. You can't," I said over and over, until it sounded like a prayer. "Please come, Otto. Please."

I tried to fight pain with pain, clawing and scratching at my thighs, slamming the heel of my hand against my skull and tugging at my hair.

"Mrs. Mykasintos?" I held on tight to the doorpost, not daring to get closer to the stairwell. As I stood there, the pain seemed to snap me in two. Warm liquid began to run down my legs, brownish water with a smell that was dark and raw.

"Mrs. Mykasintos!"

At last I heard footsteps. Halfway, she stopped and scowled up at me, wondering what all the noise was about. "Farida?" She charged up the last of the stairs, turning to hurl abuse at the children who had clambered up behind her.

"Doctor," I begged her. "Please, fetch me a doctor."

She pressed a rough palm to my forehead, then lifted my chin to get a good look at my face.

The glint of panic in her eyes made me realise that it had started. "It's not my time yet." Leaning on her strong arms, I stumbled back into my room. "Fetch a doctor. Doctor."

Mrs. Mykasintos nodded and bellowed instructions through the open door. I hobbled through the room like a wounded animal, looking for a sheltered corner with no light, hoping the pain might not find me there. Now that someone was with me, I was able to sink deeper into myself. There were hands that brought cloths, put a steaming pan of water on the table. Hands that brought twigs and splintered wood for my stove.

Suddenly a man with thick, horn-rimmed glasses was standing in the middle of the room. I can't remember much about him, except the stark impression that he did not belong there. "This woman is already in labour." It was a snarl, an accusation. "She needs a midwife." He turned to go but Mrs. Mykasintos blocked his path, astonished that he would want to leave. She formed an immovable barrier that left him no choice.

I was bundled onto the bed. Someone helped me out of my skirt, placed towels under my buttocks. Two fingers were stuck in my vagina. I looked up at the man with the horn-rimmed glasses. "She's too far gone." Another wave clenched my body, left me hunched up on the bed. "Fetch a nurse!"

I wanted to lie on my side but someone kept forcing me onto my back.

"How many months?" the doctor asked.

"E-eight," I stammered. "Nearly eight."

"More towels," he commanded. "Clean towels." Every clean towel in the house had already been used. "Then bring me a newspaper, that's the most sterile thing we have." Before long, someone came dashing in with a paper and the pages were stuffed under my backside. The waves welling up from deep inside grew fiercer, more impatient, more forceful.

What happened next is a blur. A black robe at the bedside, nimble hands as cold as tools. A crucifix dangling close to my face. I wanted to turn but the cold hands held me down. I can't remember her talking to me or looking me in the face. It was as if the nun was performing an emergency operation on me and I was no part of it. I was to follow orders and disturb no one. I heard the doctor swear. "It's coming already. I can feel it coming."

Out of nowhere, a flannel was pressed over my eyes. A rough, wet flannel. The world turned pitch-black. No matter how I turned my head or tried to wriggle free, the blindness held. Head pressed deep into the pillow, arms pinned to the mattress. Choking, no strength to resist. "It's coming, it's coming." A voice from another world. I pushed myself inside out. There was pain, there must have been pain, but it's the panic I remember most of all. Panic and the agonising release as flesh and bone slithered out of me.

The room must have gone quiet.

My thighs were trembling, but not from the cold. My mind was racing. I turned my head and the flannel fell from my eyes. No one was holding my arms or my legs and yet I could hardly move. Specks of black and white were flickering in front of me and the glare from the window hurt my eyes. Black robes beside me, the nun wrapping something in a cloth. Two feet sticking out. Two tiny feet.

"There you are," I moaned.

The nun saw me looking and quickly covered them

with a corner of the cloth. She turned her back and skirted past the bed, around the table, and towards the door. I wanted to go after her but my body held me down. Tossed on some shore with waves washing over me, I had been saved from drowning and lay abandoned in the surf. The doctor was nowhere to be seen, but voices were coming from the other side of the door. I recognised one of them.

"Otto!" My voice was too feeble to reach the landing, if it came out of my mouth at all. I cramped up again, it felt like something else was coming out of me.

There was a creak of floorboards and the nun came back into the room. Otto appeared at her shoulder, the chill of the day still clinging to his coat. He pushed past the nun and came to me. "Oh, Elfie. Elfie, my poor lamb."

"It started all of a sudden." My teeth were chattering. "I couldn't make it stop."

"Don't worry. That's all right." His lips brought warmth to my forehead.

"Where's the baby?" I asked.

"I haven't seen it yet."

Once again, my whole body began to judder. His hands stroked a few strands of hair from my face. "Oh, Elfie. I'm so glad to see you."

"Why isn't it crying?" My own words came as a shock to me.

"I don't know, Elfie."

"Shouldn't it be crying?"

He pulled the sheet over me, to protect me.

"Otto?"

He hushed me with smiles that got smaller and smaller.

"Excuse me, sir." The doctor was standing by the half-open door. "I must ask you to leave the room."

Otto got to his feet. "Is everything as it should be, doctor?"

"Sister Anna is waiting for you."

"I'll be right back, Elfie." Otto left. And he never returned.

I tried to struggle to sitting. "Lie down, miss!" the doctor said. I think they were the first words he had directed at me. "You're not finished here." It was as if some harm had been done and I had to stay behind until it was all cleared up.

"We need to get this out of you." He wrapped a towel around the bluish-purple cable between my legs and pulled with so much force that his face contorted. "But it won't budge."

"Doctor?"

He leaned over and prodded me, first with the heel of his hand, then the point of his elbow. My belly was still swollen and huge, but the emptiness inside meant it yielded a little. "Be careful, please," I said. I had been so protective of it for so long. Perhaps there was another baby to be born. The doctor continued to pull as if he was trying to win a tug of war, as if someone needed punishing.

I squeezed my eyes shut and again I saw the two tiny feet, before they were covered by the cloth. A glimpse in the space of a heartbeat. A pale, waxy substance in the creases. Toes curled, shrinking from all the cold in the world. Years passed and the image grew clearer. Until I could picture each toe, trace each line against the darker blood beneath the skin.

Two tiny feet seeking comfort in each other.

"Your placenta." The doctor shook his head. "It won't detach. Ruptured, probably."

"Where is my baby?"

He raised a bloodied hand in the air so as not to dirty anything as he walked through the room.

"When can I see the baby, doctor?"

He turned the wash-basin tap, but no water came out. "And in conditions like these ..." He shook his head.

"Doctor?" It felt like I had to keep interrupting him.

"It's not as if you could have brought up a child here, now is it?" For once it didn't sound like an accusation, more like a lament. Perhaps he even meant to console. His eyes scanned the floor, looking everywhere except at me. In the end he wiped his fingers on the sheet.

"Doctor? Please." These were the only words that came. I would have tugged at his sleeve if I'd dared. Another convulsion. With every aftershock, I could feel liquid gushing out of me. "We need to get you to a hospital. There's an ambulance on the way."

I breathed out, the ceiling ballooned upwards. I gasped for air and the walls were sucked tight, pressing in on me. "Please?" I tried to prop myself up, but the least movement brought me close to fainting. "Where is it? Is something wrong?"

"I'm sorry, miss."

"What for?"

He maintained his silence.

Far, far away, at the end of this bed, lay my trembling thighs and calves, my own pale feet. The insides of my thighs were streaked with blood as if a vital organ had been pulled out of me. I could not cover myself. "I want to see my baby."

The more I said, the deeper his silence became.

"Doctor?"

Shaking his head, he turned to the nun and began to murmur. "Yes, doctor," was her answer to everything he said. And then, "Of course, doctor. I will stay."

"Could you fetch Otto for me?"

Again, no response.

'Otto!" I shouted.

The doctor picked up his case. Coat slung over his arm, he scanned the room to make sure he hadn't forgotten anything and backed out onto the landing.

White specks swarmed wherever I looked. The sister bundled the sheet into a wad and shoved it between my legs. "Please," I begged, the rush of my own blood in my ears. "Sister?" She too seemed to disappear, though she was standing right beside me. "Sister?" I grabbed at her robe, but she intercepted my wrist and brought my hand back to my body. She pressed my arm to the mattress and patted it firmly, an order to lie there obediently.

"An ambulance is on the way," she said. "I will wait with you."

# 39

"Mum," Tobias blares before I've even put the phone to my ear.

"Are you in the car?"

"I'm on the road."

"Nothing wrong, I hope?"

"No, no, everything's fine."

"Nothing the matter with Nadine?"

"No, she's great. On my way to see a new customer in Waalwijk."

"Oh, that's good to hear."

"I'm calling because I made a discovery last night."

"And what might that be?"

"About that Otto of yours." Oh, that Otto.

"What is it?" It feels odd to be talking about him with Tobias.

"Well, after everything you said about your pregnancy and that he was practically the only one who knew, I did a bit of poking around."

My mouth is dry as paper. I can feel my heart throbbing inside the cast on my hand.

"Do you know his wife's name?"

"Brigitte."

"And you're sure about that?"

"Yes, Toby. I'm sure."

"In that case, I think he's still alive."

"What's that?"

"Your Otto is still alive."

The words start to get through to me. "How could you know that? There must be any number of Ottos."

"Yes, but how many Otto Drehmanns in their nineties do you think there are?" The excitement in his voice is getting on my nerves. "I started by calling the university in Pittsburgh. The photo of the guy you said was Otto was on their website, remember? Turns out he taught there for years. From the mid-sixties right through to the early nineties."

I feel a rush of anger. Otto didn't disappear. He got on a plane and left.

"Mum? Are you still there?"

"Yes. Yes, I'm here."

"Well, listen up. This is where it gets good. Yesterday, I got a message from a Professor Bernadette Mendoza." He says the name with a thick American twang. "She knew this Otto from way back. He even supervised her doctoral thesis. And now she's due to retire herself." He's tossing in so many details that I can hardly keep up. "Anyway, she messaged me to say that she remembers him fondly. She had no idea how he was doing, but she did know that he returned to the Netherlands after he retired. Until a few years ago, she got a card every Christmas from him and his wife. And the wife's name was Brigitte. She asked me to give them her regards."

"Toby, I ... please."

"And now for the best bit."

"What?"

He inserts a pause before his big finish.

"For goodness' sake, Toby—just tell me."

"Bernadette says he came back here, to Nijmegen."
"Nijmegen?" The idea of Otto being so close almost smothers me.
"Mum, are you still there?"
"He's not at this nursing home, is he?"
"No, no. Have you got a pen and paper handy?"
"Pen and paper?"
"I've got an address for you. And ..." Tobias's voice is bright and cheerful, a proud son eager to surprise his mother with something new he's learned. "I drove past the other day."
"No, Tobias. No! I won't have it, do you hear? I confided in you but this has gone too far already. You need to stop this. Stop it, now."
"Mum, take it easy. Nobody saw me. I drove past and checked out the name on their letterbox, that's all."
It's too much. My thoughts are racing, my head throbbing.
"And what do you think?"
"Stop playing games. Just tell me, will you?"
"Otto and Brigitte Drehmann." It stings to hear Tobias say their names in the same breath.
"Did he see you?"
"Nobody saw me. And if they had, I would have come up with something. Told them I used to live next door, whatever."
"And you're sure he's still alive?"
"Well, not one hundred per cent, but ..." Tobias goes quiet, crushed by my reaction, and I can't think of anything to cheer him up. "I thought you'd be happy."
"I don't know. I just don't know."

"What don't you know?"

"It's all so long ago and it ended abruptly. He ended it."

"It's been sixty years, Mum."

"And in all that time he's never been in touch. Not so much as a card."

"Did you ever try to reach him?"

"No, but I ... How was I supposed to do that? There was no internet, not a single Drehmann in the phone book. Besides, Otto was married. He left me to fend for myself. And by the sound of things, he and his wife are still together. Things worked out fine for him."

"Mum," Tobias interrupts me. "Why are you looking at this from his point of view? This is important to you. Doesn't that give you the right to get in touch?"

"The right? I'm not so sure."

Tobias must have parked the car. It's quieter at the other end of the line.

"Are you scared?" he asks.

"Yes, perhaps I am. Though I couldn't tell you what of exactly."

"Scared of what it might stir up?"

"Maybe the birth and what followed came as a kind of relief to Otto."

"A relief?"

"That it was over."

"You mean, a relief that the baby"—Tobias lowers his voice—"didn't live?"

For a lifetime, this has been coursing wordlessly through my veins, clawing at my skin from the inside. Now that I have to speak, I need a new language. The words in my head aren't up to it.

"How could anyone feel relief at something like that?"

"I'm probably not saying it right, Toby." I'm ashamed to have said it out loud. "It's something that has popped into my head from time to time, that's all."

After the call ends, all I can think of is Otto. I have to wander through the building to walk off my restlessness. A hunched resident with bushy eyebrows and a turkey neck trundles past on his mobility scooter. "Oh, hello," he says when he catches me staring.

They've been warning of a heatwave for days. All the curtains are drawn and the sunlight through the shades gives everything an orange glow. Everyone has been told to lay low and the staff are handing out ice lollies. They're orange too. With my head full of Otto, it's hard to imagine that I'm not on his mind at this very moment.

I park my walker and lower myself onto one of the sofas at reception to suck on my lolly.

"Good afternoon, Mrs. Buitink-Tendelow." It still makes me jump when the people here call me by that name.

"Good afternoon." I wave at the lady behind the desk.

"Make sure you drink plenty today."

"Oh, I will. Don't you worry. Do you happen to know if Jamie is in today?"

"Jamie?"

"He sometimes washes me in the morning."

"Let's see ... No, he's on holiday at the moment."

"Oh, so he's not here ..." Something in me thinks I could tell all this to him.

"It's another two weeks before he's back."

"Do you think you could give me his phone number?"

"I'm afraid we can't give out staff phone numbers. Is anything the matter?"

"No, it's just ... no, I understand."

Part of me wishes I could run into Otto by chance. Glance over at an elderly gent nodding off by the aquarium one day and recognise his face. But even the thought has me in such a state that I want to find the nearest toilet and lock myself in a cubicle. I plant my half-demolished lolly in a flowerpot and wend my way back to my room.

For a second, I think someone is waiting there for me. Then I realise I've left the television on.

On the table is the notepad I used to jot down the street name: Houtlaan. Can't say it rings a bell. Louis could have pinpointed it exactly. Apart from the jumble of new developments across the river, he knew every street in the city thanks to all those years spent dropping off prescriptions for the pharmacist. I run my thumbs over the paper, then slide it under the crocheted placemat.

Despite the heat, I plop a sugar cube in a mug of milk, stir in the cinnamon, and slide it into the microwave. When it's ready, I take it over to my armchair and blow until the milk is just warm enough to drink. The ads have finished and the repeat of the news comes on. It's mostly about the heatwave and how us fossils and other high-risk groups need to drink enough water. They show a woman, years younger than me, grinning in the shade of a parasol with her feet in a basin of water. There are shots of jam-packed beaches and children splashing in a fountain.

I take a few sips of my cinnamon milk.

A little yellow root has appeared at the bottom of my cactus cutting.

"Hello?" I say to myself, just to test my voice. "Hello." All of a sudden, I'm in a hurry. I grab the telephone and key in the number for reception.

"Good afternoon, Mrs. Buitink-Tendelow! What can I do for you?"

"Could you order me a taxi?"

"A taxi? When for?"

"First thing tomorrow morning, if that's all right."

# 40

Walls so white, they almost seemed to give off light.

Opposite my bed, the setting sun made an orange rectangle of the window. "Thirsty," I heard myself groan, too dazed to realise that this body was mine. Then sleep must have dragged me under; I opened my eyes again to find that the window had turned black. The blouse I was wearing wasn't mine. I felt for my belly.

"Where's my baby?" A voice too thin to hear. "Otto?"

There was a faint hum of far-away chatter.

A tight sheet held me captive in the bed. I squirmed onto my side. "Where's my baby?" I asked, a sound too hoarse to be coming from me. My head was absurdly heavy. Nothing about this body felt like my own, as if it had been stitched together from a strange set of limbs while I slept.

I managed to loosen the sheet and raise myself a little. A tangled bun of hair was peeping above the white sheet on the bed next to mine. "Excuse me?" There were other women in beds beyond hers. I was lying in the far corner of a hospital ward.

"Excuse me, missus?"

Slow limbs shifted beneath the sheet. A woman turned to face me.

"Are you in pain?" she whispered.

"Where's my baby?"

The woman's eyelids were thick, weary contentment on her lips. "Did they have to give you a C-section?"

I shook my head and looked around for a glass of water. All I could see was a vase, flowers that I knew couldn't be for me.

"The babies are sleeping." Again, that gentle contentment on her face.

"Where?" I turned to see if there was anything on the other side of the bed. I felt a prickling in my breasts, but they were wrapped in bandages and I couldn't touch them.

"What did you have?" the woman asked. "A boy or a girl?"

"I don't know. All I saw was two tiny feet."

"I've had two boys. At last! It's been one girl after another till now—six of them." I was slow to respond, so she said, "As if I didn't have my hands full already."

"And they're sleeping now?" I asked. "You said they were sleeping?"

I began to remember. A stretcher. The double chins of the men who carried me out. Mrs. Mykasintos reaching out her hand as I passed. Children gawping. Otto! Otto had been in the room. Two feet, two tiny feet covered in a kind of salve, greyish-white.

"What's your name?" the woman asked. I had to focus hard to be sure she was really lying there. I nodded, her question already gone from my mind.

"I'm Florence," she said.

"Are you sure my baby is sleeping?"

"You're still drowsy from the anaesthetic, love. That'll soon pass. You've just had an operation. Now, try to get some shut-eye. I'm sure it all went well. Trust me, I know the ropes around here. Before I got married, I was a nurse on this very ward."

"I saw its two little feet," I said.

"Yes, twins for me," she said with a grateful smile. "They'll be along in a bit."

There was a crackling sound, followed by a sharp hiss. Bodies stirred in every bed. "The mothers should get themselves ready." The voice came from a brown, wooden speaker hanging on the wall above a desk, nothing on it but a telephone. "The babies are being brought in for their next feed." On a chair by the desk, a hunched nun was rocking back and forth, the beads of a rosary inching through her fingers.

"Are we going to feed?" I asked. "Will my baby come now, too?"

"You'll see each other soon."

Florence peered under the wide neck of her blouse and her face twisted as she felt her breasts.

She and the other women were sitting up in their beds, everyone wearing the same blouse as me. "We're going to feed," I murmured to myself. I tried to stuff a pillow behind my back like the others, but it fell to the floor. Florence had turned her face to the door. I fiddled with the buttons on my blouse. But my breasts were bound so tightly that I couldn't even stick a finger down. "Why these bandages?"

No sooner did I feel the urge to pee than it came trickling into the thick nest of gauze and cotton wads that had been swaddled around me. That trickle started a fire I couldn't touch and I groaned. My belly bulged over the swaddling pants, a flaccid cushion I could poke and prod without it offering the least resistance.

I was going to see my baby.

Florence began fussing over the mothers in other beds, telling them what to do. "I've been through this so many times," she laughed. "As a nurse, I must have seen hundreds of births."

The nun at the desk was dressed in white from head to toe. She gazed blissfully around the room. Then I saw her stiffen and realised it was because she had noticed me. She lifted the receiver and held it to her white wimple. Her finger turned the dial. She glanced twice in my direction as she spoke

Cooing rose up from the other beds. The door swung open and a parade of nuns swept into the ward, each bearing one or two bundled-up crying babies in her arms. Behind the nuns came three nurses each rolling two small beds, one in front and the other dragged behind. Scratchy, bird-like cries filled the room. I felt my breasts tingle. My eyes tracked every nun, every little bed on wheels, but none of them reached my corner of the ward. Some of the mothers were assisted by nuns, who supported the baby's head until it had attached itself to the nipple. White robes floated back and forth among the mothers, nuns' hands fluttering from bed to bed like pale, bony birds until the sound of smacking and suckling filled the room. Florence looked tortured as her baby son sucked his cheeks hollow, while a nun stood waiting by her bed, bobbing his twin brother up and down, a soothing pinkie in his infant mouth. I strained to see his little face.

"And my baby?" I asked, at last. "Where's my baby?"

The door to the ward opened again and a nurse trotted in with a little bundle in her arms. A cold-water shock rushed through my body. I sat up straight. The heels of her shoes tick-tocked across the floor. But the baby was handed to the mother in the third bed. A nun who had appeared in the doorway behind the nurse came towards me, empty-handed.

"So, awake at last, are we?" she said, as if it had been unforgivably lazy of me to sleep so long.

"Where's my baby?"

"There's no more need for you to worry. Your baby is in the Lord's care," she said. "You must be thirsty."

She left the ward and returned almost immediately with a mug in her hands. "Sage tea," she said. "It will help relieve the pressure in your breasts." The runners screeched over the rails as she pulled the curtain around my bed. Perhaps it was to spare me the sight of the breastfeeding mothers, but I couldn't help thinking it was so they wouldn't have to look at me. Her habit against the white of the curtain gave the illusion that her face and hands were suspended in midair. I stared at the steaming mug on my bedside table, afraid of the answer to the question I wanted to ask.

"Don't drink too quickly. There will be no more till morning."

"Sister?"

"You may call me Sister Thribena." She pulled me forward by my shoulders and I felt her fingers fumbling between my shoulder blades. Slowly, she began to unwind the bandages until at last my breasts were exposed. The skin was tight and red, imprinted with the weave of the cloth.

Without examining them, she began to wrap me in

clean bandages, pulling so tightly that it hurt. "It's for your own good," she replied when I told her. With every layer, she leaned in a little closer. "Your milk is no longer needed." A haze of hair gave her upper lip an ashen colour, and the scent of soap and dried flowers hung around her. For the rest of my days, the smell of dried flowers made me think of this woman.

When she was finished and had made a wad of the dirty bandages, I asked, "Where is my baby, Sister Thribena?" I don't know why my voice sounded so restrained and hopeful. Perhaps I thought it would invite a hopeful answer.

"That's not for me to say. The answer lies with the Lord." Her hands moved as if to console mine, but instead pulled the sheet firmly to one side.

"Is my baby still sleeping? Will you bring it to me soon?" One question tripped over the other.

"Miss Tendelow." The nun took a deep breath. "Have you stopped to consider that the Lord may have taken your bastard child into His care rather than entrust its soul to your keeping? This is a shame that you will have to bear. Prayer alone can right the wrong of this deep disgrace." Her wimple shielded her lips, as if these words were never to be traced back to her mouth.

"But is my baby alive?"

"Hush now. Your complaints are a stain on the happiness that new life has brought to this ward. These ladies have just become mothers." Her lips stretched in a taut line and she whispered, "You would be better off praying in silence, Miss Tendelow. Rather than bombarding me with questions."

"But can't you at least—"

With a "ssst," she sealed my lips and turned to go.

I grabbed her by the arm. "Where is it? Please tell me it's alive?" Sister Thribena froze, eyes set on some invisible mark high on the chalk-white wall. Shocked by how hard I was squeezing, I let her go. "Surely it can't be dead?"

She tugged fiercely at the curtain and left it only half-open. Her hurried footsteps pattered across the floor. The babies had been carried off and quiet had returned to the ward. Through the gap in the curtain, I saw a moth beating against the glass of the darkened window.

"Time to sleep," a voice rang through the ward. A nun led the mothers in prayer. They mumbled along obediently. "Amen."

"Amen," the ward echoed.

"Sleep well, mothers."

The soft, white light at the foot of my bed went out, the filament glowed in the bulb for a moment or two. There were whispers, movements beneath the sheets. Closer to me, on the other side of the curtain, the squeak of metal as Florence turned in her bed. "I don't know your name," she whispered. "But I'm so sorry. I had no idea that you ... that you had been visited by a black stork." She was quiet a moment. "Now try to sleep, the anaesthetic will help." Another silence. "Forget this baby. It's for the best."

That was when the sun left me.

Sleep was a dark figure stationed at the head of my bed. He was hidden from view but when I closed my eyes, his huge hands covered my face and thrust me into stifling blackness. Exhausted, I jolted awake from my pool of ink. The gloom gave no sign of how much of the night was left. My mug of tea was empty. I rolled my tongue around my parched mouth, but the dryness remained. Snores filled the ward. In my wadded pants, the trickle I could not hold in burned and burned. And in the darkness around me, two tiny white footprints appeared.

"Good morning, mothers. Prepare yourselves for the first feed of the day." I woke with a head full of concrete and the feeling that I was stuck somewhere deep inside myself. Buried in a body I could not control. Even thinking hurt.

The parade of nuns and nurses entered and a fresh mug of sage tea was placed on my bedside table. Without a word, a young slip of a nurse changed my wadded pants, then held a spoon level with my mouth. I opened and swallowed without asking.

"Would it be ..." My voice was still crumpled from the night. "Could I be placed on another ward?"

She shook her head.

"Can you tell me where my baby is?"

Nothing about her suggested that she'd heard what I had said, or even registered my voice. But before she left me, she said, "I'd take a different tack with Sister Thribena, if I were you. Behaviour like yours has consequences."

* * *

It must have been visiting hour. Out of nowhere, men appeared on the ward. Fathers. Larger than life but quiet as mice. The talk at every bedside was muted. Sometimes a timid elder child had been brought along. In a low-pitched hum, the men admired the little creature they had seen a few times at most. I turned my back.

"Excuse me, miss." Since my morning encounter with the nurse, no one had said a word to me.

"Would you mind if I borrowed this chair?" The voice sounded close. "Miss?"

I was just about to turn over, when a nun came bustling up. "Feel free to take it. This young lady is not expecting visitors."

"Do you have anyone?"

Florence's question came unexpectedly. It was afternoon nap time on the ward.

"What do you mean?"

"Anyone to go to? After this place. A friend maybe? Or the father?"

It hadn't occurred to me that there would be an after.

"I think so," I shrugged.

* * *

My breasts felt as if they were on fire.

Since the anaesthetic had worn off, there had been a smouldering, stinging sensation beneath the bandages. But now it had turned feverish, burning as if my breasts were two festering sores. To ease the pain, I felt behind my back for the knot in the bandages, but every movement had me sobbing with pain.

"I warned you." Sister Thribena appeared at the foot of my bed. "You drank too quickly." She filled my mug from an enamel teapot and stood there to make sure I sipped. There was something fish-like about her bulging eyes. The lids never quite seemed to open. I barely drank, just moistened my mouth with the bitter taste of sage.

"Are you in pain?"

I nodded.

She put the teapot down next to the folded pile of starched cloths and rolls of gauze on the trolley she had wheeled in. On the middle shelf was a steel bowl. I could not see what was in it.

"Good," she said matter-of-factly and then, with a hint more satisfaction, "Good. It's only the milk coming in."

Sister Thribena ordered me to sit up and raise my arms so that she could unwind the bandages around my trapped breasts. With the greatest of care, she peeled back the last, wet strip. It was covered in yellow flecks.

"Colostrum," she said. There was something intimate and obliging about the way she explained my bodily functions. "That's the first milk." It smelled sour. The tight skin of my breasts was shot through with blue veins and streaked red from the bandages. Everything felt hot and raw. I had expected the fire to die out once the bandages were removed, but the contact with the air sent shivers up my spine.

"Pain and suffering are grist for the soul, Miss Tendelow." From the bowl on the trolley, she produced a dripping flannel and squeezed it in her fist. For a moment, I was afraid she was going to cover my eyes. "This will cool you." She placed the flannel on my right breast. I felt the circle of skin around my nipple contract as goose bumps prickled across my tightening bosom. One pain replaced another as the flannel absorbed the heat. But as soon as she moved it to my left breast, the fire in my right flared again and yellowish drops welled from my nipple.

"Lactation." Sister Thribena continued her explanations. "There's no stopping the flow, even in circumstances such as yours." The crucifix around her neck swayed close to my face as she moved. Then she squeezed past the trolley to the foot of my bed.

"Where are you going?"

"I beg your pardon?" she asked, as if I had said something to offend her.

"I'm sorry," I stammered. "I only wanted to ..."

"I am going to fetch some cabbage leaves, and with any luck some yoghurt, on the assumption that you would rather I ease your pain and suffering than leave you to endure it. Or are you once again feeling headstrong enough to ignore my advice?"

"No, Sister Thribena."

"Your body is in thrall to your mind, Miss Tendelow. It does not want to obey."

I took it all without a word.

"In a day or two, your body will start to realise that the lactation is serving no purpose. For now, it is labouring under the misapprehension that there is a mouth to be fed."

As Sister Thribena walked away, the speaker began to crackle again. "The mothers should prepare themselves ..." More yellow drops welled up out of invisible pinpricks. My body was sure that somewhere there was a mouth to be fed.

Those two tiny feet. I knew I had seen them. I knew my baby must be somewhere.

Awkwardly, I threw back the covers and wobbled myself to standing. The floor was cold and I tried to balance on the balls of my feet. As best I could, I pulled my blouse over my head and fumbled the buttons through their holes. I had stood up too quickly and white specks clouded my vision. I scanned the floor by my bed in search of shoes. I had no memory of what I had been wearing when they brought me to this place.

"What are you doing?" Florence asked. "You have to stay put."

I staggered barefoot towards the far side of the ward, steadying myself at the foot of every bed.

"Where are you going?" said a nurse's voice. "Miss Tendelow, getting out of bed is against the rules. Even for you." I could feel everyone's eyes on me. The cloud of white specks became a fog. I gasped for breath, wiped the cold sweat from my neck and somehow managed to stay on my feet.

A hand on my arm. "Let go of me. I have to feed my baby."

I tore myself away.

"Sister Agatha!" the slip of a nurse shouted. Receiver pressed to her white wimple, Sister Agatha was already sticking a trembling finger into the dial on the phone.

"Tell me where my baby is! Tell me!"

I staggered on and had almost reached the door when someone grabbed both my arms from behind. As I tried to pull free, the fabric of my blouse scraped like sand across my breasts. I howled. Cold metal slammed into the back of my legs and I was tipped back into a wheelchair. My wrists were strapped down, a belt pulled tight around my waist. My voice veered from pleading to screaming and I struggled to loosen the restraints as the chair was propelled into the long corridor.

"This way." The soothing voice of a man I could not see. "In here."

A panelled door flew open and I was wheeled into a small room, a kind of office. For a moment I hoped that someone was going to sit down at the desk and give me answers. There was fumbling and rustling behind me, the tinkle of a metal dish.

Hands held my arm tight, rolled up the sleeve of my blouse. I felt a wasp's sting on my shoulder. "That should do it." The man's soothing voice again. I turned to see him press a syringe and pull the needle from my skin.

Before I could ask anything, I was wheeled back into the corridor. Chattering nurses on their break stepped aside. Sister Thribena approached us holding a cabbage in both hands. She slowed to a stop and looked away as we passed her.

"Otto!" I shouted, at a man further down the corridor. "Otto, help me!" It was a stranger, a young father staring through a large window into a ward full of newborn infants. A nun on the other side of the glass was holding up his baby.

"Let me look! Let me look too," I squeaked at whoever was pushing the wheelchair. We rolled on, eventually stopping by a chalk-white alcove. A door was flung open, lights clicked on. The chair turned and I was pulled backwards into a room. Before the door closed, I caught sight of a statue of Our Lady in the alcove. Her face was turned from me. The straps and belt were loosened. I wanted to fight but my arms and legs were no longer my own. I was lifted onto a cold bed. "Please," I murmured. "Please tell me ..." but I think the words were only in my head.

No one was listening in any case.

I woke to see a vase of carnations next to my bed. Almost immediately, I was thrust into a panicky sleep again, then jolted back to waking. This happened over and over until finally I was able to open my eyes a little longer. Outside it was evening, perhaps the middle of the night.

"Is somebody there?"

My throat was dry as sand.

"I'm thirsty."

I could hear the sound of footsteps. Somebody *was* there.

"Otto?"

The door was open a crack and a pale light shone in. A shadow moved a chair to stop the door closing. "Otto? Is that you?"

"Ssssshhh." Rough fingers felt my forehead and cheek, then found my mouth and covered it. "Quiet."

"Florence? What are you doing here?"

"I couldn't get you out of my mind," she said. "I've come to warn you."

"Warn me?"

"Ssssshhh."

"Shut the door."

Florence shook her head. "I can't. It only opens from the outside."

"You mean they've locked me in here?"

"You have to stop this."

"Stop what?"

"I'm sorry that a black stork came to you. It's awful, it really is, but you have to keep it to yourself. I'm warning you. Keep this up and they won't let you out of here. I know they've drugged you. Unless you pipe down, they'll say you're hysterical and put you in an institution. You could be locked away for years. I saw it happen, when I worked here. No one has patience with girls like you."

"I only want—"

"Aren't you listening?" she snapped. "Keep your mouth shut. Forget the child. You'll never find it. Do as the nuns tell you and keep quiet. Not a word. The nuns who work here aren't paid. They sweep the halls and make the tea. Their authority goes no further than the telephones and the light switches." Florence spoke softly, but hammered home every word. "And you are in their care. The sisters are the lowest of the low in this place, and they won't pass up a chance to remind you that you are lower still. You'll get nothing out of them. You have to forget that child."

"But how? How can I?"

Florence threw her arms wide. "That's up to you. You have to believe it's in a good place now." Florence got up to leave but paused by the door. She was shivering from the cold. "Listen," she said sternly, and came back to the bed. "I'll tell you what I know."

I took her hand but she pulled it away. Instead, she turned my head and put her lips to my ear. "No one can ever know that you heard this from me. Betray me and I'll tell them you tried to snatch one of the twins. Do you understand? Then they'll never let you go."

"I understand."

"Do as the nuns tell you. Keep your head down, no more hysterics. Make sure the doctor lets you go back to your life."

"I promise."

Florence looked over her shoulder. "Seven times I did it."

"What?"

"When I was a nurse. Helped them with a baby. A child that had died." She swallowed. "It was always the same routine. Mother Almeida would send for me. She dressed the unbaptised infants and kept them in a basket in her room. When there was a place, they made a call to the maternity ward. All she ever said to me was, *You can take it down now*. I had to collect the basket from her room and bring it to the cellar. Because a coffin was being closed." Her story came in fits and starts. "It meant the child would be buried in consecrated ground. Do you understand? In a coffin with someone else ... an adult. Before the lid was closed, I had to sneak the baby in ... there ..."

"Where?"

"*There*." Florence's hand felt its way down and patted my shins. "Between the calves. Then the coffin was closed for good."

"But what about the family?"

"Family?"

"Of the person who had died? Did they know?"

"No. Of course not. But it meant the baby was in a good place, a sacred resting place. Closer to God. Because if not ..." She didn't tell me what happened if not. "Your baby is long gone. No one knows where, or who with. It might be someone who died here but was buried on the other side of the country." She wiped her nose on her sleeve. Her trembling fingers stroked my cheek in consolation. "And now, forget what I told you. You promised."

I shut my eyes and saw the two tiny feet. In a cold coffin, in the suffocating darkness under the closed lid. A little bundle wrapped up tight, between the stiff legs of a cold, dead stranger.

I nearly choked at the thought.

"Your baby is in the best place possible," Florence said. "It's time to forget it. Find yourself a good man. Marry him. Have other children. Say nothing more about it. Nothing at all. Will you promise me that?"

Don't ask me how. Though it could barely be heard, I said yes.

# 41

It must have been sometime in the mid-seventies. Among the shoppers at the weekly market around Mariënburg Chapel, I recognised Florence's face. I took a sudden interest in the apples, stealing glances to the side until I was sure it was her. Her bags were already brimming with vegetables and she handed the stall holder a fiver.

"Florence?" I asked.

"Yes?" She sounded a little wary.

"It's me, Frieda."

She searched my face for a sign of someone she recognised. "Help me out, will you."

"From the maternity ward at St. Canisius."

Florence's eyes settled on the pram and I turned it round so she could take a look. "This is Tobias."

"Are you sure we met at St. Canisius? It's almost nineteen years since I left." Florence was flanked by a pair of lanky boys, her twins. They looked around listlessly, miffed that their mother had stopped to gab to yet another acquaintance.

"You weren't working there at the time."

Florence looked blank.

"You had just given birth to your twins. I was in the bed next to yours. In the corner of the ward. You came to see me one night. I had a black stork."

"Oh my," she blurted out. "Was that you? Goodness me, that was a long time ago." She took another look at Tobias in the pram. He ducked away shyly under the hood. "And now you have a son."

I nodded.

"Mine are getting taller by the day." Her lanky lads were prodded into action and gave me a half-hearted wave. "They'll be twelve soon," said their mother. "Off to big school next autumn."

Twelve.

"'Scuse me, missus," the stall holder said to Florence. "Will you be wanting this or shall I pocket it?"

"Give it here, you cheeky sod."

A bunch of coins slid from his grubby hand onto her waiting palm. Then he turned to me. "And what can I do for you, young lady?"

"Well," Florence said, and rubbed my arm briefly. "I'm glad to see things worked out for you." I hoped she might hang around so we could talk more, perhaps arrange to meet for coffee. But she was already walking away.

"Bye then." I raised my hand.

"Who was that, Mum?" I heard one of her big lads say.

"Oh, someone," I heard her reply. "Someone from long ago."

## 42

The nameplate says *Brigitte & Otto Drehmann*, just like Tobias said it would. I peer through the frosted pane in the front door. No signs of life, not even when I ring a second time. I shuffle past the front windows and try to peek in, but I'm blinded by the sun glinting off the glass. A path leads down the side of the house and round the back. I follow it and my heart skips a beat, the way it does when a deer appears out of nowhere in the woods. A woman in an enormous sun hat is there among the shrubs, bending to pluck strands of green from the soil. The oversized gardening gloves at the end of her twig-like arms look like something from a cartoon. This must be Brigitte. I wonder whether to speak or beat a hasty retreat. I'm still struggling to steer the walker with my hand in plaster. "Hello," I say, almost without meaning to, and cough to rattle the croak from my voice. "Good morning."

The edges of the flowerbeds are neatly raked. The shrubs have already been cut back, too early in the season. It's better to leave them and only pick off the blooms that are past their best.

"Excuse me?" It's only when I walk on and my shadow touches her that she looks up. "Good morning," I say again.

"Oh, hello there." She straightens up and peers at me, lifting the brim of her hat and shading her sunglasses with her hands. She must be ninety or so, around Otto's age, but her movements are so supple that they make me feel older still.

"I'm trying to get this done before the worst of the heat." Her voice is loud.

"Yes, we're in for a scorcher." She must think I'm some batty old soul who's desperate for a chat. "I've come for Otto," I say.

"For Otto?" she repeats, to make sure she's heard me right. She turns one ear towards me.

"Yes, I ..."

"How do you know Otto?" she asks.

I can't think of anything straight off the bat and fiddle with my walker to play for time.

"May I ask who you are?"

"I lived next door when we were younger," I say.

"Next door to Otto? Oh my, that is interesting." Brigitte takes off her sunglasses and picks her way through the shrubs towards me. Her eyes peep out from a crumple of lines. "Come, let's find ourselves some shade."

I manage a three-point turn and steer the walker onto her driveway.

"We can't have you baking here in the sun."

I'm afraid of what Brigitte might tell me about Otto in the shade of their home. Without asking whether I want to come in, she helps me lift my front wheels over the threshold. Perhaps she's leading me straight to him, lurking in the cool of the kitchen or dozing on the couch or under a parasol. I'm so fidgety, it's all I can do not to bump into the furniture. My plaster mitt is itching like mad. I had pictured Otto opening his front door to me, recognition slowly dawning as I introduced myself. Not me popping up in his living room, in the company of his good lady wife.

"I may have to leave you for a second." Brigitte points at her ears. "I wasn't expecting visitors, so I need to track down my hearing aids." I'm parked by the hat stand. Women's coats mostly, though there's one that might be a man's. Maybe Otto has just nipped down to the shops. Assorted walking sticks and umbrellas poke out of the basket below.

"Please, come through."

Feeling more than a little on edge, I trundle into their living room. There's no one in the armchairs. The couch is empty too. An African mask and a display of stones and crystals adorn the far wall. A tea set is laid out on the glass drinks cabinet. It seems so unreal that these things belong to Otto, to their life as a couple. Brigitte stands by the coffee table and flaps the pages of a TV guide. "Now where did I put those wretched things?" she mumbles to herself. "Excuse me," she apologises. "Let me just check upstairs. I may have left them in the bathroom."

"Don't mind me," I try to reassure her. Brigitte is already halfway up the stairs.

On the dining table, there's a single placemat and an open book of puzzles. One empty coffee cup. Even so, it feels like Otto could appear at any moment. I listen for noises in the house—a toilet flushing, the tramping of footsteps. Or the creak of the back door and the scrape of shoes on the mat. But all I can hear is the wheezing of my own breath.

I turn a corner and find myself in a kind of conservatory with a view of the garden, then stop dead in my tracks. Otto is smiling back at me from a silver frame, a black-and-white photo that could easily have been taken around the time when we were seeing each other. His curls combed flat, a streak of grey at the temples, that long nose of his. Exactly as I've remembered him all these years, only clearer, more detailed, more complete. Cautiously I lift the frame from the sideboard. Time falls away. Here he is, looking straight at me.

It's the only picture of Otto on his own. The rest show me their life together. There he stands in a later photo, arm around Brigitte in front of that mosaic church in Barcelona, two little people in an orange-brown haze. "You're bald as a coot," I say out loud. I could easily have passed him on the street without thinking twice.

There they are again with their arms around each other—Egypt this time, the Temple of Isis. I saw it on a travel show the other night. The frame next door shows Brigitte and Otto posing beside an American car, outside a house with a veranda. Another photo—the two little girls on their laps must be their daughters. Then there's a snapshot that must be from years later, the same girls on a beachfront boulevard, pained adolescent expressions and fringes stiff with hairspray. And Otto standing between his daughters, smiling broadly.

I jump when I realise Brigitte is standing at my shoulder. "Mission accomplished," she says, with a relieved chuckle. Her fingers tease a few curls to conceal the devices in her ears. She has popped in a pair of dangling earrings. With Brigitte at my side, I struggle to look at Otto's portrait head-on. "Are those your grandchildren?" I ask. A man sits proudly at the wheel of a pick-up truck, while two girls on the back hold a surfboard above their heads. Brigitte starts reeling off names as her finger traces an invisible thread from one photo to the next. It feels like an intimate game of Memory.

"Unfortunately, most of them are an ocean away. Our youngest, Ellen, moved back to the US. She's in New Jersey, these days. She was always the more American of the two, had trouble settling when we moved back here. And of course, she was old enough to make her own decisions by then. Luckily, I still have Rosa close by. She works at the university in Eindhoven. Applied physics. Followed in her father's footsteps."

"And what about Otto?" Torn between thinking he's dead or down at the shops, it's hard to know what to ask. "How has life treated him?"

"Goodness." Brigitte waves vaguely at the array of photos in front of us. "How do you sum up a life? Good, on the whole. Life treated him well."

So, Otto is gone. Yet here he is, looking straight at me. I feel sick with nerves. Afraid Brigitte will look into his smiling eyes and see how well he knows me, see that he is about to open his mouth and say, "Hello, Elfie. My dear, sweet Elfie. It's been a while."

"But here I am, rattling on as usual." We are sitting at their table. "Now tell me again, how did you know Otto?"

"Me?' I feel caught out.

"I know I asked already, but without my hearing aids I'm not sure I caught what you said."

"I knew him from way back. We were neighbours."

"The girl next door!" Brigitte says, with a smile at Otto's photo. "And what's your name?"

"Frieda." I realise instantly that I've given myself away.

"Frieda," Brigitte repeats to herself.

My name sits there on the table between us.

"No, I can't say I recall him mentioning a Frieda."

"It was such a long time ago."

"From his days on Oude Heselaan?"

I nod. "He was always so preoccupied with his moths," I say, casting around for proof that I do actually know Otto. I regret it just as quickly, unsure what I'm permitted to know about him. "There must have been a good twelve years between us, so I'm sure he hardly noticed me."

"Ah ..." Brigitte says, as if she has uncovered a secret.

"What is it?"

"You had a crush on him!"

"No," I say, too quickly, too loud. "Well, maybe a little. I was only young. You look up to older kids at that age."

"Especially the boys!" Brigitte beams. "Well, well ... Otto's childhood sweetheart. How charming." Her laughter bounces off the walls, her bright mood runs rings around me. "The girl next door turning up on our doorstep after all these years," she sighs, as if rehearsing an anecdote to dish up to her friends or her daughters. It rankles to hear her brushing me off as something so sweet and innocent, even though it's me who has dreamt all this up in the first place. Brigitte has lived a life full of Otto, and now he can't be taken from her by a past love of any description. I stare into the empty cup beside the puzzle book. Dark grains speck the milky brown dregs.

"But if you lived next door ..." Brigitte begins, suddenly turning more serious.

"Hmm?"

"Then you must have known his parents."

"Oh, not really." I have no idea what to say. "In passing, perhaps."

"But you do remember them?"

"Vaguely," I say, trying desperately to stop my lie from running away with me.

"I only know them from the odd photograph and one or two stories," Brigitte confides. "Otto always found it difficult to talk about them. Even to our daughters."

"Of course," I say. "I understand." Suddenly, I'm knee-deep in Otto's past.

"Can you remember anything about them? Did you ever ...?" Brigitte's question trails off.

"Kind people," I stammer, to fill up the silence. Brigitte nods and her eyes widen. Those two words seem to hold a world of significance for her.

"Though of course I never actually called at the Drehmanns' home."

"No, of course," Brigitte nods, though I have no idea what I meant by "of course" in the first place. There's a certain pleasure to be had from telling Brigitte something about Otto she doesn't know, even if it is made up. As if I'm staking my own small claim on him.

"I remember his father more than his mother."

"Oh, is that right?"

"He would wave if you caught his eye as he was heading off to work. Always had a funny little smile on his lips. As if he was about to crack a joke."

"Oh, my," Brigitte says.

"I went with them once," I say recklessly, curious to hear what I'm about to come out with next.

"Went with them?"

"Spotting moths down by the Waal."

"You were there?"

"Mm-hmm."

"But you were so much younger. Were you allowed out so late?"

"Just that once. It made a huge impression on me."

"I can imagine, especially on such a young girl."

"My big sister came along. The sheets and the lanterns are what I remember most. Magical, it was. His father knew them all by name, even one species that's only found there by the river. And he showed me a moth with gold powder between its wings." I grind to a halt. There's no way back, but I have no idea how to go on.

I can see the emotion on Brigitte's face, perhaps because I experienced something she missed out on. And I'm ashamed, so deeply ashamed to be sitting here lying to her across her own dining table when she has been so kind and has welcomed me into her home. I could open up now, tell her about the unforgiveable lie that hurtled past her life like a blazing comet. Just the thought makes me feel faint. Perhaps Otto did tell her something in the end. For the first time since she let me in, Brigitte and I look each other squarely in the face. There's a dullish haze across her eyes, her lower lids are two red rims. I want to make things right, but Brigitte stretches a fragile arm across the table and puts her hand on mine. "You think you haven't told me much. But I'm so happy to hear this about Otto and his father. I can't tell you what it means to me."

Brigitte gets up and heads for the kitchen. Her legs have grown stiff from sitting. "Let me put the kettle on. You'll stay for a cup of tea?"

"No, I'm fine," I say. "There's no need." I want to get out of here, but Brigitte has already taken two cups from the shelf. "At our age you can't drink too much, especially on a day like today." She holds the kettle under the tap. "Otto and I have had the good fortune to share a life together. But his oldest memories seem to be his alone. I've noticed that more than ever, these past few years." Water gushes, a drawer scrapes. I can't have heard her right. "I think Otto would enjoy revisiting these memories with you."

"I'm sorry, what did you say?"

"Pardon?" Brigitte looks over her shoulder.

"Where is Otto?"

"Brakkenstein House. You know, that big place on Driehuizerweg." Her matter-of-factness confounds me. "It's not far from here." Brigitte waves in any old direction.

"He's alive!" The kettle is coming to the boil and Brigitte doesn't hear.

"He had a fall in the spring and hasn't been home since. But he's being well looked after. The staff are ever so kind. And it's only a brisk walk away. I try to go every other day, after lunch."

Otto, Otto, Otto. A brisk walk away. At the same time, I'm relieved he's not about to come strolling into the room.

"At first, we thought he'd make a full recovery. But unfortunately, his bones aren't what they were. And his speech has been a problem for a while now. He has good days and bad." I want to ask about his memory, but Brigitte beats me to it. "He still appears to have all his faculties."

It's almost unreal to think that, at this moment in time, Otto is living and breathing in a room just a walk away. Seeing and hearing the world around him, sitting by a window, lost in thought.

"He took quite a tumble. Fell flat on his face right outside the house." Brigitte lifts the trembling kettle and fills the cups. She transfers them to a little trolley and trundles over to the table.

"Him and his moths," Brigitte chuckles. "Funny you should mention that of all things." Her voice is warmer now, as if we were already friends. "We found a chest full of notebooks down in the cellar. Page after page, nothing but tally marks. I threw them out with the waste paper a few weeks back."

"Threw them out?" It sounds more indignant than I meant it to. Brigitte doesn't seem to mind.

"Yes, I mean, what else was I supposed to do with them?" She almost sniggers as she says it. "Slowly but surely, I've been sorting through our things. We can't saddle our children with all the junk we've amassed, now can we? And I can't rattle around this place much longer. So, you understand."

"Yes," I reply. "Yes, I understand."

"Who knows what skeletons might be lurking

down in that cellar, things you'd never want your children to set eyes on!" She laughs. "That's how the strangest stories get started." Brigitte presents me with an assortment of teabags and pulls a sour face. "Those notebooks were crawling with silverfish. I flicked through the pages and thought: these can go. Otto hoarded so much over the years, whatever he took a shine to or thought might come in handy. It was fine when we were younger but it got to the stage where he couldn't bear to throw anything away. Of course, moving to a bigger house didn't help. I suppose you could put it down to losing his parents at such a young age. His reluctance to part with things, I mean. One box contained all his tax returns since 1973. We shipped two containers of stuff back with us from the States."

I've picked a teabag at random and start sopping it in my cup.

"But anyway ... there's a twist." Brigitte suppresses a laugh. I see us sitting here, two old pals trading confidences.

"I told all this to a college friend of Otto's who came by to see how I was doing, here all by myself. And he fished every last notebook out of the waste paper. Took them over to the university and it turns out"—her pencilled eyebrows shoot up in astonishment—"the biology department is only too happy to have them. Thinks they might be of real interest. You couldn't make it up!"

"Oh," I say. "That is good news."

"They're going to get a postdoc to wade through them and see what conclusions they can draw about the moth population here by the River Waal. There's a gaping hole in the record due to our time in the US, of course, but even so ..." Brigitte sips at her scalding tea, puffs steam in my direction, and returns her cup to its coaster. "Apparently it's unheard of for someone to keep records on the same area for almost eight decades. That's including his father's observations." It's as if she's cultivating an interest to make up for lost time. "So some good has come of all those evenings and nights he was away."

I lift my cup with my left hand, enlisting my plaster cast for support. "Perhaps keeping a record was enough for Otto," I say. "The simple fact that the moths had been seen."

"Oh no, he'd have given his eye teeth to find a new species."

I want to say something but my courage fails me.

Brigitte continues, "He'd have liked nothing better than to give a name to some discovery or other."

"Well, at least he got to name your daughters."

She looks at me for a second. "They had their names when they came to us."

"They were adopted?"

Brigitte pours a splash of milk into her tea. Then another. "To me they are our girls, and that's all there is to it." Her teaspoon tinkles in her cup. "And Otto feels the same."

# 43

"Good morning, Miss Tendelow." It was Sister Thribena.

Ever since Florence came to me that night, I had been meek as a lamb. Opened my mouth when a spoon was held up to it, mumbled apologies and thank yous, held my tongue until I was asked a question. I ate what was put in front of me and nodded when the doctor told me the pain in my breasts was easing, though it smouldered on and flared from time to time. I kept all this up until finally they told me I was to be discharged.

"Would you like to take these carnations home with you? They're still at their best."

"Please give them to someone else."

Sister Thribena took the vase and disappeared into the hall.

It wasn't until two days after the flowers arrived that I discovered the little envelope tucked among the stems. I took it from under my pillow. *Miss Tendelow*. The card was written in a hand I didn't know. *My dear, sweet Elfie. I'm sorry. I'm so very sorry. The baby is with my parents now. And it's time for the two of us to return to our old lives, the lives we led before we met. We cannot go on like before. I will always treasure what we had. Always. Love, O.* The card contained two twenty-five–guilder notes, paperclipped to a note that read *To help you on your way.*

White carnations. The same flowers Otto had picked out to lay on his parents' grave the first time he came by the florist's.

"Here you are." Sister Thribena handed me a small pile of clothes with a pair of shoes on top, a couple of sizes too big. I didn't want to make a fuss but I couldn't help myself. "These aren't mine."

"You may have them."

"But what about the clothes I was wearing?"

"You were barely clothed when you arrived here, Miss Tendelow. The ambulancemen carried you in on a stretcher, wrapped in towels and a sheet."

She averted her eyes while I took off my hospital gown. I pulled on the slip and the sweater, then slumped onto the bed. Being on my feet was something I was still getting used to. Bending was painful and crouching forbidden for the time being. I looked down at myself in this baggy skirt and a sweater so big I had to roll up the sleeves to see my hands.

"They belonged to someone who has no further need of them." Sister Thribena made a sign of the cross. Alone, when no one else was within earshot, her words took on a softer tone. I zipped up the anorak I had inherited.

"Are you sure you haven't forgotten anything?"

"Yes." With no belongings to overlook, there was no need to check.

"In that case, come with me."

Though every mother I had seen left the ward in a wheelchair, she let me walk to the exit. My first steps were steady enough, but as I went down the stairs, I could feel my stitches pull. The day shone fiercely through the glass doors of the main hall. A stretcher was wheeled in, bringing sounds from outside: the noisy sputter of a delivery moped, car horns blaring on St. Annastraat. It was strange to think that this was a day with a date, a moment marked by the tick of a clock. That it was the same time in Otto's life as it was in mine.

"Is someone coming to collect you?"

"Yes," I said. "Someone will be along in a while."

"Then may God speed you on your way," Sister Thribena said, and left me there alone.

We were supposed to go back to our old lives, Otto and I. The lives we led before we met. Except our love had left me no life to go back to. And what did I want with his easy money, a hypocrite's indulgence of two folded twenty-five-guilder notes? But standing at the bus stop, it dawned on me that I had no purse and couldn't buy so much as a bus ticket without his help.

I took the bus to the market square and walked to Nonnenplaats from there, stopping to catch my breath at regular intervals. I heaved myself up the stairs and put my ear to the door of Mrs. Mykasintos's room. I knocked, and when there was no answer, I tried the handle. The door swung open. There was no one there.

I climbed the next flight to my own room and walked in to find a woman wearing a dress Otto had given me. It was stained down the front. "What do you want?"

"I live here," I said.

"Not bloody likely." Two sleeping children were curled up in my bed. The tablecloth, another gift from Otto, was hanging at the window as a curtain. The cradle was gone. Sold, no doubt, or broken up for firewood.

"These are my things," I said. "I have nowhere else to go."

"Neither do we." The woman who had stepped into my old life planted her fists on her hips, ready to block my every move, except a retreat onto the landing.

"I gave birth on that bed." I felt a burning sensation between my legs—too much walking, too many stairs. "Do you mind if I sit for a moment?"

One of the children on the bed began to stir and sat up. "Ssssshhh." The woman hushed her child and pushed it back to sleep. Turning to me, she ordered, "Out, out!" Dark eyes under thick eyebrows willed me towards the door. Before she closed it, she grabbed one of my chairs and handed it to me. "Here." A moment's respite out on the landing, before I disappeared for good.

On my way downstairs, I knocked on Mrs. Mykasintos's door a second time. The room was still empty. I wanted to write her a note, but I knew she wouldn't be able to read it. Instead, I broke off a little piece of the Christmas cactus that was blooming on her table. A keepsake, in the hope that I might be able to plant it and watch it grow. It would be years before its red flowers put in an appearance. But from then on, it blossomed every December without fail.

Nothing had changed on my parents' street. I looked up at a row of tall poplars I had never really noticed, though they must have been there since before I was born. The neighbourhood no longer seemed to hang together the way it used to. It kept breaking up into details, less than the sum of its parts. I walked up the path and felt around in the pockets of a stranger's anorak for my keys. Then it hit me that I was a stranger at their door.

My heart pounded in my throat at the sound of the doorbell. A fleeting light appeared behind the frosted glass: the kitchen door opening and closing. I recognised my mother's movements. She opened the door, but only a crack, the way she always did when people rang unexpectedly. "Oh, Elfrieda." She looked at my stomach, then at my face. "My little lass, where have you been all this time ...?" She raised her hand to her open mouth, afraid perhaps of what she might say, that she loved me, that she had been worried sick. "I've just got in from the bakery. If only you'd let me know. You might have come back to an empty house." Whatever she said, I was willing to listen. As long as she let me in.

"Ma?"

The door remained open a crack.

"Can I come home?"

"You know what your father said."

"I'm alone ..."

"Oh," she said.

"There's no baby. Not anymore."

Her eyes scanned the row of houses across the street and then she ushered me into the hall.

"Oh, my poor child."

Cautiously, she pulled the zip of the anorak down over my swollen breasts. Even slipping my arms out of the sleeves was painful. She must have seen it on my face. "Come." With her hand on the small of my back, she steered me up the stairs, as if I no longer knew what lay behind each door. Flicking on the bathroom light, she sat me down on the lid of the toilet and lifted my sweater. Underneath was the slip, flecked with someone else's stains. Carefully, she pulled it up over my breasts. I shivered. My nipples were no longer leaking but my breasts looked like they were fit to burst. I had never been exposed to her like this before, though it felt more like we were inspecting an intimate wound. She put the back of her hand to my forehead to feel my temperature.

"I'll be back in a sec."

"Where are you going?"

She tugged on the cord of the heat lamp above the door, the one we never used because it ran up the electricity bill. I heard the squeak of hinges, the click of the light switch in the cupboard under the stairs, her slippers on the three-step stool, hands rummaging in the vegetable crate. Few sounds were more familiar to me.

"I'll go down to the pharmacy in a bit for some sage tea," my mother said when she returned to the bathroom, a half-full bottle of yoghurt in one hand and a cabbage in the other. She put them down, laid a towel on my lap, then held a flannel under the tap and wrung it out. "Here." She handed it to me and I wiped myself down.

"I think it was a week ago," I said.

"What do you mean?"

I looked down at the bulge of my empty belly.

"A week?" Her hand shot up to her own bosom. "You should have dried up long before now." I watched the yoghurt slide sluggishly towards the mouth of the bottle and held out my hands to receive a blob on each palm. It quenched the searing heat so abruptly that it hurt, but applying it myself made the pain more bearable. My mother tore off two cabbage leaves.

"Put these over the top."

"I know," I mumbled.

She didn't ask me how I knew. Or where I had been all this time. She brushed a strand of hair behind my ear. I rubbed my face against her hand and she briefly ran her thumb down my cheek.

Having rinsed the flannel, she picked up my sweater from the tiled floor and draped it over her arm. "We can throw away that underwear. I'll fetch you clean clothes and you can wear one of my old bras until we can get you a new one."

"Ma?"

"Hmm?" She turned to look at me from the landing. "What is it, Elfrieda?"

"How do you know all this?"

"What?"

"The sage tea? The yoghurt. And that." I nodded at the cabbage in her hands. Her eyes seemed to take in the whole room, and another place far from here. "Well," she sighed. That was all she ever told me.

Dressed in fresh clothes, I stood dithering on the landing, not knowing which rooms I was allowed to enter or if my room was still mine. I had never noticed the smell of our house before. The damp from the cellar, a hint of rubber, perhaps from the carpet. I could even smell the bitter bronze of the crucifixes above each door, or so it seemed.

On the kitchen table, a mound of soil-crusted potatoes lay on an open newspaper. Sitting on a stool next to the heater, my mother plopped a peeled spud into a pan of water. I sat down across from her and began to grate the carrots. As long as I was making myself useful, surely she wouldn't send me away.

"I prayed for you every day, Elfrieda," my mother said, without taking her eyes off the potato in her hand. "The child is with its real parents now. It's like Father Gremhaars said, all you have to do now is forget."

"Its *real* parents?"

"That's how the child will see them. It has never known anything else. And they will love it as their own, more than you ever could, knowing what it is not to be blessed in that way."

"It was stillborn, Ma."

Doggedly, she kept on peeling. Took one potato, then another from the mound, even when the pot held more than enough for three.

"Ma?"

"Then we can only be grateful."

"Grateful?"

"I prayed the Lord would not leave you alone with a child." There were tears in her eyes. "And He has taken the child to Him for your sake. All that's left for you to do is pray. Pray and forget."

We were both startled by the sound of the key in the door.

"That'll be your father."

I didn't know what to do and started to get to my feet. But my mother ordered me to stay put.

"Quiet! Not one word to him about any of this."

I recognised the weary scrape of his shoes on the mat. My mother dried her hands on the tea towel, straightened her apron and disappeared into the hall.

"Whose coat is this?" his voice boomed from the hall. It was still for a moment.

"She's come back. Alone."

Another silence, different this time.

"Our Elfrieda?" Two words, reassuring in their way. In my absence, my parents hadn't stripped me of my name. By the sound of it, I was still theirs.

# 44

The eighteenth of December was my father's birthday. That made it ten days or so since I had given birth. He had people over. Family mostly, a friend from work with his wife, and probably the neighbours on either side. The women gathered in the kitchen, my father sat with the men in a living room foggy with cigarette smoke. I could tell people were watching me, though I couldn't have told you who. My sister Emma's children were under the dining room table playing snakes and ladders. Ma and I were in the thick of it, ferrying drinks and snacks by the trayful. The men were droning on about politics and forecasting another harsh winter. They chuckled about Sinatra's kidnapped son being released for a ransom of 240,000 dollars. "I'd have paid them double to hang onto that little vandal of mine." The world and everything in it were there to be laughed at.

It was the first time I'd been among so many people since coming back home. No one asked me where I had been all these months. No one seemed surprised to see me again.

"And what about you, pipsqueak?" Emma asked out of nowhere, after rattling on about the trials of raising a big family and the never-ending chores on the farm. "Do you have your eye on anyone? Don't put it off too long," she whispered. "Otherwise you'll be stuck with the duds. Or left waiting for a widower."

I looked for a sign in the gleam of her eyes and realised that my mother had even kept it from her. I felt the urge to tell her something at least, but before I could say a word she had ducked under the table to calm her bickering kids, and once she surfaced, she got caught up in other kitchen conversations.

"Come on, gents. Drink, smoke, and be merry," my mother crowed, refilling the glasses of cigarettes on the table. "These are filter tips," she pointed out, stating the obvious to boost her hostess credentials. "These are non-filter. And here's an extra dish of nibbles. Now, anything else to drink?"

Out in the hall, my mother took me aside at the overfull coat stand. "It's your father's birthday, Elfrieda."

"So?"

"So, let's keep things light."

"Of course."

"Not a word about that business. And if anyone asks, act as if you haven't heard them."

"But doesn't Emma know—"

Ma grabbed me by the wrist. "I said, keep it light."

I gave the smallest of nods.

"That's more like it." She straightened the collar on my blouse. "Now be a love and fetch two bottles of beer from the cellar."

# 45

"Elfrieda."

After a month of giving me a wide berth, my father spoke to me for the first time. "Here." With a nervous twitch, he gave me back my key. "We can't have the neighbours seeing you ring the bell at your own front door."

"Thank you."

For a second, it seemed as if he might say something else. Then he walked out to the birdhouse for a chat with his parakeets.

It's still hard to believe that, years later, this man turned into a playful grandad who never tired of giving Tobias piggy-back rides. Every birthday, my parents arrived on our doorstep with presents so big they had to peep out from behind them.

My mother and father were besotted with Tobias, and almost as besotted with Louis. I was always on edge in their company, though I don't think anyone could tell, not even Louis. I carried on talking, kept on breathing, made sure no one had cause for complaint.

Whenever we visited my parents, Louis always wound up having a beer and shooting the breeze with my father, under the lean-to by the birdhouse.

On Saturdays, Pa earned himself a bit of extra money driving a removal van and sometimes he would call Louis if they needed an extra man for the heavy lifting. Later they even went fishing together on summer evenings, angling for perch down by the Waal. When Tobias was old enough, they let him come too.

As a grown-up, he'd say, "I always used to go fishing with Dad and Grandad." But it can't have been more than twice.

"Can we stay for dinner? Please, can we stay for dinner?" Tobias would plead sometimes when we stopped by for coffee on a Sunday. Ma would shrug that it wasn't her doing. "Tobias doesn't need any encouragement from me. As long as you know that your father and I would like nothing better."

"Uhm ..." I would say and smile at Tobias. If he'd had a tail, it would have been wagging. And so I gave in.

"Here you go, little man," I would hear my mother say, holding out a rolled-up slice of ham to Tobias when she thought I wasn't looking. I raised no objection.

"Who's Grandma's little sweetheart?"

"I am!"

"How right you are!" Ma let him chomp the ham from her hand. If she was out of ham, she would run her pinkie through the peanut butter and hold it up in front of Tobias's face. He was only allowed to lick it clean when he had told her whose sweetheart he was.

I couldn't help but hate their love for each other.

* * *

When we got home, my temper would often flare if Tobias started acting up when I was getting him ready for bed. Sometimes there would be an outburst in the car, especially if Louis began merrily tapping his thumbs on the steering wheel. If he tried to stroke my neck, I would slap his hand hard.

"What's the matter?"

"Keep your hands to yourself."

"Frieda, at times you can be so … so …"

"So what? Come on, out with it." I could have pinched him in my frustration. "Well?"

"At times, I don't know where I am with you and your moods."

The calm in his voice made me livid. Knowing Tobias was looking on from the back seat, I would chew the inside of my cheek until I tasted blood. Sometimes I couldn't contain myself and I'd scream at Louis to let me out of the car.

"Don't be ridiculous, Frieda. Just sit where you are." In the back, Tobias was already howling.

"Now!" I yelled at Louis. "Here!" And if he didn't slow down, I would tug at the door handle, so incensed that I didn't care where we were driving. "Frieda! Stop it, now!" It was the only way to make him pull over. I had to get out and walk, even if we were miles from home.

Louis had usually put Tobias to bed by the time I got home, bless him. I would find him in the kitchen with his head in his hands. If he'd have kept his mouth shut, the tension would have ebbed away all by itself. Unfortunately, Louis was a talker. I would lock myself in the bathroom, but eventually we had to face each other again.

"Frieda?"

"Leave me be."

"I honestly don't know what to make of you sometimes."

That was enough to unleash a hurricane.

"And we had such a nice day with your parents too."

"Oh, shut up," I drowned him out. "Shut your stupid mouth!"

"All of a sudden you—"

"Go and live with them, why don't you? Sometimes I wonder who you married—me or my parents!"

"Look Frieda, I—"

"Spare me the sanctimonious speeches."

"Frie, how are we supposed to carry on like this? I mean—"

"Then go! I won't stand in your way."

When we quarrelled, I would scream until my voice deserted me. At times I threw anything I could lay my hands on. A packet of cereal, dishes drying in the rack on the kitchen counter, a pan of spaghetti sauce. Once I even let fly with the dustbuster.

Louis just stood there. And he stayed.

Calm as could be, he would walk over to the cupboard under the stairs and fetch the dustpan and brush. And as always, his patience, that gentle way he had, triggered a wave of guilt. Infuriating though it was.

"Here, give me that." I would take the pan and brush from his hands and start sweeping up the cornflakes or shattered crockery. Without saying a word, I would fill the dustpan and take it over to the bin. It was always Louis who broke the silence.

"Have things been a bit much lately?"

"Yes, maybe they have," I'd reply, never stopping to think whether he was right or wrong. I was ashamed of my outbursts and most of all relieved that Louis was willing to settle for the excuses he came up with for my bad temper.

"You see," he would say in a fatherly tone that implied he knew me better than I knew myself. After a while, he would start to tease and cajole me, drag me onto his lap. "What do you say we make an early night of it?"

"If you play your cards right." I kissed him full on the lips and he countered by landing a stubbly kiss on my neck. His scratch and tickle made my shoulder shoot up to my ear and I squealed like mad when Louis poked me in the side and wriggled his fingers under my sweater.

"What are you doing?" Tobias was standing at the kitchen door.

"Nothing, love."

"I wish you would stop fighting."

"We're not fighting," Louis reassured him. "Mummy and Daddy are madly in love again."

"Yes," I chimed in. "Your mum and dad love each other." Because I knew I would find my way back there again.

Louis went to get up but I beat him to it. "Leave this to me." And I carried Tobias back upstairs to bed.

"Goodness me, you weigh a ton."

"Why were you so angry?"

"Everything's all right now."

Tobias was only reassured once he had heard me say those words a few times. He clung to me with that wiry body of his, those pudgy hands, those knees that were never free of grazes and bruises. Such a scrawny little body with a whole human being inside. I hugged him so tightly that he croaked, "That hurts a bit, Mama."

"I'm sorry, love."

I tucked the covers under his chin and sat on the edge of his bed, let him chatter away until he began to yawn.

"Time to close your eyes, Toby. School tomorrow."

Before I switched off the big light, I plucked a pair of dirty socks from the floor and a pair of pyjama bottoms that smelled of pee, bound for the laundry basket.

"And you're not angry anymore?"

"It's time you were asleep, my little lad."

And I closed his bedroom door.

* * *

A month before his eighty-ninth birthday, my father was rushed to the hospital. St. Canisius. A major heart attack, they said. I drove there in a panic. In the intervening years, I had always managed to avoid the place and I turned onto St. Annastraat to find that the broad building I knew had been razed to the ground. The site was a wasteland, little more than an expanse of sand where the first weeds were taking hold. My father was in another place entirely, a new building with brightly lit windows, out beyond Goffert Park. Propped up in a bed surrounded by tubes and machines, there was an air of seriousness about him, as if he was doing his best to concentrate on what was coming next. But there was no sense of urgency. He might have been sitting patiently at the kitchen table, waiting to see what my mother was about to dish up.

"Hello, Pa," I said. "It's me."

In the days that followed I went to see him as often as I could. Perhaps in the hope that, in his final bed-ridden hours, someone else would emerge from deep inside him, the man he had been his whole life but had never dared show us. A man who spoke his mind.

Whenever my mother left his side to fetch coffee or go to the toilet, I would take his hand in mine for a while. Without his dentures, his cheeks were hollow. It was then I noticed how much he had started to look like his own father, a man I mainly knew from photographs.

"It's me, Pa." I repeated it now and again, and gave his hand a squeeze. "It's Elfrieda." I dipped a flannel in a beaker of apple juice and moistened his lips. A sliver of tongue appeared and he smacked his lips softly. I can't remember ever having touched his face before. However long I sat with him, no hidden man emerged. Instead, someone appeared inside me. Perhaps, for as long as it lasted, I was able to be the daughter I had wanted to be.

One evening he began to murmur. I dipped the flannel in apple juice and asked if he was thirsty. Pa shook his head. I asked him if he was afraid and he answered hoarsely, "I will be with my parents again. And my little brother."

This came as a shock. I didn't even know he'd had a little brother. By then, my father was too weak to provide answers. He held on longer than anyone expected, but those were his final waking moments. There was sometimes a faint squeeze of the hand when he sensed I was there to relieve my mother, but no words as he breathed his last. One morning, after hours at his bedside, I took my mother by the arm and we walked to the machine to get coffee. And my father found a way to die.

I had to take the bus home that afternoon. Louis was still at work and my sister had come by to pick up my mother. I got off at the market square. After days cooped up in the hospital, I felt the urge to walk for the sake of walking. It was one of those clear days in early December when I half-expected to run into Otto. The city was bristling with cyclists and all manner of sounds. I walked down Grotestraat, keen to get a view of the river. Without even thinking, I turned down a side street and got lost in my own home town. Nothing around me made sense. I recognised the curve of the street, but every house was new.

A bike rattled past with a tatty student in the saddle.

"Excuse me, could I ask you something?"

"Sure, knock yourself out." The boy slammed his feet to the ground and screeched to a halt. No brakes.

"I'm looking for Nonnenplaats."

"Well, you don't have to look far," he said with a laugh and pointed to a sign a few metres away. Only the steps remained, though the crumbling stone was now brand-new brickwork. There was no trace of the house where I had given birth. The room might have been floating in mid-air for all I knew.

A few years after my father, my mother passed too. It was Emma who found her, still in bed. The church service was a re-run of my father's. After the mourners had paid their respects and downed their coffee and cake, I walked back to the car park, arm in arm with Louis. Tobias had his own car by then.

"You know what, Frieda? I think it's exactly what your mother would have wanted."

"What do you mean?"

"You know, going in her sleep like that."

"Do you think so?"

"Isn't that what everyone wants?" Louis kissed my cheek. "Lights out and it all fades away, just like that."

It all faded away.

In the end, even Otto's name attached itself to someone else, a young chap who started working alongside Louis at the pharmacy.

# 46

But those two tiny feet never left me. Never.

# 47

"Good morning." A girl with a bouncy ponytail is doing the rounds with a thermos of coffee. "Can I help you?" Without missing a beat, she feeds a resident a forkful of rhubarb flan. Someone's had a birthday.

I scan the room and see only women. "I'm looking for Otto Drehmann."

"Over there." She mimes that he's sleeping. Otto is parked with his back to us, in a high-backed wheelchair at a long, empty table. "Feel free to give him a nudge."

I shuffle over at a snail's pace.

A wreath of thin hair with a tuft sticking up. Not stubborn or stiff, more like gravity has lost its hold on the little he has left. A couple of small wounds on his scalp look like they might never heal. Head bowed, as if he's inspecting his lap.

"Mind if I join you?"

Otto springs to life like a computer screen when you touch the mouse. "Of course," he says hoarsely and waves at the chairs all around him. "Be my guest." He looks at me, gives a friendly smile, then gazes out the window at the trees across the way. I recognise him from Brigitte's photos: the man who looked nothing like the Otto I remember. He has the body of a complete stranger. His skin looks too big for him, as does his checked jacket. A little orange ribbon is pinned to the lapel, in honour of some worthy pursuit he has kept up for a lifetime. I sit down opposite and can't help but stare.

"Are you new here?" Otto coughs to clear a rumble in his throat. "Or just visiting?"

"Otto," I say, softly.

A shake of the head. "Have you come to see me?" He doesn't appear to have full control of his body.

"It's me. Elfie."

Otto looks straight at me and tears spring into his eyes. His chin begins to judder. He looks out at the trees, then back at me.

"Do you know who I am?"

Otto nods, almost violently. His hand moves towards me but his fingertips barely reach the table. I heave myself to standing and, leaving my walker where it is, make my way to his side.

"Elfie," he murmurs. "Elfie, Elfie, Elfie. Here you are." Otto's fingers find my good hand. The words and phrases I've heard myself say through the years, the things I wanted to be true, the abuse I wanted to hurl at him, they all shrivel to nothing. Our hands search for a way to hold each other. "Here you are." He raises my thumb to his mouth, presses it to his lips. "Elfie. Oh, Elfie." The same words over and over. "Here you are." As if we'd agreed to meet in this place at the end of our lives and, after waiting so long, he was worried I might not turn up.

"Here I am." They're the only words that come to me.

"I'm sorry," he says. "Sorry you have to find me in

this state. I can't even offer you something decent to drink."

"It's all right, everything's all right."

"How did you find me?"

"My son. He got in touch with the university. In Pittsburgh. All that way. A woman you worked with sends her regards. Said you used to send her a card at Christmas." All of a sudden, I'm rambling. "She told us you'd come back to the Netherlands."

"Your son? You have a son?" Otto seems out of breath, his glasses fogged and greasy. He takes them off and pulls me closer so that he can still see me. They leave red imprints along his temples, on the bridge of his nose.

"Give them here." I polish the lenses with the thin fabric of my skirt and pop them back on for him.

Otto closes his eyes. "How did you manage?" he asks. Almost sixty years too late. "How are you doing?" And, without waiting for an answer, "Did you get my flowers?"

"Your flowers?"

"I brought you flowers at the hospital, handed them in at the desk." He makes it sound like it was only weeks ago, like I'm supposed to say they looked lovely on my bedside cabinet and lasted a good ten days.

"Why did you disappear, back then?"

Otto sniffs long and hard. "I have no right ... to ..." He waves a hand at the tears on his cheeks.

"I'm sorry, I should have let you know I was coming."

"No, no. It's me, I ..." Otto makes another wordless apology for his tears, his sudden inability to speak. I lift his teacup from the table and raise it to his mouth.

He takes a few sips. Gradually his breath begins to settle. "It's so good to see you. I often thought of you." He hammers his temple with a crooked finger. "I often wondered, 'How did Elfie get on?'"

"I did all right," I say. Sudden tears well up in Otto's eyes again.

"I'm glad," he says, and he means it. He tries to caress me. Runs his fingers over my arm, my shoulder, brushes my cheek. To brush back time perhaps, rekindle a connection through our skin. I give him a potted history: Louis of course, our son, my work at the nursery garden, my life here in Nijmegen. "And for a while now, I've been on my own again." Strange to hear it coming out like that. "Louis died. It was all rather sudden."

I can't really tell if he's following everything I say.

"And you?" I ask. "Brigitte told me you were here. I called at your home."

"Brigitte?" Otto straightens up in his chair. "Does she know who you are?"

"I told her I lived next door to you when I was a girl."

Otto rubs his palms on his thighs.

"Does she know who I am?" I ask.

"No," he says. "I never told her."

"She was very kind. We sat at your dining table and talked."

"We've had a good life together," he says, answering a question I didn't ask. "Always made the best of things." We tumble into another silence. Odd that we have so little to say to one another. Swapping facts from afterlives that did not touch at any point.

"And you have two daughters," I say. Otto doesn't

reply, runs a finger and thumb from the corners of his mouth to the middle.

"I was afraid," he says. We are face-to-face, but his eyes look beyond me. "The longer I stayed away, the more difficult it became to come and see you. More than anything, I was afraid."

"Of what?"

"That you would be angry."

"I was angry. Sometimes."

"Oh, I'm sorry. So very sorry. For everything." We are leaning towards each other. Otto's fingers even stroke my plaster cast. Thick veins crinkle across the back of his bony hand, his pink nails are neatly clipped. Our three hands and my concrete mitt form a tangle of fingers, crowding in around a flickering fire, shielding flames from the wind.

"I think about it so often," Otto says. "And these past few years ..." He shakes his head. "My mind starts wandering and suddenly it's right here in front of me." Otto tightens his grip and whispers, "I took it to my parents ... I didn't know what else to do." He has my wrist in a stranglehold.

"No, don't say that." How I hated those words. "I don't believe that, Otto. I never have."

"But it's true."

I pull free of his grasp, of this pious consolation he's granted himself.

"I had to get rid of it, the sister told me to."

"Get *rid* of it?"

"Don't be angry."

"Where did you take it?"

"The sister thrust a shoebox into my hands. I had to take it."

"A shoebox?"

"She'd put it in a shoebox."

Otto searches for my hand again, but I do not want to be touched. "I was in such a panic, Elfie. I drove around and around. And the whole time it was right there." His right hand indicates the space in front of the passenger seat.

"Where did you go?"

"First to the beaches by the Waal. But I couldn't bring myself ... I thought of the foxes digging and I ... I couldn't leave it there. The wind, the cold rain that soaks the sand." His words falter, clump together, then suddenly race along. "I drove to a hospital." It was so late in the day that he had to ring the doorbell. A nun answered, listened and asked him one question: was the child baptised? She held out her hands to receive the box but he couldn't hand it over. "I asked what they would do with it. But she refused to tell me."

Otto dwells on every detail. Holding the box close, under his coat. The nun telling him he could go to a cemetery, but that the child would not be buried with the Lord. Standing there helpless on the hospital steps at twilight, as the nun closed the door, slid the bolt, drew the blinds. Driving out to the cemetery, the place where his parents were buried, ringing the sexton's doorbell. How it was the only place he could think of and how, though the sexton did not recognise him, he listened, nodded, and asked a few brief questions. Over the sexton's shoulder, Otto could see the family at dinner in the kitchen at the end of the hall. He had wanted to pay but the sexton refused his money and told him the gate was a short walk away, one hundred metres to the right. The sexton said his son had almost finished his meal and would meet him there.

"I fetched the box from the car. A boy appeared on the other side of the gate. A youngster, sixteen at most. 'Good evening, sir,' he said. The gate was locked." Otto stops, searches for words. "I had to hand our baby over then and there. In that old shoebox. 'Don't you have a nice cloth or something?' I said. 'A cloth?' the boy asked. 'Something clean to wrap the baby in.' And the boy said 'I'll have a look' and stuck his hands between the spikes on top of the gate. 'Are you sure you know what to do?' I asked. 'Will you take good care of it?'"

Otto's head is wobbling on his neck.

"So, you see Elfie, I had to." He raises his hands. "And that young lad took it from me." Otto's movements suggest someone walking away. "That was all."

"Where did he take it?"

"I pulled myself up on the gate. I could hear his footsteps on the gravel. The lamplight among the trees gave me an idea of where he was. But ..." Otto shakes his head, bites back his sorrow.

"And you didn't think to ask?"

"I had to go back to Brigitte. I had to go home. I stopped to call her. I needed to speak to her before I saw her. She was worried, of course. I told her something bad had happened. 'An accident?' she asked. 'Yes,' I said. 'An accident. But I wasn't involved.' 'Oh, thank goodness,' she said. I was sobbing down the phone, I had to say something. So I said, 'There was a little one. A baby ...'"

I keep waiting for Otto to return to our baby, to the

flowers he left at the hospital. To tell me he went back to the cemetery. But he keeps talking about Brigitte. "And that, more than anything: her trust in me. That's what hurt most of all. Without a moment's hesitation, she believed that awful lie of mine." Otto shakes his head, looks down at his lap. "I never found a way to tell her," he whispers. "Instead, I've spent a lifetime trying to make things right."

Otto looks at me as if he wants something. Understanding perhaps, confirmation that he did what he had to do. I pat him on the arm, and regret it straight away. Slowly it dawns on me that our baby has always been somewhere. And that Otto knew, all this time he knew.

"Did you look?" I ask, as calmly as I can. I have to ask, though a shake of the head is all I can hope for.

"Look?"

"In the shoebox."

His face crumples, sorrow in every crease. "When I left your room ..." Otto stammers. "It was lying on the kitchen table." He whispers, as if we might wake it. "Wrapped in a stained towel. The nun came in with the box. Then she sent me away, told me to forget what I had seen."

"So you did see the baby?" I hold him by the chin, make his eyes meet mine.

"Only for a second. All I saw ..." Otto lifts the corner of an invisible towel. "It had the thinnest eyebrows," he says. I can barely hear him. "Its shoulders were so very small." He holds up two crooked thumbs. "It was ..." Eyes tight shut, Otto feels his way over an invisible face, gently, afraid to touch the memory. "It was beautiful, Elfie. So beautiful."

"Was it a boy? A girl?"

"I didn't ..." Otto shakes his head, seems incapable of forming words. "In the car ... I didn't dare take another look."

Anger so fierce, it almost makes me gag. A sorrow that forces its way up through my throat. I bite it all back to hear what he has to say. I want him to describe every hair, every eyelash. But my hands are filling with rage. I want to punch him, drag him to the floor. Wring the images from his eyes, things he has seen his whole life, things that have never been mine. Never.

"How could you?"

Otto glances away, nervously.

"You should have come looking for me!" I spit the words at him. "I saw nothing. Nothing. My whole life. Those two tiny feet, that was all. Two tiny feet. And you ... you knew all this time, you've always known."

"I only wanted the best ..."

"The *best*?"

"I had to. She told me."

"Who told you?"

"The sister, when she gave me the box. She told me you had to forget. I had to promise not to tell. It was the best thing for you."

I have to, can't spend another second here with him.

"Elfie?" Otto pleads. He reaches for me. Across the room, a couple of residents gawp in our direction. The rest jolt awake when my chair clatters to the floor behind me. I round the end of the table, release the brake on my walker and start rolling away.

"Stay," Otto begs. "Please stay, Elfie. I'm desperately

sorry. For all of this. I couldn't help it. Please, come back."

At the far end of the room, the doors swing open and the girl with the ponytail comes in, pushing a lady in a wheelchair. "Everything all right?" she asks as she passes. "That sounded rather intense."

I flee through the swinging doors and into the long corridor. I'm not even sure where I'm going, all I know is I need to get out of this place. Before they strap me into a wheelchair, lock me away where no one will ever find me.

"Excuse me!" Footsteps behind me, coming down the corridor. I can't go any faster. "Excuse me?" Her hand on my arm.

"Let go of me!"

"All right, all right." The girl raises her hands to show that she doesn't plan to try again. "Can you explain what just happened? Mr. Drehmann seems to be very upset."

The corridor is long; we are standing halfway.

"Why don't you come back with me? Just for a moment? Perhaps it would be better for both of you. To part company on better terms."

I shake my head.

"Can I get you a glass of water? A cup of coffee, perhaps?"

"I need to go." I start walking again.

"What's your name?"

"Elfie."

She keeps pace with me, questions in her eyes.

"We knew each other once."

That seems to do the trick. She stands still and lets me walk on.

"Are you sure?" she says.
"What?"
"That you don't want to come back for a while?"
"Tell him I might come and see him again."
"All right. I'll let Mr. Drehmann know."
I don't know if I'll ever be able to stomach it.

# 48

We're on the early side.

"In one hundred metres, take the exit." The sat nav lady sounds so familiar, it's like there's three of us in the car. "Take the first exit."

Tobias turns onto the dyke. Swallows swoop low and welcome us like old friends. The church steeple is decked out in a ruffle of green; only its peak and the golden cockerel on top are visible above the treetops nowadays. Late summer light glints off the river beside us. Astounding to think of the water that has flowed through this land all these years, never ceasing. On a river meadow, the colourful bustle of a campsite comes into view. A couple of kids come skating over the asphalt towards us.

Tobias peers over his shoulder and turns onto a road that leads down from the dyke. We pass a cemetery. "That's where we're headed in a little while, Mum. The man we're meeting is a volunteer, not the man who used to work there. You know that, don't you?"

"Yes, son, I know." Tobias keeps trying to spare me a disappointment, ever since he called to tell me he'd spoken to the woman in charge of the cemetery. We were welcome to visit any time, she said, and Wednesday afternoons were best, when there was a volunteer who could tell us more about the place.

"He can show us the way to the memorial."
"That's more than enough for me."
"Shall we stop for something to drink?"
"Yes, that would be nice."

We rumble through the narrow, cobbled streets of the medieval town centre. Not the kind of place that changes much, but I can't say anything looks familiar. "Are you sure we're allowed to drive here, Toby?"

"As long as you have trouble walking, we're allowed to do anything around here."

The buildings all lean forward a touch, as if they're vying with each other to see who's coming. A smattering of antique shops and a stall that sells sweets from grandma's time rub shoulders with the glare of a drugstore. We pass a huddle of tables and chairs on the pavement outside a small café.

"Here," I command. "Stop here." Tobias swerves into an empty parking space.

"A bit of warning would've been nice." He gives a growling cyclist an apologetic shrug. "Sorry, sorry."

This might be the hotel, but it's hard to tell from this angle.

"Why here, Mum?"

"It looks like a nice spot for something to drink." I fling open the car door to avoid further questions, but can't get out without his help. "Come on," I say. "My treat."

At a table by the window, I wait for our coffees to arrive. There's nothing here I recognise. Bare, whitewashed walls, young people everywhere. Perhaps it's the wrong place after all. Tobias comes back from the toilet, weaving past tables. He glances at his phone, then pops it back in his inside pocket.

"Everything okay with Nadine?"

"Couldn't be better."

For a second, I worry he's expecting further reassurances that I can't wait to see their impending daughter. My grandchild.

"Mum?"

"Mmm."

"Can you keep a secret?"

"Course I can." I turn my best ear towards him.

"We've decided to call her Lou."

"Loo?"

"After Dad."

"Oh ... yes, of course. Lou!" I recite it to myself a time or two. "Lou. Lou." More a sound than a name if you ask me, but I throw in an approving nod to keep the peace.

"Nadine loved it too. As soon as she heard it."

"Your dad would be very proud."

"It's so hard to choose something that will be with her for a lifetime. What's in a name, eh?"

"Lou," I say softly to myself. "Little Loulou."

"Dad would have made a wonderful grandad."

"Yes, love. He would have." Suddenly I miss Louis intensely, here on the empty chair at our table. On all the empty chairs in this café. I see us sitting here waiting for him. He's just dropped me and Tobias at the door and will come hurrying in any minute, cheerily complaining about having to park at the far end of the village.

"What would I have been called if I'd been a girl?"

"Oh ... uhm ... I can't say I remember."

"You didn't think about names before I was born?"

"Yes, we did. Louis came up with Tobias, I remember that much. And I liked it immediately."

"To-bi-as." He tries out his own name for size.

"And I always liked the name Odile."

"Odile?"

"I think that's what you might have been called."

"But I'm nothing like an Odile ..."

"Here we are," says a boy with his hair in a bun and a tray balanced on his fingertips. With a flourish, he sets two cappuccinos in front of us on the table. Two glasses of water on the side.

"Now, can I get you anything else?" He holds the tray like a breastplate in front of his chest.

"No," says Tobias. "Thank you."

He drums his fingers on the tray and turns towards the bar.

"Actually ..." I call after him. "Young man?"

He makes a squeaky half-pirouette. "Yes, madam?"

"Did this use to be a hotel?"

"It did indeed. Still is, in fact."

"Oh ..."

"We've been here three years now." The boy with the bun points out which walls they knocked through and proudly announces the advent of a lift. Gutted by fire years before, the place stood vacant for a while. The open kitchen, he explains, is where the hotel reception used to be. Kitchen staff dressed in white are whizzing around preparing a wedding dinner.

"Ah, yes," I pretend. "Now I recognise the place."

"And we still have rooms upstairs. If you ever fancy an overnight stay, we'd be happy to accommodate you."

"Well, who knows." I thank him with a smile. "I'll bear that in mind." It strikes me that the stairs are in the same place.

"Have you really been here before?" Tobias asks when the two of us are alone again.

I spoon a dot of froth from my cup.

"Mum?"

"Yes?"

"Why the cheeky smirk?"

"Cheeky? What a word to use about your mother."

"I've never seen you smile like that before."

"Well, Room 14. What can I say?"

"Room 14?"

"A room full of memories."

"Mum ... please ..."

"Well, you did ask."

"So, you were here with that Otto fella?"

"Mm-hmm."

"Room 14," Tobias chuckles, shaking his head. He looks down at his watch. "Oh."

"What is it?"

"We have to be there in fifteen minutes." Our cappuccinos have gone cold and we sip without speaking. Tobias signals for the bill. I place my bag on my knees and dig out my purse.

"Now don't get your hopes up, Mum."

Tobias lets me tickle him behind the ear. That always used to calm him when he climbed into our bed at night, shaken by a bad dream or a clap of thunder. I can't remember the last time I touched his face or ran my fingers through his hair.

"Thank you, son. For doing all this for me."

# 49

The cemetery gate is open and the taxus hedge has had a decent trim. I feel a restless tingle in the backs of my knees. A tall, thin fellow is loitering with intent, wheelchair at the ready.

"That'll be him, don't you think?" Tobias asks. He raises a tentative hand and the man waves back. He has a ring binder clamped under one arm and with the other he points out a parking space in the shade. Tobias turns the car smoothly and the engine goes quiet.

"Here we are," I say.

Tobias pats my leg. "Back in a sec, Mum." He yanks his door handle and gets out.

In the mirror, I watch them say their hellos and strike up a conversation. Backs half-turned, it looks like they're cooking up a scheme I'm not allowed to be privy to. Tobias points in my direction and the man nods a few times. Then Tobias takes command of the chair and steers it over to my side of the car.

"It's a bit of a trek, so this gentleman has been kind enough to provide transportation." Without waiting for a response, Tobias helps me into the seat. I keep my handbag on my lap.

"Good afternoon," the man says. He looks like a retired history teacher. He holds out his right hand and I shake it rather clumsily with my left. Harmelink?

Huiveling? I can't quite catch his name and fiddle anxiously with my hearing aids, so as not to miss the rest of what he has to say. They give a nasty shriek but, once that's over, the wind in the plane trees comes through loud and clear.

"Your son has given me a brief account of what you have been through. I am very sorry to hear it." His eyes are friendly, full of understanding.

"Thank you," I stammer, unused to this kind of sympathy, especially from strangers.

"I'm afraid there are no headstones, no names on the graves. But you can be sure that your child is buried here."

By the sound of things, I need to lower my expectations another notch.

"Shall I take you to the memorial?"

I press my lips into a wan smile.

"We'll need to stick to this side of the cemetery," he continues, addressing Tobias. "There's a funeral ongoing in the north section."

We make our way along the gravel path, follow him as he takes a wide bend to the left. We pass a couple of giant mole hills, topped by little wooden crosses. Fresh graves awaiting a headstone.

"It's quite a distance," Tobias says.

"The unconsecrated ground was at the very end of the cemetery, along the hedge."

"And you're sure my baby is still buried there?" I ask.

"I think it's safe to assume that, yes. This site has never been cleared, unlike standard graves after a number of years. Five years ago, it became a place of remembrance."

"And before then?" Tobias asks.

"It was where we kept the bins." The man sighs and looks a little sheepish. "Until someone discovered that it was where the unbaptised children were buried."

"How many?" I ask.

"What do you mean?"

"Children. You said children."

"Based on what we can gather from the written records, two hundred is our best estimate."

"Two *hundred?*" Tobias says in a loud voice.

"It's important to remember that this practice went on for decades." The man's face clouds over. "Sometimes three or even four children were brought here in the space of a month. And that's this cemetery alone."

I'm not sure these are things I want to hear.

Bark that has fallen from the plane trees by the path crunches under my wheels.

"Nearly there," our guide says. We have to pass through a long, shadowy lane that seems to stretch to the very end of the cemetery. Tobias says hello to a couple walking arm in arm in our direction. A young woman is crouched by a marble slab with a pail of soapy water. We arrive at an old stone wall that borders on a supermarket car park. Shopping trolleys rattle, cars turn and reverse, a truck beeps as it lowers its tailgate.

"Mrs. Buitink?"

"Hmm."

"We're here."

Tobias slows his pace but keeps pushing me forward. Ahead there's an opening in a taxus hedge that's too tall to see over. It looks like the entrance to a small maze.

"After you." The man motions for us to go in first. Tobias wheels me slowly through the opening. I had expected a special place, a place that might speak to me somehow. But it feels like any old patch of grass, wider than it is long, hemmed in by the dark green of the hedge. It could just as easily be a picnic spot or a place for kids to play. A statue stands in the far corner, two stone hands enclosing a baby made of white marble. A teddy bear is slumped against the plinth and someone has left a little vase of tulips. Our guide walks past us, onto the grass. Tobias starts pushing me after him. "No," I blurt out. "Stick to the side. I don't want to go over the grass."

"There's no need to worry." The man's voice is quieter now, the soul of discretion. "You can come this way. All the children are buried by the hedges."

Even so, Tobias waits, his warm hand on my shoulder. "Mum?"

"All right, but not too close to the hedge."

Tobias pushes me further and parks the wheelchair beside the statue. We stay there, gazing into space for a while. The man stands solemnly, holding his binder to his chest. Tobias has folded his arms. I try to think about what might be lying there, under the grass by the hedge, but I can't really picture anything. My back is damp with sweat, sticking to the artificial leather of the wheelchair.

"Excuse me, Mrs. Buitink?"

"Hmm."

"Back at the car park, I mentioned to your son that the sexton often noted the names of the parents whose child was handed in here."

"Oh." I straighten up in my seat. "Where did they do that?"

"In a simple notebook. We discovered it a few years back in the archives." He pats the binder, still clutched to his chest. "Your son mentioned December 1963. Is that correct?"

"Yes, that's right."

"If you like, I can take a look for you."

"Yes, I'd like that."

"I should warn you beforehand: I know from experience that these unofficial records are not complete." He pulls a well-thumbed notebook from a plastic sleeve. The cover is curled at the corners. "What was the name of the person who brought the child here?"

"Drehmann. Otto Drehmann."

"And he was the father?"

My nod must be all but invisible, because Tobias answers, "Yes, that was the father."

"Drehmann," the man mumbles to himself and flicks through the book, then stops and runs his finger down one of the pages.

"December 1963?" he asks to be sure.

"Mm-hmm."

He shakes his head slowly, turns back a few pages. "I'm sorry."

"What do you mean?"

"I'm afraid there's no entry with that name. But"—he shuts the notebook and gestures to the grass—"you can rest assured that your child is buried here." This is all he has to offer me.

A shrill bickering scrambles my hearing aids. Sparrows chasing each other through the hedgerows. They gather in a treetop along the way.

I have had enough of this place, more than anything I want to leave it behind me.

"It's a small comfort, I know, but you are not alone. In recent years I've spoken to several people here who knew for certain that their baby had been handed in, yet no name had been noted."

Tobias was right, I shouldn't have got my hopes up. And now that we're here, I can't help thinking we should never have come.

"I'll give you a moment, shall I?" he asks, tucking his binder back under his arm. "To be alone with your thoughts." He's a kindly soul, I'll say that for him.

"That would be nice," Tobias says. "Wouldn't it, Mum?"

"I'll wait for you at the main entrance." He backs away. "I can offer you a cup of coffee before you go."

"Why isn't my baby's name written down?"

"Excuse me?"

"Mum, this gentleman has already told you. He doesn't know."

The kindly soul pipes up again, in that patient voice of his. "That's anyone's guess, I'm afraid. Your son has told me a little about your circumstances at the time. It could well be, because the child was born out of wedlock, that it was handed over anonymously. We will never know for certain. The sexton was not always home. And this is the only cemetery we know of where a written record was kept."

"Can I look for myself?"

"In the notebook?"

"Yes."

"Why, of course." I see him hesitate. "Only I wouldn't want you to be upset, seeing all these names for yourself."

"It's what I want."

He flaps open his binder and slides the notebook from its plastic sleeve a second time. "Here you are." He places it reverentially on my lap. The square on the front for a child to write their name and subject at school has been left blank. He steps sideways to block the sun and give me shade enough to read. I open the book carefully, have to hold it up to my face to see.

"Can you make it out, Mum?"

Row after row of names in a neat and patient hand, intended to be read for years to come.

"This is the year 1961. Do you mind …?" Carefully, he pinches a couple of pages by the corner and turns them. The paper is fragile, on the verge of tearing from the string that binds it at the spine. It could be a list of names in someone's telephone book, only without the crossed-out addresses of friends who have moved or family members who have died. It's more like a marriage register. A register of sorrows.

Each line begins with a date, followed by the name of the couple and whether the child was a son or daughter. Sometimes I see the word *twins*. Then a note of the approximate location along the hedge. Most of the people listed are long since dead and gone. Every now and then, only the woman's name is given. June 1963. I read on and see August of the same year. October, November. I can hardly bear to turn the page, but I do it anyway.

It leaps out at me.

On the left-hand side, halfway down.

"Here."

"What does it say, Mum?"

I hardly dare touch the paper, afraid my damp finger will erase the pencilled letters forever. *7th December 1963*. Tobias and our guide move closer, light and shadow ripple across the page. I look and look again. And still it's written there.

"Oh, Mum." Tobias kneels beside me, pulls my cheek to his ear.

"Would you look at that." My tears won't stop. I move my hand, shade the words from the sun. "Here she is."

*7th December 1963 – Born to Mr. and Mrs. Tendelow – A baby girl.*

# Thanks

I would like to thank a number of people without whom *Afterlight* would never have existed. First of all, Gezina van der Wal, the first female gynaecologist in The Hague, for telling her stories. Laurie Faro, who allowed me to call whenever I needed to: thank you for your expertise and enthusiasm. Jos Joosten for sharing his impressions of a Nijmegen that is no more but lives on in his mind. Midwife Marie-Louise Klösters who told me so many intimate stories and whose work deserves more admiration than we can give. Janneke Peelen for her book *Between Birth and Death* and Wim K. Steffen for his photographs of the city. I am also indebted to the book *Een engeltje zette de wereld stil* (An Angel Made the World Stand Still) by René Oomen and *Zodoende was de vrouw maar een mens om kinderen te krijgen* (Why a Woman Was Only a Person Who Had Children), a collection of letters compiled by Marga Kerklaan.

I would also like to extend a special thank you to Hans Peters, Frank Eliëns, Andrea Voskens, Stichting Novio Magus, and Nijmegen City Archives, with its endless depot and its helpful treasurers. And to psychologist Inge Land, who was kind enough to work with me on a small-scale model of the family relationships in the book.

Thanks to my tireless editor Ad van de Kieboom. To my publisher Nathalie for her trust in me. And not forgetting Marja, Welmoed, Rebecca, Nienke, Martijn, Jolijn, correctors Meike van Beek and Akkie Strijk, and everyone at publishing house De Geus & Singel Publishers. It's thanks to them that you and I are able to hold this book in our hands. I would also like to thank my manager Michaël Roumen for his trust and his friendship, and for helping me regain that most precious of commodities: the time and the peace of mind to write.

Thank you to my dearest Suus, who deserves a line all to herself.

And to our dearest Lucy and Midas: without you, this book might well have been published years ago, but never in its present form.

Lastly, Patrick and Piekie. And, of course, my parents; always, my loving parents.

Jaap Robben

The translator would like to thank Michele Hutchison for her kind support, expert guidance, and the gift of the perfect title.

**DAVID DOHERTY** studied English and literary linguistics in Glasgow before moving to Amsterdam, where he has been working as a translator for over twenty years. His literary work includes novels by award-winning authors Marente de Moor, Peter Terrin, and Alfred Birney. *Summer Brother*, his translation of Jaap Robben's *Zomervacht*, won the 2021 Vondel Translation Prize and was longlisted for the International Booker Prize.

Book Club Discussion Guides on our website.

World Editions promotes voices from around the globe by publishing books from many different countries and languages in English translation. Through our work, we aim to enhance dialogue between cultures, foster new connections, and open doors which may otherwise have remained closed.

Also available from World Editions:

*On the Isle of Antioch*
Amin Maalouf
Translated by Natasha Lehrer
"A beguiling, lyrical work of speculative fiction by a writer of international importance."
—*Kirkus Reviews*, *Starred Review*

*About People*
Juli Zeh
Translated by Alta L. Price
A novel about the social and very private consequences of the pandemic, written by Germany's #1 bestselling author Juli Zeh

*Fowl Eulogies*
Lucie Rico
Translated by Daria Chernysheva
"Disturbing, compelling, and hearbreaking."
—CYNAN JONES, author of *The Dig*

*My Mother Says*
Stine Pilgaard
Translated by Hunter Simpson
"A hilarious queer break-up story."
—OLGA RAVN, author of *The Employees*

*We Are Light*
Gerda Blees
Translated by Michele Hutchison
"Beautiful, soulful, rich, and relevant."
—*Libris Literature Prize*

## On the Design

As book design is an integral part of the reading experience, we would like to acknowledge the work of those who shaped the form in which the story is housed.

Tessa van der Waals (Netherlands) is responsible for the cover design, cover typography, and art direction of all World Editions books. She works in the internationally renowned tradition of Dutch Design. Her bright and powerful visual aesthetic maintains a harmony between image and typography, and captures the unique atmosphere of each book. She works closely with internationally celebrated photographers, artists, and letter designers. Her work has frequently been awarded prizes for Best Dutch Book Design.

The cover photo, entitled 'Mimesis – Ornithogale Vénusiaïs', was shot by French photographer Seb Janiak as part of his *Mimesis* collection. The *Mimesis* photomontage project depicts the wings of insects as the petals of flowers. Janiak is interested in the mechanisms behind mimicry in nature, where an organism develops appendages, textures, and colors that directly mirror its surroundings. To create each artwork, Janiak scoured antique stores and taxidermist shops to find examples of wings which he then photographed at extremely high resolution. The pieces were digitally edited and pieced together into flower-like forms. Cover designer Tessa van der Waals rotated the image to give it more speed.

The fonts used on the front cover are Fonseca Black for the title and Neutraface Display Bold for the author's name. Fonseca was created in 2019 by Nasir Udin, a type designer based in Yogyakarta. Fonseca is a modern font inspired by art deco and typography posters from the early 20th century.

Neutraface was designed by the American type designer Christian Schwartz for House Industries and released in 2002.

The cover has been edited by lithographer Bert van der Horst of BFC Graphics (Netherlands).

Euan Monaghan (United Kingdom) is responsible for the typography and careful interior book design.

The text on the inside covers and the press quotes are set in Circular, designed by Laurenz Brunner (Switzerland) and published by Swiss type foundry Lineto.

All World Editions books are set in the typeface Dolly, specifically designed for book typography. Dolly creates a warm page image perfect for an enjoyable reading experience. This typeface is designed by Underware, a European collective formed by Bas Jacobs (Netherlands), Akiem Helmling (Germany), and Sami Kortemäki (Finland). Underware are also the creators of the World Editions logo, which meets the design requirement that “a strong shape can always be drawn with a toe in the sand.”

Printed in the USA
CPSIA information can be obtained
at www.ICGtesting.com
JSHW021112010424
60342JS00004B/4